"MISS FALK," BETHANY SAID, "CASSIE LEFT."

The key wanted to stick in the lock, and she wriggled it back and forth, trying to work it free. "Her grandmother came for her?"

"Uh, I don't know. I mean, I didn't see her."

A tingle of alarm traveled the length of her spine in a fraction of a heartbeat, and she turned, the key forgotten, her eyes taking in the playground, the other kids, and yes, there were only seven.

"Bethany, this is very important," she said, struggling to keep calm. "You didn't see her leave?"

Bethany shook her head. "Only . . . one minute she was there, and then she wasn't."

Danielle felt her pulse quicken. A rush of adrenaline sent a chill through her veins. She ran towards the street, her legs threatening to give way with every step. Her heart was pounding now, she could feel it—but oddly, not hear it—as she searched for any sign of Cassie in either direction along the street.

There was nothing to be seen.

"Don't jump to conclusions," she whispered.

For a moment she felt light-headed and nearly paralyzed by indecision: should she look through the neighborhood or call the police? Precious seconds were passing, time which could never be reclaimed.

The notion of a ticking clock sent her at a run back to the school. Fighting to keep the fear out of her voice, she called to the children to come inside, and for once there was no dissent.

"Cassie," she murmured as she surveyed the playground one last time before closing the door behind them, "where are you?"

DARK INTENT

PATRICIA WALLACE

ZEBRA BOOKS
KENSINGTON PUBLISHING CORP.

ZEBRA BOOKS are published by

Kensington Publishing Corp.
850 Third Avenue
New York, NY 10022

First Printing: September, 1995

Printed in the United States of America

For Andy
and
with thanks to
Jill Morgan,
who listened to me rant and rave,
far beyond the call of duty.

And
for all the kids
who never came home..

And there is even a happiness
That makes the heart afraid
— *Ode to Melancholy*

FRIDAY

One

Danielle Falk shielded her eyes against the sun and took a quick count.

Eight. The final bell dismissing classes had rung forty-five minutes ago, and there were *still* eight children who hadn't been picked up. A private academy for gifted elementary students, Northcliffe offered no bus service, requiring the parents to arrange for transportation to and from school.

Indeed, today as every other day, an orderly line of cars had passed through the circular drive fronting the school. Au pairs and housekeepers, older brothers or sisters with driving privileges, as well as harried mothers and distracted fathers showed up en masse each afternoon to collect their charges, siblings, or offspring, whatever the case might be.

Inevitably there were scheduling conflicts, missed connections or other unavoidable delays. The staff took turns providing adult supervision until the last ride arrived. Usually that meant staying after an extra fifteen or twenty minutes; today, with eight little darlings left unclaimed, she might very well break the school's long-standing record of an hour, five minutes, thirty-three seconds.

Of more immediate concern, however, was that three of the kids were wreaking havoc.

"Justin! Scott! Todd!" she called across the playground. A spirited game of kickball was in progress, the main objective of which appeared to be to see who could most accurately kick the ball into another's face, while making it seem accidental.

Danielle blew the whistle and admonished them: "Cool it, and I mean now!"

There was a barely perceptible lessening of mayhem, but given that there were scarcely two weeks left until the last day of school, it would have to do. One of the first lessons she'd learned as a teacher was that as the school year waned, so did her influence over the students. With the promise of summer in the air, their wild little hearts resisted being civilized.

And summer was near. The sky was a deep, intense shade of blue, the air clear enough to see, in sharp relief, the mountains to the east. The breeze caressing her bare arms was warm and scented with lilac from the trees that bordered the property. The blush of sunlight on her skin made her feel drowsy, almost languid.

If she were to close her eyes and just listen to the sounds of children playing, to the rattle and creak of the swing-set chains, it would be easy to imagine that she were one of them, again.

A hand tugged at her skirt.

"Miss Falk, guess what?" Cassandra Wilson said excitedly, pointing towards the pyracantha bushes near the entrance to the school grounds. "We have butterflies! See them? Aren't they beautiful?"

Danielle smiled and rested her hand briefly on Cassie's head; the child's jet black hair was hot from the sun. "They certainly are."

"Can I go— "

"You know the rules, Cassie." The children were not allowed beyond the turnaround.

"Not even for one minute?"

Seven years old, and the very picture of wide-eyed innocence. Never mind that she had an uncanny knack for breaking the rules. "Sorry, I don't think so. Why don't you go play with the other girls?"

"Please? Just this once?"

Danielle sat on her heels so that she could look into Cassie's face. She noticed a brass button on the child's denim bib overalls was undone, fastened it, then straightened the slightly frayed collar of the white blouse Cassie wore underneath. "Cassie, honey, it isn't polite to pester someone who's already told you no, regardless of how much you want to do something. Now, I know your Grandma taught you better . . ."

Cassie looked down, digging the toe of her tennis shoe in the short-cropped grass. "Yes, Miss Falk," she said with a sigh, and walked away.

Danielle watched after her for a moment, hoping that Cassie would approach one of the other children and ask to play. But, as she had all year, Cassie kept to herself, not even glancing towards the others.

Perhaps she ought to talk to Evangeline Wilson about her granddaughter's emotional detachment from her classmates. Then again, she'd hate to add to the poor woman's burden, what with a son in prison, and being called upon to raise his child . . .

Aware all at once of a curious silence, she turned to the boys, who now had abandoned all pretense of playing a game and were taking dead aim at Melissa and Melanie. The twins were lost in mutual self-absorption, whispering and laughing, their blond heads nearly touching, excluding the rest of the world.

Justin braced himself and drew back his right foot, ready to kick.

"Justin!" she called sharply, crossing the yard. "Don't even think about it, young man."

Caught in the act, the boy had the grace to give her a sheepish grin. Todd and Scott each took a step backwards, as if that small distance would be enough to establish their nonparticipation in Justin's misdeed.

"What's gotten into you kids?" she asked, confiscating the ball.

"I wasn't gonna hit 'em with it," Justin said, "just kick it over their heads."

"I feel *much* better knowing that."

Scott nodded vigorously, he who had a nasty if colorful bruise forming above his left cheekbone as a result of their earlier game. "That's the truth, Miss Falk. Honest, we were just goofing around."

Todd remained mute, no doubt on standing advice of counsel; his parents were senior partners in Booth, Clay & Rierdon, La Campana's preeminent law firm.

"Fine. But in the interests of disarmament, I'll keep the ball."

A chorus of protests followed her, which she ignored, instead sending a glance heavenward. And people wondered why teachers were brought to their knees at the prospect of year-round school.

Back at her usual observation point, the soccer ball tucked safely away, she looked again towards the entrance of the drive and tried to will someone to show up for these kids.

That isn't the most nurturing of attitudes, now is it? she could imagine Principal Rifkin saying. Maribeth Rifkin was a world-class nurturer.

"Give it a rest," she said *sotto voce*, and determinedly turned her attention elsewhere.

Across the road, directly opposite the school and just north of the city bus stop, a dark green van was parked in the shade of a sycamore tree. The afternoon sun, filtered through leaves and branches, cast a changing pattern of light and shadow, making it all but impossible to see if anyone was inside.

Danielle frowned. Hadn't she seen the van there earlier today?

Her classroom faced Hillcrest Street, and it was her habit to stand at the window, gazing out, as she recited the words for the weekly spelling test, which she'd given in the late morning, right before lunch. She had seen the van then, she was almost positive.

There was, at most, a moderate level of traffic on Hillcrest, which dead-ended at a long-abandoned dairy farm a mile or so to the south. Several small businesses operated out of refurbished houses across from the school, including an insurance office, a medical billing service, an antique store, a television repair shop, and the like. And while it wasn't unusual to observe people coming and going throughout the day, it seemed odd that anyone would spend *four hours* parked on their quiet street.

A glint of light flashed within the van's shadowed interior, and Danielle took a step to her right, intending to walk to where she might catch a glimpse of the license plate. But she got no further than that: a high-pitched scream spun her around, and she saw Sarah hop off the swings in mid-howl, bright red blood dripping from her right hand.

Danielle ran to the kindergartner's aid, but Sarah was in the throes of a full-fledged, white-faced panic, as only a five-year-old can be. The child continued to wail at the top of her lungs, at the same time cradling her injured hand, and turning violently away every time Danielle attempted to have a look.

After a few failed efforts, Danielle knelt in the sand and took Sarah firmly by the shoulders, forcing the child to stand still. "Hush now, let me see."

"I was pushing her on the swings, and her finger got pinched in the chain," Bethany offered helpfully.

"That hurts, I know," Danielle soothed, carefully prying Sarah's hand away from her chest. There was blood all over, and it took a few seconds for her to find the source of it, a ragged cut on the fleshy pad of the right index finger. The cut wasn't terribly deep, nor did it appear severe enough to require stitches, but it continued to bleed profusely. As she watched, fat drops welled from the wound and fell to the sand.

Lower lip trembling, her screams quieted to hiccoughing sobs, Sarah whimpered, "It ouches."

"I'm sure it does, sweetie." Clearly, the bleeding wasn't stopping on its own. Danielle found a clean tissue in the pocket of her skirt, folded it, and carefully applied pressure to the wound. "Come with me to the nurse's office, and we'll put a bandage on your finger."

"No, no, it'll hurt."

"I promise it won't." She got to her feet and gently urged the five-year-old forward, at the same time scanning the playground for another count. Seven, and Sarah made eight.

"Bethany," she said to the fifth grader who was standing solemnly by, "I want you to keep an eye on the others. Can you do that for me?"

"Yes, Miss Falk."

". . . don't use that brown stuff," Sarah was saying. "It stings."

They were in the nurse's office just long enough to clean the blood off with antiseptic soap— no brown stuff— rinse with warm water, apply a sterile compress, and secure it with adhesive tape. On Monday, the nurse would check for swelling or other signs of infection; tetanus was not a concern, since state law required children to have their DPT boosters before starting school.

Sarah's sniffles echoed through the empty halls on the way out.

"Keep your hand above your heart, and your finger won't throb," Danielle reminded the little girl as she held the door open for her, then set about locking up.

"Miss Falk," Bethany said, "Cassie left."

The key wanted to stick in the lock, and she wriggled it back and forth, trying to work it free. "Her grandmother came for her?"

"Uh, I don't know. I mean, I didn't see her."

A tingle of alarm traveled the length of her spine in a fraction of a heartbeat, and she turned, the key forgotten, her eyes taking in the playground, the other kids, and yes, there were only seven.

"Bethany, this is very important," she said, struggling to keep calm. "You didn't see her leave?"

Bethany shook her head. "Only . . . one minute she was there, and then she wasn't. And, you know, if her grandma came for her, they'd be waiting over at the bus stop, like always."

Which they weren't; the bench within the plexiglas shelter was unoccupied. "Where was she, when you saw her last?"

"There." Bethany pointed towards the pyracantha bushes, as Cassie had earlier.

Butterflies. The pyracantha bushes so close to the street.

The deserted bus stop.

And the green van was gone. Danielle felt her pulse quicken. A rush of adrenaline sent a chill through her veins.

Danielle ran towards the street, her legs threatening to give way with every step. Her heart was pounding now, she could feel it—but oddly, not hear it—as she searched for any sign of Cassie or the van in either direction along the street.

There was nothing to be seen.

"Don't jump to conclusions," she whispered, but even as she sought to find some other explanation, one question repeated itself over and over in her brain: *They haven't found the other little girls, have they?*

For a moment she felt light-headed and nearly paralyzed by indecision: should she look through the neighborhood or call the police? Precious seconds were passing, time which could never be reclaimed.

The notion of a ticking clock sent her at a run back to the school. Fighting to keep the fear out of her voice, she called the children to come inside, and for once there was no dissent.

"Cassie," she murmured as she surveyed the playground one last time before closing the door behind them, "where are you?"

Two

Det. Matthew Price stepped over the yellow police line tape and approached the uniformed patrolman standing guard nearby. "They inside?" he asked, indicating the school building.

"Yes sir. Front door's open."

Price nodded in acknowledgment, then hurried across the yard to the cement stairs, which he took two at a time. The door opened as he was reaching for it. Another cop, this one decked out in urban camouflage—a refugee from the SWAT squad?—held the door for him and motioned down the empty hallway.

"Fifth door on the left."

Walking down the hall, he glanced through a small window in the door of an empty classroom, at pint-sized desks in neat rows. Numbers and the letters of the alphabet, cut out of brightly colored construction paper, formed a border around the blackboard.

In one corner of the room, a translucent plastic rainbow seemingly came in through the ceiling, terminating above a six-foot-long aquarium which was populated— he supposed appropriately—with goldfish.

This was alien territory, a landscape as foreign to him as the dark side of the moon.

Sometime in his life he must have done time in a

room like this— no doubt champing at the bit to get the hell out— but he recalled almost nothing of his childhood. Nor did he care to.

When he reached the fifth door, Price paused, cleared his mind of minutiae, and went in.

The office was fronted by a long counter, behind which sat the secretary's desk, nearly buried under paperwork. To his right were two hammered glass doors; the designations Principal and Vice Principal were painted on the glass in bold black letters. The doors were partially open, and from the veep's office he could hear the distinctive olive-pit-in-the-disposal growl of Capt. Rudy Salcedo. So the brass was out on this, although that hardly qualified as a surprise on a big-ticket item like a child abduction, much less one that was the third such case in as many months.

To his left was an alcove which evidently served as a kitchenette, complete with a miniature refrigerator and hot plate. A hand-held Motorola sat on the counter, and though the volume was turned down to almost a subliminal level, he caught an exchange on Tach One between officers discussing a search grid within the city.

Standing at the Mr. Coffee, spooning grounds into the filter basket, was the latest, and by far greenest, addition to the Detective Division, Major Crimes Unit.

Gaetke had beat him to the scene; six months out of uniform and the rookie still drove like he was in perpetual hot pursuit.

Price cleared his throat and said, "I had no idea you were so . . . domestic."

"Hey, Matt," Billy Gaetke said with the easy familiarity that had accelerated his rise through the ranks. He slid the basket into place and pressed the Brew button; a second later coffee began to drip into the glass carafe. "I'm glad you're here."

"What've we got?"

"One hell of a mess." Gaetke flashed his trademark cocky grin, but his eyes gave him away. Billy Boy was in over his head, and knew it.

Price allowed himself half a smile. "Succinct, not terribly informative. The kid's still missing?"

"Still missing," Gaetke confirmed. "There hasn't been a ransom note or any calls."

"I didn't think there would be." Money wasn't what this creep was after. "Another little girl?"

"Right." Gaetke consulted his notebook. "Seven years old, name of Cassandra Wilson— "

"Has the Center been advised?" Recent departmental policy required they notify the National Center for Missing and Exploited Children of any abduction within the first few hours of a case.

"Dispatch handled it. Plus we got a recent photograph of the kid from the school's records, and that's being faxed to the case manager at the Center for national distribution."

Price nodded his approval. "Go on."

"There's not a lot else." Gaetke opened a cupboard, poked around, and pulled out a short stack of styrofoam cups. "As far as we know, no one actually witnessed the kid being grabbed, but the teacher said she'd noticed a van parked across the street— "

"That figures." Price had a theory that if Detroit stopped selling vans, the crime rate would take a sudden nosedive.

"— which evidently took off about the time the kid disappeared."

He accepted a cup of coffee and took a sip; it wasn't half-bad. "Got a make on it?"

"A color's what we got. Dark green, if that'll do it for you. But no make, no model, not even a partial on the plate."

"So much for the rewards of clean living," Price said absently, his attention drawn to the school principal's office. He could now see the young woman inside, although her back was to him. She was slender, perhaps five foot four, and dressed in a dark-hued peasant skirt, pale blue blouse, and tan suede boots. Her honey-brown hair was neatly plaited into a French braid that left bare the nape of her neck.

He noticed her hands clenched into tight fists that didn't quite hide the fact that she was shaking. In shock, he guessed, or maybe just frightened. Fear did that to people; fear cut through every facade.

"Is that the mother?" he asked, well aware that the rookie was watching him.

"Nope, the teacher. From what I gather, the mother's missing in action; she ran out when Cassandra was still in diapers."

From the vice principal's office came the sound of quiet weeping. In response, Salcedo's voice dropped to a whisper; Price couldn't make out individual words, but the overall tone was reassuring, as in, the cavalry is here. "Who's in with the captain?"

"Grandma. The grandmother's raising the little girl, because, get this, dear old Dad got tagged on a murder one. What we're dealing with here is your basic dysfunctional American family."

"If you say so," Price said with a frown. "What's the father's name?"

Gaetke thumbed through his notebook. "I wrote it down here somewhere . . . ah, right. Lewis Natchez Wilson, currently a guest of the California Department of Corrections at San Quentin."

"A local boy?"

"Born and bred."

The name was vaguely familiar, but he couldn't put a face to it. "How long's he been in?"

"Three years, more or less."

That definitely put it on his watch. He made a mental note to pull Wilson's jacket. "All right. Anything else I should know?"

"Well, if you want to run the gauntlet of some very vocal, pissed-off parents, they've got the other kids down in the cafeteria— "

"Any of the other kids see anything?"

"That I don't know. Dr. Harper's talking to them, or so I've heard."

Lauren Harper was the department's psychologist; if anyone could soothe a child's tender psyche— or a cop's for that matter— she could. Unlike most civilians, she had an inkling of the emotional battering that coming even within spitting distance of evil inflicted on the human soul. "Is that it?"

"That's it. Except I'm glad you're the primary on this, and not me."

He shrugged. "Like the song says, some guys have all the luck."

Price rapped on the glass with one knuckle and, without waiting for a response, eased the door open. "Excuse me, Captain . . ."

Salcedo, who years ago had taken a bullet in the neck which had necessitated the surgical fusing of his cervical spine, executed a stiff quarter-turn, his expression changing in an instant from annoyance at being interrupted to total, unequivocal relief. "Matt, come in."

"Sorry to— "

"Not at all." Salcedo stepped awkwardly to the side as he said somewhat formally, "Detective Price, this is Mrs. Evangeline Wilson, Cassandra's grandmother and legal guardian."

Evangeline Wilson didn't look like anyone's grandmother. An inch or so shorter than his own six-foot
height, she moved agilely, sleek and graceful as a big
cat. Dressed in dusty jeans, a denim shirt, and what
were probably steel-toed work boots, the woman looked
as though she could hold her own on any construction
site.

Her age was indeterminate: her short-cropped black
hair showed a scant hint of gray, and her creamy brown
skin was as smooth as a young girl's. Her eyes, though,
were red-rimmed and anguished, and the naked pain
in them established without doubt her kinship with
the missing child.

"Mrs. Wilson— "

"Evangeline, please."

She had a slight accent, and as he nodded to acknowledge her request, Price tried to place it. "I know
this is difficult for you, but there are some questions
I have to ask."

"Of course."

"If you'll pardon me," Captain Salcedo said, "I've
got to get back . . . but let me assure you, my dear,
you're in excellent hands— "

Price noted a flash of irritation in those dark eyes
at Salcedo's paternalistic tone.

"— so I'll leave you to it."

"Thank you for your kindness and concern," Evangeline Wilson said, matching the captain's earlier formality.

Price had it then: it wasn't as much an accent as
a manner of speaking which seemed to originate at
the back of the throat, guttural rather than breathy.
Native American, he thought, although linguistically,
he hadn't a hope in hell of narrowing it down further than that.

He sought and found confirmation in the woman's

bone structure, her broad forehead, and high, strong cheekbones. Having nurtured throughout his career a modest gift for determining ethnic origins, he decided that her face was too angular to be full-blooded.

"Have I passed inspection?" she asked after the door closed behind Salcedo.

Busted. Not that being caught in the act of staring was unusual for him; it happened all the time. He was beyond making excuses, so he didn't answer, asking instead, "Is there any possibility that someone in the family could have taken Cassandra?"

"All things are possible, Detective Price. But it isn't likely. No one in our family would have a reason to grab her off the street."

"Understand that I have to ask. The news coverage is always sensational when it happens, but abductions by strangers are exceedingly rare." That in fact was true, but he felt absurd saying it, knowing what he knew. "Tell me about the child's mother."

"Alyssa?" Tiny lines bracketed her mouth when she frowned. "What do you want to know?"

"Her full name and whereabouts— "

"Alyssa Reid Wilson, although I don't suppose she uses the Wilson anymore. I can't tell you where she is, because I don't know."

"Is there, or has there been, a custody dispute?"

"No. *I* am Cassie's legal guardian, and have been since she was nine months old."

"Alyssa hasn't seen Cassie since then?"

Evangeline started to speak, paused as though she'd thought better of it, and then said carefully, "From what little I've been told, Alyssa has put the marriage behind her and wants only to get on with her life. No, she hasn't seen Cassie."

His impression was that she was being truthful, but

he would have to check the mother out regardless. "What about your son?"

"I'm sorry?"

"Your son had no objection to having you appointed legal guardian?"

Again, she hesitated. "How could he?" she said finally. "There isn't a court in this state foolish enough to give the child to Lewis to raise."

He wasn't so sure. The California courts had issued some bonehead rulings in the past. A few of the judges he'd dealt with over the years were certifiable, Prozac-popping flakes.

"And if I hadn't taken Cassie in, they'd have sent her to foster care."

"Your son's been in prison before?"

"Lewis has, yes. Several times." There was a touch of defiance in the lift of her chin. "My younger son is finishing law school. Zeke will graduate at the top of his class."

"He live at home?" Price asked, deliberately keeping his tone neutral and nonaccusatory, while reflecting on the percentage of sexual abuse cases that occurred among family members. Blood might be thicker than water, but it often ran hotter as well.

Evangeline Wilson wasn't fooled. "It would be a long commute between here and Harvard."

"He's in Massachusetts now?"

She gave a curt nod. "He'll be flying out later this evening. You can check on him, of course. Make sure he didn't cut class and race three thousand miles across the country to kidnap his own niece for whatever vile purpose you have in mind . . ."

"I'm sorry, Mrs. Wilson, but everyone is a suspect at this stage. Everyone."

Tears glistened in her eyes, but didn't fall. "I can

live with that, Detective Price, if it will get my Cassie back."

As much as Price wanted to reassure her— and he was the cavalry after all— he couldn't. Not with the smell of death lingering in his head, staging a continuing assault upon his senses.

The reason he'd been late to this scene was because shortly before ten A.M., the body of the first little girl, who'd disappeared back in March, had been found in a culvert just inside the city limits. A poodle on a morning walk had slipped its leash and began to whine pitifully as it dug through the leaves and branches under which the body was hidden. The horrified dog owner, after losing his breakfast, called the police.

Eight-year-old, redheaded, blue-eyed Lucy Bosworth was in an advanced state of decomposition. The cause and time of death could not be determined pending an autopsy, which was scheduled for tomorrow morning at seven.

He would be there. He'd stand silently by as the forensic pathologist removed, weighed, examined, and took tissue samples of the internal organs. Every injury, however slight, would be detailed centimeter by centimeter and photographed in the search for answers as to how the girl had died. He would stand there, and breathe in particulates— microscopic bits of bone dust— when the saw cut into the child's skull.

It was part of the job.

There were worse things, such as having been the one sent to break the awful news to Lucy's parents that the body of their daughter had been found. Even as he swore that they would find Lucy's killer, he'd heard and been chastened by the mocking echo of hollow words.

Now, there wasn't anything he could say, no promises he could make, no comfort he could offer.

So he said nothing.

By the look in her eyes, he could tell that Evangeline Wilson understood the nature of his silence, and knew too well the mortal danger her granddaughter was in.

Three

"One final question, Melissa, and we'll be through. Did you see *anyone* near the schoolyard this afternoon? Anyone at all?"

As expected, Melissa looked at her twin before shaking her head in silence.

Dr. Lauren Harper stifled a sigh, regretting that she hadn't insisted on interviewing the girls separately. But their mother, shaken and somewhat wild-eyed at her daughters' close encounter with a fate worse than death, demanded shrilly that they be allowed to stay together, to give each other comfort and support.

The problem was, together Melissa and Melanie functioned virtually as one. As often happened with twins, the two were able to communicate without speaking, finding answers in the other's eyes.

Melanie had already said no, she hadn't seen anyone lingering near the school. Of course, Melissa's response would be the same.

"Okay, that's it. Thank you."

"Can we— " Melanie began, then fell silent, allowing Melissa to finish "— go now?"

"Of course." She watched them leave, mirror images, and wondered with more than idle curiosity if one of them had been taken, whether the remaining girl would sense where her sister could be found.

An interesting question, but she hadn't time now to waste on a hypothetical situation.

Time was the enemy, of that she had no doubt.

"Is that it?" a male voice asked. "The kiddies are gone?"

"Yes," Lauren said without looking up from her notepad, which was precariously balanced on her knees. The tables in the school cafeteria folded up into the walls, and she'd been forced to sit on an undersized plastic chair to conduct her interviews with the seven children who'd been on the grounds when Cassie Wilson disappeared. "Can't you feel the chill in the air?"

"Did I hear you right . . . chill?"

"You did." She glanced at Detective Gaetke, who was standing in the doorway. "The parents were pretty steamed about not being allowed to whisk their kids out of harm's way. It got pretty hot and humid out there, but— " she smiled wryly "—everyone's gone now and the temperature is falling."

Gaetke smiled faintly. "It could happen, I guess. So . . . did you get anything?"

"Afraid not." She capped her pen, closed her notepad, and stood up. "One of the boys, Todd, thought he might have seen a man crossing the street, but he's quite suggestible, very much in need of attention, and in any case, he wasn't able to give a description."

"Too bad."

"That depends on how you look at it." She slipped the strap of her bag over her shoulder. "If he *had* seen the man, he'd likely be frightened out of his wits.

Children at his age are so amazingly egocentric, he'd convince himself the bad man would be after him next."

"It might help us, though," Gaetke maintained.

"It might, if he were able to come up with a description specific enough to actually identify or eliminate anyone." She crossed to where he stood, the click of her heels echoing off the hard surfaces in the room. "Poor kid'll probably have nightmares as it is."

"Won't we all?" The young detective held the door for her, pulled it closed with a loud metallic clang, and fell in beside her as she started up the hall. "Matt's talking with the teacher. He wants you to have a look at her, tell him what you think."

"Think about what?"

"Well . . . he didn't exactly say, but I'm guessing he's worried the lady's about to flip, if you'll excuse me for intruding on your area of expertise."

"Flip, right, a time-honored psychological term." Lauren had introduced herself to Danielle Falk when she first arrived at the school. Although markedly pale, the young woman seemed in control of herself. "Anyway, after what happened with the Gennaro case, I sure don't blame him for wanting backup, if you know what I mean."

Lauren stopped dead in her tracks. "Matt isn't obsessing over that again, is he?"

Gaetke turned to face her, looking at her with raised eyebrows. "Again?"

She caught the inference, that the operative word should be *still*. "He told me—"

"—whatever he had to, to get back to the job." Gaetke's grin was disingenuous. "Don't take it personally, it's no big deal."

"Like hell it isn't." She remembered quite clearly the last session she'd had with Det. Matthew Price, how candid he'd seemed to be when he reported finally sleeping through the night without waking violently in a cold sweat. The auditory "ghosts" and sensory distortions had ceased as well, or so he'd said. She didn't consider herself naive, but evidently he did. "Son of a—"

"Whatever. For now, the man's waiting." The rookie gestured down the hall.

"Can't have that, can we?" she said under her breath, and went along.

Lauren was grimly amused to note Detective Price's frown at the icy stare she gave him upon entering the room. Then she put it aside— there would be a better time and place— and focused on Danielle Falk, who was sitting on the edge of her chair, hands gripping her knees so tightly her knuckles were white.

Lauren went to stand by a window, glancing only briefly at the police cars which blocked the street. A couple of the vehicles still had lights flashing, casting their red and blue warnings in the gathering dark.

Gaetke closed the office door, and leaned against it cop-style, his arms folded across his chest. In the outer office, he'd shed his coat jacket, revealing his shoulder holster and the wood grip of his Smith and Wesson .38 Chief's Special.

He meant to be intimidating, Lauren knew.

Price, on the other hand, looked casual and comfortable sitting on the edge of the principal's desk, facing the pretty young teacher. He made quick work of introductions, finishing with an avuncular smile. "Relax, Danielle. We're all on the same side."

"I know. I'm just a little . . . nervous."

"That's perfectly understandable. Dr. Harper"— Price nodded in her direction— "has talked to all the kids, and I asked her to stop in for a minute before you go downtown to give your statement, so we could see if the pieces fit, those we have so far.''

That wasn't precisely true, as she understood it, but Lauren offered what she meant to be a reassuring nod to Ms. Falk. On a clinical level, she noticed only that the pallor she'd observed earlier was still present . . . and fine tendrils of hair worried loose from the teacher's French braid clung to the damp skin of her neck.

Nervous, yes, but who wouldn't be?

She listened absently to the Q-and-A, recognizing various elements of the stories the children had told, but concentrated on classifying the young woman's so-called affect. Aside from the physiological signs— her coloring and the marked diaphoresis— there were mannerisms to look for and other less quantifiable nuances such as tone of voice, which could help determine whether or not Danielle Falk was being totally forthcoming.

Not that any police officer worth his salt couldn't arrive at that conclusion on his own; the best of the best were walking lie detectors, in blue. And while polygraphs were inadmissible in a court of law, *instinct* zeroed in on the bad guy more often than coincidence allowed.

Which led her to believe that Price was on to something, although she couldn't fathom what. True, she detected a moderate level of anxiety and even guilt in the teacher's demeanor, but that was to be expected, Danielle Falk had been responsible for watching the children, and keeping them safe. It was only natural that she would blame herself for failing to do so.

Feeling responsible and being culpable, however, were different matters entirely.

Then again, perhaps Gaetke was right, that Price's

main concern was the possibility that under pressure, Danielle might flip on him.

"— only inside with Sarah for a couple of minutes," the teacher was saying, her voice subdued but under control. "When we came out . . . it was already too late. Cassie was gone."

Price and Gaetke exchanged a look, after which Matt gave a slight nod.

Gaetke cleared his throat. "And you did what, again?"

"I . . . I ran to the street, to see if I could spot her or the van, but the street was deserted. There was no one else around."

"Anything else?"

Danielle Falk closed her eyes briefly, as if trying to remember. "I can't think . . . but the strangest thing, it was so *quiet*. Unnaturally quiet. For a few seconds, while I was standing there on the street . . ." the words trailed off to a whisper, "there wasn't a sound."

Lauren recognized the fading, breathless voice as symptomatic of underlying shock. The reality of what had happened this afternoon was sinking further in, along with a growing awareness of what might be Cassandra Wilson's fate. The potential consequences were so horrible for Danielle Falk to consider, that her thoughts had the power to force the very air from her lungs.

"What is it?" Lauren asked, speaking for the first time since entering the room.

There was a pained wistfulness to the teacher's expression that suggested her composure was slipping. She didn't answer immediately, instead tilting her head as though listening, and then frowned. "Did Cassie cry out, do you think?"

"I don't know," Lauren said carefully. Catching a

questioning glance from Price, she shook her head to warn him off.

"Sarah was whimpering over her cut finger and water was running in the sink, but . . . I should have heard Cassie. If I had, I could have stopped this."

"Danielle— "

"He wouldn't have dared take that child, if I'd come running. He'd know I had seen him, and he would have to let her go. If only I'd heard Cassie cry . . ."

"Let her go home," Lauren urged as the three of them stood in the outer office a moment later. "She's told you what she knows, she can give a formal statement in the morning."

Price ran a hand through his graying dark hair. "I don't know . . ."

"Don't forget the blood," Gaetke said, hitching his thumbs through the leather straps of his shoulder holster. "We gotta collect the evidence."

"What *evidence?*" she asked.

Matt Price shrugged. "Oh, she's got a couple of drops of blood on her skirt— "

"—and on her boots— "

"—and her boots," Price finished with a mild look of irritation at his partner.

"From Sarah's cut finger," Lauren said.

"Probably. But we have to check it out— "

"— do a blood-type, ABO, and PGM," Gaetke clarified, which drew another annoyed glance.

"If only as a means of elimination, and in the interests of expediency— "

"Wait a minute," Lauren said. "Time out. I've talked to the kids, remember? They all agree that the teacher was inside the school building with Sarah when Cassie disappeared. How could you possibly consider Danielle Falk a suspect?"

"Not a suspect, no. But at this point in the investigation—"

"—there's no telling who might be implicated," Gaetke said earnestly. Then, aware no doubt of Price's growing impatience at being interrupted, he winced before offering a conciliatory smile. "Sorry."

"Implicated my ass," Lauren hissed. "What do you think, she's scouting for some damned pedophile?"

Gaetke appeared taken aback, while Matt Price looked down and shook his head.

"The woman's no more implicated than I am."

Price surprised her by laughing. "Well, Lauren, now that you mention it—"

"Send her home, Matt. As a matter of fact, I will personally drive her home. If you want her clothes as evidence, I can wait while she changes, and bring them to you." As a sworn member of the police department, she had the legal standing to be the first link in the chain of custody.

"Okay, if you feel that strongly, it's your call."

Lauren Harper was acutely aware of a near-suffocating darkness as she turned onto Danielle Falk's street, but it took a moment to comprehend that it wasn't because the night was closing in. The lights were out.

"Looks like a power failure," she said, flicking on her high beams. Judging by the rustling of the branches of the trees which lined the street, the wind was up, blowing rather briskly.

Danielle had been silent since they'd left North-cliffe, staring out the side window, but she stirred, and spoke softly, "I never used to mind the dark. As a child, I mean. Now . . ."

Lauren heard the melancholy in that single word, and understood that just below the surface lurked an uneasy fear. In spite of herself, she shivered. "I'm sure the lights will come on in a minute."

"That's my driveway on the left, just beyond the fire hydrant."

Lauren slowed and, although there was no cross traffic, signaled her intention to turn. The blinker put her in mind of a metronome, and she had a sudden flash of herself as a child, sitting on a piano bench in a sun-drenched parlor, running a finger slowly down the white keys.

The memory was so clear, she could hear the tinkling notes.

She'd never learned to play, however much her parents wished it, and had in fact forgotten until this very moment the time she'd spent supposedly learning the scales.

Memory was like that; selective, imprecise, mercurial at best . . . and yet.

And yet?

Last fall she'd attended a workshop on memory at the University of Washington in Seattle. It wasn't a subject that had attracted much of her professional attention in the past, but with the recent emergence of so many repressed memory witnesses in criminal trials, she'd thought it prudent to check it out.

What she learned about the stages of memory, its acquisition, retention, and retrieval, was fascinating. One workshop did not an expert make, but there was a possibility that she could help Danielle remember more than what she had so far—

A horn honked behind her.

Startled out of her reverie, Lauren pulled into the driveway. She parked so her headlights lit up the front door of the small stucco house. After engaging the parking brake, she glanced across at Danielle Falk.

"I know you want to help Cassie," she said. "Would you be willing to undergo hypnosis?"

"Anything," the young teacher said. "I'll do anything."

Four

Standing on the bus stop bench, Dakota Smith had a clear view of the detectives as they left the school building. She raised her Sony and taped them walking towards the street. The lighting wasn't the greatest, but with any luck at all, she could use the footage with an energetic voice-over, and no one would notice that there was nothing in the least bit dramatic about the shot.

Funny thing about television news: give 'em a stunning visual and nobody complained about the incoherent narrative that accompanied it, but the reverse wasn't true. The most insightful copy ever written couldn't rescue a dull, fifteen-second loop of, say, cops leaving a building.

But what the hell, she'd never set out to be a cameraman.

Through the viewfinder, she noticed Detective William Gaetke notice her. She waved. He came to a dead stop for a second or two—the press had that effect on people—then caught up with Detective Price and, ever helpful, pointed her out.

Bad light and all, she could read Price's lips, for which she blessed whomever had invented the autoᵐatic zoom lens. "Temper, temper," she said aloud, and then, feeling charitable, shut the camcorder off.

With practiced nonchalance, she slipped the Sony in its soft-sided bag. The zipper stuck momentarily, and she tugged gently at it even as she heard footsteps, as expected, coming in her direction.

"What are you doing?"

"My job," Dakota answered as she worked the zipper loose before glancing in his direction with a grin. "How's it hanging, Detective Gaetke?"

"You know you shouldn't be here."

"No, I don't know." With as much self-assurance as she could project, she slung the camera bag over her shoulder and stepped down off the bench. Which she immediately regretted, since she now had to look *up* at him.

"Who are you working for?" Gaetke persisted. "If you're really working."

Dakota shook her head. "Doesn't make any difference. I've got a press card, and— "

"Come off it, Dakota. You've been fired from every station in town."

"Details, petty details." She pulled a crumpled pack of Marlboros from the inside pocket of her Levi's jacket and extracted a slightly bent cigarette. "That promotion must have gone to your head; you never used to be such a stickler for details. Got a light?"

"I gave it up."

"Shit, that's no excuse. Cops on TV are always flicking their Bics for some handcuffed, lowlife scum."

Gaetke snorted. "So go try Hollywood."

She jammed the cigarette back in the pack, not caring, in the heat of the moment, if it broke. Across the street, Detective Price had finished talking with the solitary patrolman standing guard— a reincarnated Nazi storm trooper who'd run her off earlier— and now was headed for his city-issued Ford Taurus. "Maybe I ought to try your *compadre*," Dakota said.

"He might just accommodate you, provided he could handcuff you first."

"Ooh, kinky. In a pathetic, older-man, white-bread kind of way."

"And don't keep changing the subject. For the last time, who was crazy enough to hire you after what happened at Channel 7?"

Dakota felt the color rise in her face and was glad for the cover of darkness. "That's a cheap shot, and you know it. That could have happened to anybody. How was I to know we were still on the air?"

"Tell it to the FCC."

"I did, many times. Besides, what difference does it make? I told you I'm working. And I've got a valid press card."

"Damn it—"

"Oh oh, *now* you've gone and done it; your date's leaving without you." The beige Taurus was approaching, and as it neared, she saluted Price smartly, the way her daddy had taught her.

Faster than he looked, Gaetke caught her wrist on the out-swing. "Come with me."

"Okay, okay," she said, trying unsuccessfully to pull free. "I won't make you beat it outta me. I'm freelancing for a guerrilla station, KOUT."

"What?"

"You know, a low-watt wonder. Local stuff, with a broadcast range of a mile or two." She smiled wanly. "How the mighty have fallen, huh?"

"Tough luck," Gaetke said, and let go.

"A master of understatement, as always." Dakota rubbed her wrist. "That hurt."

"It was meant to."

"Huh. You break it, honey, you bought it. Be making payments to the Dakota Smith Foundation for a good long time."

Gaetke laughed. "I'll say this much for you, you *are* fresh."

"Hey, don't I know." She ducked her head slightly and favored him with the only coy look in her repertoire. "So . . . anything new on the little girl?"

"No comment."

That was more or less what flirting usually got her. It took every iota of self-restraint in her body not to whack him with the camera bag. Instead, she sighed. "You know, I went to that school. It's kind of scary—"

A burst of unintelligible static erupted from the mobile radio Gaetke was carrying. "Listen, I've got to go." He took a few steps backwards before turning away from her. "Keep your chin up."

"Oh, no you don't." Dakota hurried after him. "I told you my dirty secret; you owe me."

"Doesn't work that way."

"Then at least give me a ride." She yanked on his coat sleeve. "Please? There won't be a bus along here for hours, if ever."

"What happened to your car?"

"I stopped making payments. The bank took exception to that for some reason, and repossessed it. I know what you're thinking— how incredibly rude!— but I marched right down there and closed my Christmas account. Eighty-two dollars and fifty cents, a not inconsiderable amount. That ought to teach them, don't you think?"

Gaetke made a sound in his throat. "What I think is that I'll live to regret this . . ."

"No, you won't," she said.

* * *

Dimly lit and musty, the narrow stairwell leading up to the television station gave Dakota the creeps. Bad enough that the stairs creaked and groaned beneath her, but even worse, it often seemed she could hear footsteps other than her own going up.

Climbing the stairs, she half-expected to feel a hand close around her ankle and yank her down. On a night like this, with the wind blowing, the streets deserted, and a sex-crazed maniac on the loose, it was easy to imagine cold, clammy fingers reaching for her, imbued with superhuman strength . . .

"Now you're being silly," she chided herself, with a nervous look over her shoulder, and took the last of the stairs two at a time. At the top, she turned left, but then executed a quick three-sixty to make sure she was alone in the hallway.

Which, thankfully, she was.

The studio door was locked, as usual. Dakota rapped on the window—she could see Freddy at the video replay machine in the glass-walled editing room—but after a minute or two, she gave up chivalry for dead, and fished her keys out of the camera bag.

"Freddy," she fumed once inside, "you craven coward, I could be dead right now."

Freddy appeared in the editing room doorway, gnawing on an apple. "What?"

"Suppose someone followed me up here—"

"Like who?"

"—I'm cornered at the door, trying desperately to get in, and this killer has a butcher knife!"

"You got a key," Freddy said around a mouth full of apple.

"Right, and I'm supposed to calmly unlock the door, while this guy's carving me up like meat on a hook? I think not, Galahad."

He seemed to reflect on that while he made a loud

sucking sound, evidently trying to dislodge a piece of the fruit from the gap between his front teeth. "What's your point?"

"Open the door when I knock, okay?"

"Whatever." He pitched the core into a nearby wastebasket— a three-point shot— and slunk back into the editing room.

"I feel safer already," she muttered, heading for her own tiny workspace, an eight-by-eight cubicle conveniently located next to nothing and no one.

She liked it that way.

Absorbed in the effort of making sense of the fragments of information she'd scavenged at the scene and over the police scanner, Dakota was only marginally aware of voices in the hallway. When she saw the shape of someone standing behind her on the video monitor, she nearly jumped out of her skin, rising to her feet so quickly that she sent her chair crashing into the wall.

"Didn't mean to scare you," a voice said.

"Jesus, Mr. Avery!" Dakota held her hand over her thundering heart. Deleting the expletives, she asked, "What are you doing here?"

Simon Avery pursed his fleshy lips into a cryptic smile. "I had an equipment failure this afternoon— "

"Not again!"

"Yes, again. Your boss said I could pick up a tape of your six o'clock newscast. Freddy's leaving on his dinner break, but he said you'd make me a copy."

She made a face. "If you insist, but I don't know why you bother." The six o'clock wasn't much more than a teaser for her gig, the scintillating if unimaginatively named Late News.

"Gotta make a living." Simon ran News On Demand, La Campana's only media transcription service, out of a wing of his home, an old antebellum mansion on a densely wooded three-acre lot on the south side of town. He'd inherited both the business and the house from his mother, Katherine, a local philanthropist who'd died last Valentine's Day.

Dakota remembered it well, having attended the funeral and covered the solemn occasion for Channel 7. Simon had flung himself on the casket, cutting his chin and bleeding all over the place. His loss— or maybe the sight of his blood?— had thoroughly freaked him out.

Whatever the cause, Simon was indisputably his Mama's boy, and the funeral had ended with him whimpering as if his heart would break.

The incident made for good TV. Back then, she'd worked with a cameraman, but it had been her idea to close with a shot of blood-spattered white roses. The station manager had been impressed.

Very visual, the station manager had said, and— better yet— visceral. The kind of graphic image that lingered in the mind.

Later, he'd been the one to fire her.

"All right," she said, feeling kindly towards Simon as the source of a past triumph. "Come with me."

Dakota slipped the three-quarter-inch master tape into the playback machine, and patched it to a standard VHS recorder loaded with half-inch tape. "While I'm at it, is there anything else?"

"I don't know," Simon Avery said, "what else have you got?"

"Not a lot," she said absently, watching the fractured images of a week's worth of six o'clock broadcasts in fast-forward. "It's been a slow news week."

"Until today."

She glanced at him as she turned the dial to slow the tape. "A terrible thing, isn't it? Those poor little girls . . . and, my God, their parents."

He didn't answer, his hooded eyes seemingly fixed on the screen.

"Here we go." She froze the frame, hit Record on the VHS, waited a second to allow for a lead-in, and resumed playback in real time. The familiar up-tempo KOUT news theme music filtered into the room.

"Good evening," the silver-haired anchor said. "Police are searching this evening for seven-year-old Cassandra Dawn Wilson, who they fear was abducted from a schoolyard late today . . ."

Dakota shook her head at the anchor's monotonal fill-in-the-blanks style. "Come on, put some juice in it," she said under her breath.

A photograph of the missing child took his place on screen. This was the first time she'd seen the photo, and it made her heartsick. Cassandra was a gorgeous young girl, with big brown eyes and an impish grin.

"According to a police spokesperson," the anchor said, "they are looking for a dark green van in connection with the kidnapping."

Beside her, Simon Avery exhaled softly.

"Tonight, the police aren't saying whether this is connected to the separate disappearances earlier this year of Lucy Marie Bosworth and Rachel Elise Kraft."

Cassandra's photo was downsized to allow for those of the other young girls.

Not of a type, Dakota thought, looking at the three. Cassandra was dark-skinned and somewhat exotic, while Lucy had flaming red hair and freckles, and Rachel was a blond pixie.

"This guy's an opportunist," she said.

For the first time since the tape began playing, Simon Avery turned his eyes away from the screen. "What makes you say that?"

"Don't you see? He's not after the same little girl every time."

Clearly confused, Avery frowned. "Well, how could he be?"

"Not the same girl, but the same *type*. You know, the way Ted Bundy preferred girls with long dark hair." It occurred to her that for someone whose livelihood depended on the news, Avery wasn't terribly well-informed. "It's quite common with serial killers."

"Is it?" His attention returned to the newscast, which had switched to footage of a deputy coroner loading a stretcher bearing a velvet-shrouded body into the back of a white van.

". . . police have not released any information on the badly decomposed body found today near Blue Canyon," the voice-over said, "pending identification. A source in the Coroner's Office has confirmed, however, that the body is believed to be that of a female."

"Have to be a pretty small female," she said, thinking out loud.

"An autopsy is scheduled for tomorrow. In other news . . ."

The phone rang. "Excuse me," Dakota said, taking off her headset and placing it on the control board. She crossed to the console and punched the flashing button, noting that it was the station's private line.

"Dakota Smith," she said into the receiver.

"Turn on Channel 7, the news brief!"

She recognized Freddy's voice, although she'd seldom heard him this excited. "Why? What's going on?"

"You know that body they found this afternoon? Guess who it is?"

"This isn't the time to play twenty questions,

Freddy," she said crossly. Stretching the phone cord, she reached a second set and turned it on, cycling through to KNNX. Freddy was yapping at her, but she didn't hear him, overcome for a moment by a sense of *déjà vu:* Channel 7 was showing near-identical footage of the Blue Canyon site.

And then the photograph of the little redheaded girl replaced the crime scene.

Feeling sick, she turned the sound up.

". . . parents are in seclusion tonight," said KNNX's silky-voiced female co-anchor. "Lucy Marie Bosworth, who disappeared while walking home after attending her best friend's birthday party, was eight years old."

Dakota closed her eyes briefly.

"Such a shame," Simon Avery said.

"Okay, Freddy," she said into the phone as she walked back to the console. "I'll get on it." Without waiting for his response, she disconnected him, and dialed the police department.

"Umm, I know you're busy," Avery said, "but . . . could I have my tape?"

Listening to the line ring, Dakota went through the motions, and in short order handed him a cassette. Just then the desk officer answered and, wanting to keep the call private, she turned away.

When she hung up a few minutes later, Freddy had returned with a grease-stained bag of tacos and Simon Avery was gone.

Five

Billy Gaetke made a left turn into the alley that ran between Fourth and Chestnut. At one time the alley had been paved, but only crumbled chunks of asphalt remained, and the ruts were deep enough to justify his concern about bottoming out and cracking the oil pan.

He drove slowly out of consideration for the car, an unmarked Taurus which was his first—and so far only—perquisite as a detective. And to keep from raising a cloud of dust.

Not that the denizens of the alley needed dust to alert them to his arrival; this particular element of the human race had a sixth sense in regard to the cops. If they even *were* human, which he frankly doubted, imagining them as the angles of a kaleidoscope, ever-shifting fleshy shapes that rearranged themselves, when necessary, to imitate human form.

Only among others of their kind, Gaetke suspected, did they show their true faces. Small wonder they sought out places like the alley in which to congregate; the dark suited them.

There was a carport up ahead on the right, with a sagging roof and graffiti-ravaged walls. At the back of the carport sat a grimy bench seat someone had taken out of an Olds Cutlass, which for years had sat rusting on its rims in the vacant lot across the way.

That seat was the exclusive domain of Enrique Tackett, the self-described "prince of the night." From that unlikely throne, he held reign over others of his ilk.

Enrique had served seven years of a twenty-five-to-life sentence for a double homicide down in Los Angeles. A blade man of long-standing, he had eviscerated two biker brothers in a bar fight, bad actors who he claimed at trial "needed killing and then some." Since making parole in 1990, Enrique had stayed straight . . . or more likely, he'd gotten better at hiding his criminal enterprise.

Gaetke eased to a stop, keyed the radio mike, and gave his location to Dispatch, ending with, "Give me a call back in ten."

It was a standard safety measure; the dispatcher would flag his car number and check in on him after ten minutes. If she was unable to raise him, she'd broadcast a Code 30— officer needs assistance— and his fellow officers would swoop down on this place like a swarm of ravenous locusts on a Kansas wheat field.

"Victor Eight," the dispatcher acknowledged, "ten-four on your call-back."

He killed the lights but left the engine running, got out, and made a deliberate show of reaching inside his jacket to unfasten the leather strap of his holster, a not-so-subtle warning.

A fire burning in an old oil drum provided minimal illumination. He couldn't make out individual faces, but he felt them study his every move. And he sure as hell could *smell* them, that peculiar alcohol-tinged sweat of chronic boozers, commingling with the scent of marijuana and plain old body odor.

It was a long shot, coming here, but the word from Salcedo was to leave no stone unturned. Which meant socializing with the slimy creatures that dwelled beneath said stones.

"Enrique," he said to the slimiest as he crossed behind the car. "It's Billy Gaetke."

"Long time," Enrique said from the shadows. "To what do we owe this honor?"

He heard the disdain in the ex-felon's voice. Evidently the others did, too; a ripple of derisive laughter passed between them. "You hear about the kid who got grabbed this afternoon?"

"I may have heard a thing or two."

Gaetke was close enough now to see Tackett, lounging with his arms extended along the back of the seat. For a punk with a big mouth, Tackett had small, babylike teeth. A pointy chin and high-arched eyebrows gave him a satanic look. The mustache, pencil-thin and precisely groomed, was new.

"What, exactly, would that be?"

Enrique laughed, a vaguely suggestive sound. "You can't expect me to betray a confidence. I do that, and nobody'll tell me nothing."

"She's seven years old, pal."

"Hey, I was seven once, getting the snot slapped out of me on a daily basis by the old man, wasn't anyone coming to my rescue, to try and save my scrawny little ass. Unless—" Enrique stroked his chin as if in contemplation, "— some shit-for-brains cop went to the wrong address . . . day after day after motherfucking day."

Appreciative laughter from the entourage, no surprise there. "You're breaking my heart," Gaetke said.

"And that's a bad thing?"

He could feel what patience he had slipping away. "You ought to try stand-up, Tackett, you're a funny guy. I have to ask, though, would you be as funny spending the night in the tank."

"On what charge?"

"I'll think of something," he promised.

"Sounds suspiciously like false arrest to me."

"Or an honest mistake," Gaetke shrugged. "Whichever it is, you can be sure your dance card will be full while you're in."

"There ain't a cop in this city with a sense of humor," Enrique sighed. "Okay, fun's over. You still haven't said what's in it for me."

"My eternal gratitude."

"My attorney would call that 'deliberately nonspecific and unactionable.' You can do better, no?"

Gaetke shook his head. "Not until I hear what you have to say."

"Well," Enrique said, drawing the word out, "not much, really. I can offer an opinion, for what it's worth. The guy who's grabbing these girls probably isn't one of the old guard."

"How do you figure?" In fact, they were already sweeping the city, talking to the usual suspects, registered sex offenders and known pedophiles, as they had after the Bosworth and Kraft disappearances.

"Picking kids off the street isn't the style. As sick as it is, the chickenhawks like to *seduce* a child; they claim the chase is half the fun. This guy's either late to the party, or he's got a lot of pent-up desire—"

"You know they found the first girl's body today," Gaetke said, a hard edge to his voice. "This isn't some prom he's taking them to."

"That's the point I was making." Tackett offered a sardonic smile. "You're wasting your time *and* mine. He's not a known player, which means he isn't predictable. And that, my friend, means you won't catch him unless or *until* he makes a mistake."

As much as Gaetke hated to admit it, there was a good chance Tackett was right.

* * *

Back at the Division— which was virtually deserted, with everyone out hitting the streets— he wrote a brief Field Contact Report regarding his conversation with Enrique Tackett. He tossed the duplicate in his Ongoing basket, and paper-clipped the original to the embryonic Wilson file, which he found on Matt Price's desk.

He couldn't help but notice that Matt had pulled the file on the little girl's father, Lewis Natchez Wilson. He glanced through it, counting five pages of priors which started with a breaking and entering at a public school at the tender age of eleven, and ended with a first-degree murder conviction at twenty-six, three years ago. A lot of it was relatively penny-ante stuff— joyriding, vandalism, drunk and disorderly, and assorted misdemeanors— but even so, it served as an accurate predictor of Wilson's inevitable slide into hard-core crime.

Felony assault, burglary, armed robbery, resisting arrest, attempted murder, and then, voila, the punk hit the big time with murder one.

Taken altogether it revealed Wilson's blatant disregard for the law and the rights of others. And that was only what he'd been charged with.

Gaetke closed the file and picked up a photocopy of Cassandra Wilson's school picture from a stack on the corner of the desk. Her sweet smile and hopeful eyes nearly broke his heart. "Poor kid."

Having forgone dinner, he took the elevator to the basement where the vending machines were. Surveying the selection while he dug into his pocket for a handful of change, he didn't turn at the sound of footsteps behind him. Not that he needed to; he could see Dr. Lauren Harper's reflection in the glass.

"You're working late," he said.

"I stopped by to pick up a book from my office." She stood close beside him, her arm brushing his as she reached in front of him to put quarters in the slot. "I'm buying. What'll you have?"

"Cheetos . . . and a Diet Coke."

"Very nutritious," Dr. Harper said as she pushed the button for the Cheetos, which dropped into the tray. At the soft drink machine, she fed assorted change to it until the red digital display totalled seventy-five cents. Handing him the can, she smiled and shook her head. "Fat and fake sugar, the essence of life."

Gaetke popped the top and took a long swallow of ice-cold Diet Coke. "It'll do in a pinch."

"Listen, I'm glad I ran into you. I want to apologize for biting your head off earlier."

He shrugged. "No harm, no foul."

"Still, I *am* sorry."

"Apology accepted." He tucked the unopened bag of Cheetos into his jacket pocket, and turned to leave. "Thanks for dinner."

"Billy, wait."

He looked at her curiously; she had never called him by his first name before. He was surprised she even knew what it was, for that matter.

"I want to talk to you," Lauren Harper said, "about Detective Price."

"Sorry, Dr. Harper, but I can't help you," Gaetke said. "If you have a question about Matt, you'd be better off going straight to him."

"I think it's fairly obvious he prefers not to confide in me."

"That doesn't make it my business."

"What I'm trying to avoid, Billy, is having to go over his head."

He hesitated, wondering if this was for real or a bluff, but she met his gaze unflinchingly, seemingly resolute. Then again, anyone who spent a lot of time around cops perfected "the look" sooner or later.

"Is this about Gennaro?" he asked. "Because if it is, I honestly can't help you. I was in uniform when that went down. I know less about it than you do."

"But you said— "

"I know what I said." He glanced out the door at the empty hall beyond, assuring himself that they were alone, that there was no one to overhear. "I was out of line. That business about Gennaro was my personal interpretation of the situation, period."

"Matt didn't mention— "

"No, he did not," Gaetke said, cutting her off. Then, thinking better of it, he favored her with a smile. "Look, I blew it, okay? It was a rookie mistake, running my mouth like that. It won't happen again."

Dr. Harper frowned. "What if this were to remain just between us, off the record?"

"It doesn't matter whether it's off the record or not. I have to work with him, you know?"

"Yes, but— "

"What it comes down to," he said, "is that I'll deny saying anything if anyone asks."

Her eyes flashed at that. "I understand that you might think that what I do is irrelevant, but I want you to know I'm on Matt's side."

"I can tell." He drained the Diet Coke and tossed the can in the recycling bin.

"Do you honestly think he should be on duty, if he's still having flashbacks?"

"He's a good cop, he can decide that for himself. Now, if you'll excuse me, I've got work to do." Gaetke headed for the stairs, hoping she wouldn't follow, but, of course, she did.

"It's not that simple," she called after him, the words echoing in the stairwell.

"Yeah, well, nothing ever is."

"Billy, wait— "

He ignored her, taking the stairs two at a time.

At the door to the Division offices he ran his ID card through the access reader and punched in the code. The lock disengaged and he was reaching for the door handle when she caught up.

"Billy, listen to me for a minute," Lauren Harper said, her gray eyes serious. "If you think I want to cause trouble for Matt, you're wrong. I know he's a good cop, but he's only human. Death has an effect on all of us— "

"I'm not trying to sound like a hard-ass, but it's part of the job. Shit happens, you know? It happens and you deal with it."

"But he's *not* dealing with it."

The lock had reengaged. Exasperated by her persistence, he fumbled his ID through the reader a second time, then drew a total blank on the code. "I can't think straight with you harassing me."

"Because you know I'm right. Matt could be endangering himself, risking his life, or yours. Or, god forbid, that of an innocent bystander on the street."

"You talking about me?" a familiar voice asked.

Billy Gaetke hit the doorframe with his fist, then leaned forward to rest his head on his still-clenched hand, closing his eyes momentarily while trying to convince himself that it wasn't Matt asking the question.

But it was.

Matt had gotten off the elevator and was walking

down the hall towards them, a manila folder in his hand. Even at a distance, Gaetke could read the name on the file: Wilson, Zeke Juarez.

"What's the problem?" Matt asked.

The man did not look happy.

"I'm outta here," Billy Gaetke said, raising his hands as he backed away.

Six

Zeke Wilson stood by the window, gazing out at the street where he'd spent practically every summer day of his youth. The houses in the neighborhood were small by current standards, but the yards were big and there were lush, full-grown maple trees lining the street that kept it tolerable even on scorching hot afternoons.

Not a bad place to live, though most folks in La Campana considered it to be on the wrong side of the tracks, figuratively speaking. The racial mix had always been eclectic; he'd learned to curse in Spanish from a Cuban neighbor, mastered chopsticks at his best friend Mike Choi's house, and fractured the little finger on his right hand helping Carlos Guiterrez install the hydraulics in his lowrider, a candy apple red Chevy Bel Air. His own mixed pedigree— Shoshone Indian, African-American, and Scots-Irish— blended right in.

A working-class neighborhood, striving to move up and out, although almost no one had, yet. On the other hand, of the kids he'd grown up with, only his big brother had strayed from the straight and narrow.

Leave it to Lewis to buck the trend.

As tenacious a woman as their mother was, Lewis's escalating troubles had nearly broken her spirit. Cassie's disappearance— and what probably was the child's ultimate fate— might finish the job.

But not if he could help it. "Damn the son-of-a-bitch who did this."

"I'll second that."

Zeke closed the curtains before turning. "How is she?" he asked.

Doc Bigelow shook his head. "The woman amazes me. Fifty-nine years old and strong as a Kentucky mule. Of course, it figures she's stubborn as one, too."

Zeke did his best to smile. "Wouldn't take anything, would she?"

"No. She said she'd sleep when the good Lord let her. She promised to stay in bed for a while, though, and rest." Doc rummaged through his black bag and extracted a strip of blister-packed tablets, pink in color, which he placed on the coffee table. "I'll leave these with you anyway, just in case."

"Thanks."

Dr. Bigelow started for the door, but then hesitated. "How about you, Zeke? How are you doing? Still got that headache?"

Zeke pinched the bridge of his nose between his index finger and thumb, and winced. He could hear the soft *whoosh* of his pulse in his ears, and feel his heartbeat in the follicles of his scalp. "More like it's got me. Jet lag, I guess."

"Want something for it?"

"Nah. What I need is some fresh air. Maybe I'll take a walk around the block— "

"I gather the reporters left?"

"They must have; I didn't see anyone outside just now." The wind direction had shifted during the evening to an on-shore flow, changing the weather from balmy and mild to damp and downright bone-chilling.

The cluster of reporters who'd assembled at the end of the driveway had scattered into the night.

"Not even the police?"

Zeke made no attempt to disguise his cynicism. "Not even a meter maid."

"Well, I guess it's better that every available officer is looking for Cassandra."

Zeke nodded but reserved comment. Only months and a bar exam away from being an attorney, he considered himself on the same side as law enforcement more often than not, but he had doubts as to the quality of the local police department's effort thus far.

He couldn't shake his recollections of several high-profile kidnappings in recent years, in particular that one up north in Petaluma, wherein an army of patrolmen had feverishly prowled the streets, going door to door, and the detectives in charge more or less set up a command post in the family's home.

Was it only certain victims who merited such an all-out endeavor? Certain photogenic, blue-eyed victims? He hated to think so, but . . .

"Call me," the good doctor said, "if you need anything, you hear?"

"You'll be the first."

The house was unnaturally quiet, to the extent that he felt obliged to make the odd noise as he wandered through the silent rooms. He rapped his knuckles on the mahogany dining-room table, picked up— and quickly muted— the brass cowbell in the kitchen that his mother had used to call Lewis and him to dinner when they were boys. In the family room, he turned on the television set to find the late news ending.

"Join us tomorrow morning on our A.M. edition, when we'll have more on this evening's top story," the anchor said. "The discovery of the body of Lucy Marie Bosworth in the wake of yet another disappearance— "

Zeke switched it off before they mentioned Cassie. He wasn't superstitious, really, but all things considered, he'd rather not tempt fate by hearing his niece's name spoken by a stranger.

He went to the back bedroom to look in on his mother. She was facing away from him, but her deep, even breathing at least mimicked sleep. He watched her for a moment, taking comfort in her nearness.

He was by no means unbiased, but in his eyes, his mother was a most remarkable woman. Born into poverty, she'd worked hard all of her life, starting out as a fifteen-year-old piecework seamstress at a sweatshop garment factory in Oklahoma. After moving to California three years later, she took a job as a domestic, and basically spent her twenties and thirties on her hands and knees, scrubbing and waxing rich folk's floors.

At twenty-eight, she'd married their father, Calvin, of whom she said little except that even good men suffered temptation. Woefully tempted, Calvin Wilson had drifted in and out of the marriage before he died of peritonitis in a jail cell in Tiajuana, Mexico. Zeke never knew the man; his mother was pregnant with him when she got word she'd been widowed.

Then, at forty, when Lewis was ten and he was six, she went back to school for a high school diploma, after which she enrolled in a trade school, where she studied interior design. By the age of forty-five, she had started her own business, Custom Corner, which might have afforded the family a better standard of living had not Lewis gotten into trouble so often and at such great expense.

Always a hands-on type— the woman could knock down a wall in a New York minute —she'd been work-

ing at the site of a kitchen refurbish this afternoon.
The building inspector had been late for their one-
thirty appointment, and then had taken his sweet-ass
civil service time checking and signing off on the elec-
trical and plumbing. By the time he left, she'd missed
her crosstown bus.

She had never learned to drive— cars were about the
only thing he knew of that intimidated his mother—
and so had little alternative but to call a cab, which she
didn't have the cash for, or wait for the next bus.

By the time she arrived at Northcliffe Academy, Cassie had disappeared.

Pausing at the door to the second bedroom— Cassie's
room now— which he'd once shared with his brother,
he wondered why he didn't *hurt* more. Whether from
simple exhaustion or jet lag or emotional overload, the
fact was, he felt distant from it all. Numb.

And guilty as hell because of it.

In the kitchen, the phone rang. The answering machine would pick up if he let it, but grateful for the
distraction, Zeke headed that way.

"Is this the Wilson residence?" a slightly nasal voice
asked.

"Yes."

"Any relation to the little girl?"

Zeke frowned. "We'll have a statement first thing
in the morning, but right now we're not talking to the
press. If you— "

"I'm not the press. Who are you?"

His initial impulse was to hang up, but he didn't.
"I'm Cassie's uncle. Who are *you?*"

The man laughed nastily. "I'd have to be crazy to
answer that now, wouldn't I? Considering that I've got
the girl."

A prank call, he thought, but what if it wasn't? The police had pretty much dismissed the possibility that Cassie had been taken for ransom, but Northcliffe was an exclusive school, and the kidnapper might have figured any kid who went there had to come from money.

In which case, he had no choice but to play this through. "What did you say?"

"You heard me. You know where Fielder's Park is?"

"Yes."

"I'll meet you there in fifteen minutes. You'd better come alone."

"But— "

"You've got fifteen minutes. Don't call the police, don't even think about it."

"I have no money— "

"This is a *negotiation*, my friend. Fourteen minutes and forty-five seconds. And I meant what I said about coming alone. We'll be watching."

The phone went dead.

Zeke pressed the switchhook and got a dial tone. He punched out 911, but hung up before the connection was made and the line started to ring.

Clever of them, he thought, to give him so little time to react. Or to *think*, for that matter. On a gut level, he suspected that this might be a trap. Or an elaborate hoax, devised solely for the sick satisfaction of the caller. Some people got off on other folks' misery.

Trap or hoax, he couldn't play it safe at the risk of Cassie's life. He had to go.

Fielder's Park was halfway across town; if he didn't leave now, he'd never make it there in time. As it was, fourteen minutes wouldn't allow him to observe the niceties, like obeying traffic signals and speed limits.

※ ※ ※

He wheeled his Suzuki out of the garage and down to the street before starting it, in what was probably a vain hope that his mother wouldn't hear.

The engine caught but sputtered, and he gave it a little gas, revving until the stroke evened out. He hadn't been on a bike since his last visit home, at Christmas, but riding was second nature to him, and after gliding to the end of the block, he roared off into the night.

His helmet visor was tinted, giving the city a surreal look. Friday night or not, there wasn't much traffic, and he made good time on the freeway.

Nearing the exit to Fielder's Park, he had a moment to consider what might be awaiting him. The location was ideal from the kidnapper's point of view, since there was only the one road in or out, and that curved down into the valley. He would doubtless be watched every inch of the way.

On the other hand, a police blockade of the road near the top would trap all of them. Except, of course, he hadn't called the police.

Ignoring the icy sensation in the pit of his stomach, he drove onto the park grounds. The parking area was gravel, and he slowed, his tires crunching rock. There were four light poles at even intervals, casting an eerie purplish light on the vacant lot.

Zeke saw no one, but parked anyway. He took off his helmet and propped it on the handlebars, then ran a hand over his sweat-drenched face.

There was a baseball diamond nearby, complete with wood bleachers. He thought he saw movement up on the top row. He got off the bike, engaged the kickstand, and walked slowly in that direction.

"That's close enough," someone said from off to his left. "Stop where you are."

Zeke stopped. "Where's Cassie?"

"I'll ask the questions, if you don't mind."

He started to turn towards the voice, when he heard the rustle of footsteps through drying grass ahead and to his right. So there were two of them, at least. The chill in his belly sent a shiver through him. This was not looking good.

"And watch your eyes. Don't look at us."

"Whatever you want," he agreed, staring straight ahead. "But . . . is she all right?"

The second one snorted and said, "Yeah, she's just dandy. We're, like, running a day camp. She's having the time of her life."

"Shut up," the first guy said.

Zeke caught a glimpse of him from the corner of his eye. On the short side and kind of stocky, he wore dark clothing and a ski mask, and was carrying a base-ball bat. "What do you want me to do?"

"It's pretty simple. Give us a hundred thousand dollars, and we'll give you the kid."

"A hundred thou— there's no way!"

"There better be a way, my friend."

Until this very moment, he had never considered violence to be a justifiable response, whatever the provocation, but it took every ounce of self-restraint in his being not to give into the urge to try and cram that "my friend" down the bastard's throat.

"You don't understand," he said instead, calmly. "If I had it, I'd give it to you, but— "

"Hey, we're not idiots. You ain't got that much money sitting around the house, but we'll give you maybe a week to raise it. Borrow the money or steal it, I don't give a fuck which. To save the little girl's life, no? A bargain, I'd say."

His mouth went suddenly dry. Despite a partial scholarship, he owed close to forty thousand dollars in student loans, and had only a single credit card which he'd nearly maxed out booking his airfare to come home. His mother's house was mortgaged to the hilt, and there was even a lien against it filed by Lewis's attorney, for unpaid costs related to his last appeal.

". . . or you know what you could do?" the second guy was saying. "You could go on one of those shows. Oprah or Geraldo, you know? Cry a little, give 'em a sob story, and people be sending you buckets of cash."

And the two of them laughed.

For the first time in his life, he understood what it meant to see red. Zeke lunged sideways and swung without thinking, his logical mind having shut down. He struck the first one a glancing blow to the side of the head, and spun to kick at the other.

He should never have turned his back on the bat.

The first swing caught him in the ribs, which sent white hot splinters of pain racing along the bone to his sternum and spine. Before he could move, the bat smacked into his right shoulder, numbing it like an externally applied dose of Novocaine.

He dropped to his knees and raised his left arm to protect his head.

The second guy kicked him in the stomach, hard. Zeke tried for the guy's leg, hoping to grab it and put him on his back, but wasn't fast enough.

Guessing that the stocky one would swing at his now-unprotected head, he fell face forward onto the gravel, and tried to scramble away. Only there was nowhere to go; a third man had joined the others— had he been watching from the bleachers?— and he was trapped.

The beating played out in slow motion, accompanied by the sound of heavy breathing. Mostly kicks now that he was on the ground. He stopped fighting, primarily to keep them from finding cause to kill him, drew his body into a fetal position for protection, and tried to will himself into unconsciousness.

Eventually they stopped.

Only then did he pass out.

When he came to, they were gone, and so was his bike. His pockets were turned inside out and emptied. Somehow he got to his feet and immediately regretted it; he was nearly overcome by a wave of dizziness and nausea, and began to shake.

He tasted blood, and smelled it. He could feel it oozing from his nose. Running his tongue around the inside of his mouth, he was surprised not to find loosened teeth or worse. He spit on the gravel; the purple light made the blood appear black.

"Damn," he swore softly, and bent over at the waist. It took a minute, but his stomach spasmed and he vomited the bitter remains of the airline dinner. A case of dry heaves followed.

When his belly quieted, he straightened up and used his shirttail to wipe his face. He took a couple of slow, deep breaths, and gingerly ran his fingers over his skull. Not finding any apparent lacerations was small comfort, given that his entire body was a tender mass of abrasions and contusions.

The muscles of his back were tight as a drum, and he had a dull ache in the vicinity of his kidneys, which probably meant he'd be pissing blood for days. His spine was sore as the devil right above the tailbone, and he had what felt like a pulled hamstring in his left thigh.

That was the good news.

The bad news was he had to somehow get home from here, or at the very least find a phone to call the police. Good thing 911 calls were free; they hadn't left him twenty cents to call anyone otherwise.

What had he said to Doc Bigelow about fresh air

and a walk? He'd had a fair measure of the first, and had an uphill allotment of the second to look forward to.

"Hasn't done much for my headache so far," he said, and started to walk slowly towards the road.

Seven

Simon Avery retrieved his nylon gym bag from the back seat of the Caprice and set it on the hood of the car, where he wouldn't overlook it on the way into the house. Using a flashlight, he searched under the seat for anything he might have missed when he had removed the plastic shower curtain from the floor up front.

Nothing that he could see, not as much as a broken button or wayward thread.

He closed the back door and locked it, then slipped into the front passenger seat and reached over to his cleaning supplies in the blue bucket atop the console. He removed the cap from a bottle of 409, adjusted the nozzle, and sprayed the dashboard half a dozen times, not much caring that it dripped onto his month-old floor mats while he unwound a few paper towels from a roll.

His mother had always sworn by Formula 409.

He worked methodically, spraying and wiping every surface several times, tossing the soiled paper towels onto the garage floor. Humming all the while, he used an old toothbrush to get into the tight spots— another of his mother's cleaning tips— until the interior was as spotless as it had been this morning.

When that was done, he unlocked the glove box, and removed a sealed plastic Glad-Lock bag— "yellow and blue make green"— which contained one of his monogrammed handkerchiefs. When he'd taken it from his dresser drawer this morning, it had been an immaculate white, ironed just so, and neatly folded. Now it was crumpled into an unsightly wad, and there was a faint stain where the liquid, although colorless, had dried.

Since he knew next to nothing about how sophisticated the police laboratory was at testing for residual substances, the handkerchief would have to be destroyed. Wasteful, but hardly a tragedy, since he had a hundred or more exactly like it. His dear departed mother, may she rest in eternal peace, had considered a boxed set of handkerchiefs as the ideal gift for any and all occasions; slap a bow on the box, and that was that.

"The perfect gift should be personal and practical, without being presumptuous," Mother would always say, quite unintentionally alliterative.

He took a cautious sniff at the seal of the bag, but smelled nothing. Even so, he figured, better to be safe than sorry, so he placed the Glad-Lock inside a wax-lined paper bag that he'd saved from his last deli take-out and rolled it up; in a week or two, after allowing for evaporation, he would toss bags and handkerchief in with the yard trash and burn them. For now, he slipped it in his rear pants pocket. That way, if there were any lingering fumes, they wouldn't drift up to his nose.

You could never be too careful with ether, he knew. While it wasn't a notoriously fast anesthetic, it was an effective one. Of course, its flammability and reactivity to light was something of a drawback, but it was relatively safe for his purposes, and more to the point, he hadn't found anything he liked better.

The side effects were a tad unsettling— nausea and vomiting, excessive thirst, headache, plus all that drooling— but since *he* wasn't the one suffering from them, he thought it tolerable.

After closing the glove box, he took a final look around and ran through a mental checklist. The shower curtain *cum* catch-sheet had gone through the washing machine with extra detergent and bleach. The lap blanket that he used as cover during transport was even now tumbling in the dryer.

All surfaces which might hold a fingerprint had been wiped clean. Tomorrow he'd take the Caprice— which didn't in the least resemble the "suspect" dark green van the police were mistakenly searching for— in for its regular monthly car wash and carpet shampoo . . . and, of course, he'd replace the floor mats.

Yes, okay. Check and double check.

Roger, wilco, et cetera and et cetera.

He returned the cleaning materials to the bucket, which he placed in the deep sink at the rear of the garage, near his mother's old wringer-washing machine, which he'd had the audacity to replace with a top-of-the-line Maytag washer and dryer. He collected the used paper towels and threw them in the garbage can.

Finally, he locked the car, grabbed his gym bag, and started up the stairs to the kitchen door. There he paused again, unable to resist a last look to assure himself that he had indeed restored order. Thus reassured, he turned off the garage light and went inside.

Simon Avery walked silently down the hall that led to the News on Demand offices in the west wing of the

U-shaped house. The second shift of typists worked from 3 P.M. to 11 P.M., and everyone was long gone, but even so he did not wish to make any unnecessary noise.

If one made it a rule to be quiet always, being quiet came easily.

Another of his mother's charming homilies.

To which he would add: quiet or loud, a healthy touch of paranoia makes it that much more difficult for your enemies to get to you.

At the door to NOD— a fitting acronym if ever he'd heard one— he put his ear to the wood and listened for a few seconds, before pulling the keys from his pocket. After unlocking both dead bolts, he pushed the door gently, letting it swing inward.

Nothing stirred.

The cassette he'd picked up earlier this evening from KOUT sat exactly where he'd left it, on top of the computer at the first desk. Tomorrow morning, his weekend girl, Sharon, would watch and listen to the newscast and prepare a printed transcript of that tape, as well as the usual Saturday dreck.

It never ceased to amaze him how many people were willing to pay good money for transcripts of the most inane material; one of his longtime subscribers was an absolute sucker for human interest stories, the kind of sappy, syrupy, feel-good stuff Charles Kuralt had done so incredibly well, and his legion of imitators did not.

Human interest wasn't his cup of tea, to be sure, but there was no accounting for taste, Avery thought, and took the KOUT cassette into the next room.

In this room beat the heart of NOD, a bank of forty VCRs, each loaded with a six-hour extended play tape. Each VCR was programmed to record selected channels at scheduled hours throughout the day and night, although four of the machines were "dedicated" solely to CNN, and another three to the hot rage, Court TV, taping every precious minute of every broadcast.

One of the VCRs, a Panasonic, had eaten its tape, thus necessitating his jaunt earlier this evening over to KOUT. The Panasonic was off-line, its distinctive blue LED dark, but the repairman would be by on Monday. Until then he'd parceled out its programming, half an hour here, half an hour there . . . a messy but adequate accommodation.

NOD also had a video editing machine, albeit a less advanced model than KOUT used. He sat at the console and inserted the cassette in the source slot. He'd brought his own master tape— which he hid from prying eyes in the fireproof safe in his office— and he carefully fed it into the "B" slot.

Not quite as adept at this as Dakota Smith was, he dithered and fumbled a little before hitting Play on A and Record on B. Then he sat back, watching the images he was transferring. The monitor was black and white, which gave the footage a newsreel quality that he found unexpectedly appealing.

It felt like . . . history.

This was actually volume two, chronicling the news coverage since the beginning of his exploits. Volume one, which he'd shot himself with his Fuji Hi8 8mm Camcorder was more . . . intimate . . . in nature.

He hadn't allowed himself to really enjoy either tape yet, or view them all the way through. He struggled daily to build his character through rigorous self-denial, but one day soon, he intended to *indulge* by sitting down with a big bowl of buttered popcorn and a Dr Pepper poured over shaved ice, and luxuriate in every glorious moment of his little adventure.

Until then, well. Anticipation, drawn out to the edge of sweet agony, could be every bit as delicious and satisfying as indulgence

For a while, anyway.

Avery smiled at his faint reflection in the monitor screen. Wouldn't his mother be astounded at what he'd done? At the nerve and initiative her "meek little mouse" of a son had shown?

Horrified is more like it.

Avery flinched, but it hardly came as a surprise that The Good Simon would want to put in his two cents worth. The Good Simon had never been shy about criticizing aspects of *his* personality.

The Good Simon did not subscribe to the If-you-can't-say-something-nice theory of human relations. The Good Simon had no qualms about hurting any-one's feelings.

To put it mildly, The Good Simon was a nudge.

Avery chose to ignore him, and started humming, which for reasons unknown shielded him from unwelcome intrusions into his brain. Gershwin tunes worked well, but the early Beatles songs were by far the best.

Rap and hard rock, by comparison, were so full of hatred and savagery that they elicited in him a sense of deep self-loathing, which, of course, was playing right into The Good Simon's hands.

Couldn't have that.

He'd reached the end of the KOUT tape. Humming "Yellow Submarine," he stopped the VCRs and hit both eject buttons simultaneously.

Avery replaced his master in its padded case, and took the KOUT tape back to the transcriber's desk. A minute later he locked the door and headed for the living side of the house.

One last task before bed . . . no, actually two.

Positioned at the center of the property, the house was a fair distance from the streets surrounding it.

Street noise only rarely could be heard from inside, and he knew from the stereo experiments he'd done that no sounds from inside would ever, ever reach the street.

The windows were triple-paned, which provided a measure of soundproofing closer in. And in March he had recaulked the windows and applied smoke-colored reflective film to the glass for added privacy.

Of course, privacy could be assured in other ways: there were no windows in the basement "guest" room, and the entrance was concealed behind a heavy built-in bookcase in his bedroom, formerly his father's study. It had been a wine cellar once upon a time— the Avery family tree was rife with closet drinkers— and he guessed his father, too, had sought solace in a bottle, out of view of his mother's disapproving eyes.

Mother, quite naturally, disapproved of a good many things. The use of spirits or tobacco. Wagering on games of chance. And, most of all, what she referred delicately to as "men's urges."

But Mother evidently hadn't known the cellar room existed; even now he got a tingle of pleasure at that naughty fact. He'd come across it by accident, while climbing the bookcase to retrieve a dog-eared pornographic magazine he'd hidden from her on the top shelf.

He'd been sixteen then, he was thirty-three now. The secret he'd kept for more than half of his life was serving him well.

He meant to keep it that way.

Avery went out with the flashlight and walked the perimeter of the estate. It was cool tonight, the wind brisk enough to bring tears to his eyes. Head lowered, he made his way from corner to corner, shining the light along the eight-foot-high cinder-block wall to check for anything amiss.

At the front of the property, he went into the gatehouse, which in his great-grandfather's day had been manned from dusk to dawn by a guard. Now there was a security panel at car-door level, the transcribers alone had the code, which was changed frequently. All others had to announce themselves via the intercom, and be buzzed in through the wrought-iron gates.

It was his practice to lock down the system at night, so the code wouldn't work and no one could get in. Sometimes it seemed like a bother, since he had to make sure to get up early in the morning to turn it back on before his first employee arrived at seven.

However, tomorrow would be no problem; he didn't expect to get any sleep tonight. For that matter, he hadn't slept more than a couple of hours a night since March.

Since before.

The bookcase swung ponderously away from the wall, revealing the tiny vestibule which fronted the stairs. Avery switched on the light and pulled the bookcase closed again, securing it from the inside with a thick brass hasp. He turned the swivel plate and inserted a padlock, but didn't lock it.

If he were as light on his feet as felt in his heart, he would have danced down the stairs—

Like a paunchy, pasty-faced, balding Fred Astaire, The Good Simon said.

"Shut up, shut up, shut up," he chirped, and began to hum "Penny Lane."

Another door at the bottom, with a one-way glass inset that allowed him to see into the guest room without being seen.

It was dark in there, with only plastic Little Mer-
maid nightlights plugged into wall outlets, but he saw
the child roughly where he had left her, on her side
so fluid wouldn't pool in her lungs, a trio of pillows
propped behind her on the bed. She appeared to be
unconscious still, or perhaps merely asleep.

Avery slowly opened the door; the child didn't move.

He took a cautious step into the room, and breathed
the same air she did. He felt almost giddy, as if he
might swoon, but found the strength to take another
step closer to her.

What a dazzling child! Much prettier than the others, he'd outdone himself this time. That tawny skin
and the lush fullness of her lower lip. To think he
might not have found her at all. Going to Northcliffe
Academy this afternoon had been a dangerous impulse, but—

His little treasure groaned, startling him. Her eyes
remained shut, but the muscles of her slender throat
moved spasmodically, as if on the verge of vomiting.

Avery had no desire to witness that. Bad enough
that he'd have to clean up after her in the morning,
if she were to be sick.

Regretfully, he backed away.

Eight

Cassie waited for what seemed like a long time after the door closed, before opening her eyes.

There wasn't much light, but her eyes had adjusted and she could see fairly well, well enough to know she wasn't anywhere she'd ever been before, nor anywhere she wanted to be. The room was bigger than her bedroom at Grandma's, but not as nice.

There was no white ruffled canopy over the bed, no hand-woven rug on the floor, no dollhouse in the corner. Her stuffed animals weren't here to cuddle with, and there wasn't a window seat, lined with comfy pillows, from which to look out on the backyard.

There wasn't even a window, unless you counted the one in the door.

There was, instead, one of those portable toilets partially hidden behind a bamboo screen. Even from here, the smell was so strong it made her wrinkle her nose. The smell was all the worse, because she knew she'd have to use the bathroom soon.

On a table sat a pitcher of water, next to a large glass bowl. A wrapped bar of soap. a stack of hand towels, and washcloths folded into triangles were arranged beside the bowl.

A ceiling fan turned lazily overhead.

A row of wooden pegs high on one wall served as the

closet, she guessed; a dark-colored sweater hung from one of five pegs.

The bed was kind of small, like a cot she'd slept on the summer Grandma had taken her back to Oklahoma to visit the family, before the bad times began. All the cousins had slept on cots, lined two deep on Great-gram's screened-in porch.

And that was it.

Except for the man. She hadn't looked at him, not even a peek.

Cassie was scared of him, but angry, too.

He was the one who'd brought her here. She had noticed him on the street in front of the school, looking into a cardboard box and laughing to himself. It was then she heard a kitten meowing.

Oh, but she had to see!

A glance over her shoulder confirmed that no one was watching. She didn't know where her teacher had gone, but it didn't matter.

She approached the man hesitantly, and might have kept her distance except that he picked up the box and took it to his car. The meowing seemed to grow louder as he put the box in the back seat. He was about to shut the door, when he saw her standing there.

"Want a look?"

He had a nice voice, quiet and friendly. His smile reached his eyes, unlike some grown-ups she knew. He wasn't mean-looking, like the men she saw the time Grandma took her to visit her daddy in prison.

There was a little sweat on his forehead and upper lip, but it was a warm day . . .

Scratching sounds from inside the box, like a kitten trying to climb out.

Cassie couldn't resist.

Her last memory was of looking into the box and seeing one of those toy kittens, the kind with batteries that could

*walk and meow. Then the man put his hand over her mouth
and nose.*

*Something wet in his hand. She drew in her breath to
scream, and everything went black.*

The man had brought her here.

*He'd taken off her tennis shoes, but not her socks or any-
thing else.*

*Cassie sat up. Her head hurt. Her throat felt raw and
scratchy, and her tummy ached. She wanted badly to go
home, but knew in her heart that the man wouldn't let her,
whether she asked nicely or not.*

*Mrs. Rifkin, the school principal, had talked to her class
about staying safe, after those other little girls had disappeared. They'd watched a short movie that had warned
against getting in a stranger's car or letting anyone in the
house, if you were home alone.*

*There'd even been a part of the movie where a man asked
kids on a playground if they would please help him find his
lost puppy, Scamp. There wasn't a puppy— like there hadn't
been a kitten— even though the man had shown the children
a picture of the puppy, and its leash, and had given them
dog biscuits to feed poor hungry Scamp.*

*All of that was pretending, Mrs. Rifkin said, to fool the
kids into going off with the man. And what were they to do,
if someone tried to fool them?*

Run and scream.

Cassie hadn't done either.

*Her Grandma always told her she was a smart and brave
little girl. She had been scared lots of times and hadn't cried,
mostly because crying never really changed anything. And
she was smart, or she wouldn't be at Northcliffe, which only
took gifted kids.*

*Somehow, she would have to get out of here, away from
the man.*

Sitting on the narrow bed, worrying her loose front tooth with her tongue, she tried to do as Grandma had taught her, and think it through.

SATURDAY

Nine

Price stood up to put on his jacket and leave, when the phone rang. An unwelcome interruption, the most recent of many. He grabbed the receiver before the second ring. "Major Crimes Unit, Detective Price."

"Are you in early this morning," Captain Salcedo asked, "or did you work all night?"

Same difference, he thought, but said, "What can I do for you, Captain?"

"A couple of things. We have a press conference set for noon—"

"Tell me I don't have to be there."

"You don't have to be there," Salcedo said. "But I need you to bring me up to speed on Wilson."

"Right." Price yawned as he pressed his thumb and forefinger against his eyes, which burned and itched from the lack of sleep. At the same time, he was carrying quite a buzz from an excess of caffeine. The combination was unsettling, if not totally unfamiliar.

"We released the crime scene," he said, "if you can call it that. The techs went over the area with a fine-tooth comb, didn't find much of anything. No gum wrappers, no candy wrappers, not even a stray cigarette butt to test for saliva."

"Damn."

"Exactly." Evidence collection techniques and analysis had improved over the last few years, but the techs couldn't collect or analyze what wasn't there in the first place. "If this sick, sorry bastard was hanging around the neighborhood for as many hours as the teacher claims, he was uncommonly neat about it."

"Or she's mistaken."

"Or she's mistaken," Price agreed, "and this was a grab-and-go, which is certainly well within the realm of possibility. Regardless, we've got virtually no physical evidence."

"And no witnesses, again."

Price chose not to disabuse him of that notion, although he knew Lauren Harper believed that Danielle Falk might have seen more than she remembered.

"Can this guy be that lucky?" Salcedo asked.

"Maybe, but luck can run out," Price said dryly. "And his is bound to, sooner or later."

"Pray it's sooner," the captain sighed. "Anything else I need to know?"

"Well . . . there was a bogus ransom demand."

"That we don't need." The irritation in the captain's voice matched his own. "Damned bloodsuckers are coming out of the woodwork these days. You'd think they were reporters. So what's the damage?"

Price treated him to an abbreviated version of Zeke Wilson's ordeal. Wilson had been brought in by a patrol unit shortly after being picked up; an elderly woman had called in to report a suspicious man "lurking" in her neighborhood at 1:00 A.M.

Though bruised and battered, Wilson had given a lucid and cogent three-page statement— to the utter amazement of them all— detailing what was obviously a blatant attempt at extortion. He'd subsequently been driven home after refusing Gaetke's offer of a ride to

County General's Emergency Room for medical treatment.

"Thinks he's Superman, does he?" Salcedo asked with a gravelly chuckle.

"I doubt if he does anymore. He got his ass kicked." Loathe as he was to admit it, Price had been moderately impressed by Evangeline Wilson's younger son, Harvard law student or not.

"Gotta wonder, don't you, what the world's coming to. Civilians trying to do our jobs."

"I suppose. Not to change the subject, but the Bosworth autopsy is this morning . . ."

"You'll be there?"

"I'm leaving as soon as I get off the phone."

"I want to hear from you on the preliminary findings, understand?" Salcedo, fellow street cop, had reverted in an instant to Salcedo, top brass.

"Yes sir," Price said.

The forensic pathologist assigned to the Bosworth post was Dr. Peter Soo, a whip-thin Korean who rollerbladed to work each day in fluorescent Spandex bicycle shorts. That was, however, his only personality quirk; on the job Soo had a reputation for being thorough and meticulous. Nothing got by him.

Ever.

Equally as important, Soo made an excellent witness in court, one of the few pathologists Price had worked with who was able to bridge the expert/layman gap that separated scientist from jury. Soo also had the rare ability to impart dignity to the victim after death; his testimony often moved the jurors to tears.

Drawing Soo felt like a good omen. Lucy was in kind, caring hands.

Nevertheless, Price wasn't looking forward to this.

He scooped a dab of Vicks out of its distinctive blue jar with his little finger, and applied it under his nose. It would, in theory, take the edge off the ripe autopsy smells . . . and maybe clear his head.

The postmortem exam began promptly at seven o'clock.

"The body," Dr. Soo said, his accent barely detectable behind his mask, "is that of a Caucasian female child, whose remains are consistent with the stated age of eight. Weight at autopsy is approximately forty-two pounds and length, that is, height, is fifty-one inches. On visual examination, we find that decomposition is in an advanced stage, with significant loss of soft tissue resulting. There is marked skeletonization of the extremities, and most of the small bones of the hands and feet are missing . . ."

Price stood at a distance from the stainless-steel table on which the child lay. He closed his eyes briefly. This wasn't the first time he'd been present at a child's autopsy, and it almost certainly wouldn't be the last, but invariably he had to remind himself that the child's suffering was long over.

"The hair is straight, red, and shoulder-length. It is matted with soil and organic detritus, particles of leaves and twigs. In the hair, two centimeters above the helix of the right ear, there is a blue plastic and white metal, um, clip—"

"Barrette," Price said quietly. "It's called a barrette."

"Barrette, yes."

Soo went on, but Price was only half-listening, thinking instead of the matching barrette, which he had in Evidence. It had been found at the scene of the abduction back in March, on the sidewalk, around the corner and down the block from the child's home.

Within shouting distance, he'd thought at the time. Evelyn Bosworth had asked for the barrette, then, and he'd had to refuse her. He would have to refuse her still if she asked again, even now that her daughter had been found. Lucy's personal effects would not be released until after the trial . . . assuming that they ever caught the guy who did this and it went to trial.

"External evidence of injury," Dr. Soo was saying, "is hindered by the degree of decomposition and the, um, evident infestation of various types of insects, both in larval and pupal stages, and the predation by scavenger animals and/or birds."

Price averted his eyes momentarily, and shook his head. Dead or not, no one should be left the way Lucy was, in a culvert like so much trash. He would get this bastard, or die trying.

"There is, however, enough tissue remaining on the face to detect the presence of a significant number of petechial hemorrhages— "

Those were pinpoint, dark red spots caused by the rupture of capillaries, Price knew.

"— perhaps indicative of acute anoxia."

"She was strangled?" he asked, not bothering to disguise the anger in his voice.

Dr. Soo didn't look up. "There are no ligature marks, nor do I see fingernail marks that would be consistent with manual strangulation. Suffocated perhaps, it's too early to tell. Be patient, Detective."

"Do I have a choice?"

"No," the pathologist said. "And neither do I. It takes as long as it takes."

* * *

It took ninety-odd minutes to finish the autopsy. Price waited in Soo's office, while the doctor went to the lounge to change into a fresh set of surgical greens.

"Well?" he asked when Dr. Soo came into the room, "what do you think?"

Peter Soo sat behind the desk. "What I think is the child died of acute anoxia or traumatic asphyxiation. Petechial hemorrhages were present within the pericardium membrane of the heart, and, of course, the lungs. There was also right-sided cardiac congestion, and some indication of venous engorgement, which is characteristic of asphyxia, as is the cyanosis . . . so yes, Detective, I think we can conclude she was suffocated."

"By what means?"

The pathologist shook his head. "I can't be sure, but due to the absence of bruising or other contusions, and since the hyoid wasn't fractured and the larynx and trachea weren't crushed . . . I would guess a pillow or other soft object, held over her face."

"Was she awake when he killed her?"

"I have no way of knowing, but if so, she would have lost consciousness rather quickly. It wouldn't have taken long, smothering a child that age. And in this kind of thing, there's always the possibility that she might have been drugged."

"Son of a bitch."

"You'll have my complete report by Wednesday, although the toxicological results won't be available for several weeks— "

"Can you tell if he assaulted her?"

"Sexually?" Dr. Soo frowned, leaning back in his chair. "Not at this late date, no. The body was too decomposed to evaluate for specific tissue damage."

"How about a time of death?"

"By which I hope you mean the approximate *date*

of death. The best I can do is estimate . . . between four and six weeks."

"He had her for a month, then. Lucy was alive for at least that long."

Dr. Soo inclined his head in agreement. "Yes, so it seems."

"And afterwards . . . he found another one," Price said, thinking of the Kraft girl. "He took Rachel to replace Lucy. And now he has Cassandra, which probably means that Rachel is dead, too."

The pathologist stood. "I don't envy you your job, Detective."

Price squinted at the bright sunlight as he walked across the morgue parking lot towards his car. Someone fell in step behind him. He didn't turn to look; he knew damned well who it was.

"Detective Price," Dakota Smith said, "if I could have a moment of your time?"

He'd been warned that members of the press were in the vicinity, and hoped that leaving by the rear exit would allow him to avoid them. No such luck. "I'm busy."

"No shit."

Price smiled, but kept walking. "Call the Department, if you want a statement."

"I'd rather talk to you."

"Except I've got nothing to say." Nearing the car, he reached for his keys.

Ms. Smith maneuvered her way in front of him, insinuating herself between him and the car. "Come on, pretty please with sugar on top? A couple of minutes is all I need."

"That's more than I can spare." He eased her aside.

"You wouldn't want me to be derelict in my duty now, would you?"

"I wouldn't mind, if it'll get me a story."

"You *are* corrupt," he said, but laughed anyway at her apparent candor.

"What can I say? I'm shameless. I have to be."

His brain obviously was softening in his old age; he was almost tempted to answer a question or two. Almost. Price unlocked the car door and got in. "The official statement will be out at noon."

"Not even a hint?"

"Sorry."

She held onto the car door, which kept him from closing it. "I've been wondering, you know, about what this means for Rachel."

That stopped him cold. "Rachel?"

"Is she dead, do you think?"

In his mind, he heard his own voice say: *He took Rachel to replace Lucy. And now he has Cassandra, which probably means that Rachel is dead, too.*

It didn't require a leap of logic to come to the conclusion Dakota Smith had, but it struck him as an eerie coincidence that she would ask that particular question only moments after he'd said what he had to Peter Soo. If it was a coincidence . . .

For the first time, Price looked directly into her eyes. "Rachel Kraft has a mother and a father, and a little sister. Her family loves her and misses her. They've been in agony since the day she disappeared. I don't think it is right or for that matter *decent* for anyone to add to their burden by speculating in a public forum about what might have happened to her. Am I making myself clear?"

"I . . . but I . . ."

"But nothing. You know about being innocent until

proven guilty . . . well, I'm operating on the premise of alive until proven dead."

Dakota Smith, looking stricken, let go of the door and took a step back.

"And that," he added grimly, "is not for release."

Ten

"I'm sorry I kept you waiting," Dr. Lauren Harper said, ushering Danielle Falk into her office. "But I had to take that call."

Which was true, in spades. In fact, she'd spent the last fifteen minutes pacing her way through a conference call with Rudy Salcedo and an assistant district attorney, doing her utmost to talk them into giving the go-ahead for this morning's hypnosis session. Contrary to his reputation for being conservative, Salcedo was all for it, but the ADA professed to having reservations in regards to Ms. Falk's eventual appearance in court.

There was the requisite back-and-forth over rules of evidence and statutory requirements, plus a surprisingly heated discussion of the police department's guidelines for the use of hypnosis as an investigative technique. Her own qualifications to conduct the exam were also discussed at length, but since she'd been trained under the auspices of the American Society of Clinical Hypnosis, even the ADA had to admit she had the expertise required.

Salcedo finally ended the argument in his usual gruff, decisive way.

"All of that is bullshit," the captain had said. "Detective Price tells me there's a strong possibility that the Wilson girl is still alive. If it comes down to a choice between saving her life versus guaranteeing the admissibility of fucking testimony, we're damned well gonna do whatever it takes to find this kid, and you lawyers can go straight to hell. Do I make myself clear?"

"Absolutely," the ADA said.

Lauren could have kissed Salcedo for that; maybe she would the next time she saw him. In the meantime, in the privacy of her office, she'd pantomimed a victory cheer, knowing all too well that in this male-dominated profession, it wouldn't be wise of her to gloat over a triumph, no matter how delicious.

Now she sat at her desk, contemplating the woman across from her. Danielle Falk was dressed casually, in acid-washed Levi's, a peach-colored blouse, and Italian sandals. Wearing her hair down and sans makeup, she looked young enough to pass for a college freshman, instead of an elementary schoolteacher.

"Before we get started," Lauren said, "I must advise you that it's department policy to tape these sessions. I trust that's not a problem."

"Not at all."

Lauren reached down to the control panel, located in the well of her desk, and turned on the remote camera which was hidden in the ceiling. Out of sight, out of mind, the logic went. She also engaged the backup tape recorder, in case the camera failed.

She next took the clipboard with the consent form she'd prepared earlier, and handed that and a pen to Danielle. "If you'll read this and sign here . . ."

"Of course," Ms. Falk murmured, quickly did so, and passed it back.

That took care of the legalities. "How are you this morning?"

Danielle Falk smiled slightly. "Better, I think."

Noting the young woman still looked pale, she asked, "Were you able to sleep?"

"Yes, a little."

"How were your dreams?"

As fragile as her smile was, it faded instantaneously out of existence. "I only had one dream, and it wasn't pleasant."

"Was Cassie in it?"

"Just . . . her cries."

Lauren nodded sympathetically. "Would you like to tell me about it?"

"There isn't much to tell . . ."

There was generally more to a dream than the dreamer was consciously aware of, but it often took specific and persistent questioning to reveal any relevance to what was going on in real life. For the time being, however, she did not want to risk cueing the patient at any level, so she settled for an innocuous approach: "Did you have this dream more than once?"

"No. I woke up with my heart pounding, and never got back to sleep."

"Where were you, in the dream? At school?"

Danielle shook her head. "I don't know, it didn't seem to be anywhere I was familiar with."

"Describe it for me."

"I . . . okay." The teacher closed her eyes briefly, her expression that of pained concentration. When she looked at Lauren a moment later, her brown eyes were filled with dread. "It was at night, I think. I was in a long, dark hallway, and there was a lot of glass . . . I remember that because I could see my reflection in the glass, as I walked down the hall."

"Were there doors?"

"Yes, but they were closed, I think locked."

"Did you try to open any of them?"

"No. There wasn't time. I heard Cassie crying, and I . . . I'm looking for her."

Lauren took note of the change from past tense to the present, but didn't want to interrupt, given the urgent tone of Danielle's voice.

"I *have* to find her."

"Why isn't there time?" Lauren asked, although she thought she knew.

"Because he's there."

"He?"

"The man who took her."

Precisely what she had expected. "Can you see him, Danielle?"

"No." Danielle frowned and shook her head vehemently. "No, I can't."

"All right." She made a note to ask that question again later, during hypnosis, but for now she let the answer stand. "Go on."

"There's a sound, behind me. I—" Danielle faltered, clearly uncertain. "I can't, no wait . . . I'm sorry, it gets kind of . . . frantic?"

"You're doing fine."

"I don't know why I'm so nervous."

"I'd worry if you weren't," Lauren said, matter-of-factly. "You heard a sound and . . ."

Visibly bracing herself, Danielle went on. "I remember turning, to see what that sound was, and all of a sudden there's this bright light coming at me, and I can hear someone running, breathing hard, and . . . and I woke up." She licked her lips. "That's it."

"An interesting dream," Lauren said.

"It terrified me."

Lauren recognized that as a simple statement of fact, and not a bid for sympathy. Quite possibly the young woman's deep sense of guilt left her feeling unworthy of consolation— and consequently unwilling to accept comforting— at the very time she needed it most. "I imagine it would terrify anyone."

Danielle looked away.

Time to move along, Lauren thought. "Okay, before we continue, do you have any questions or concerns about undergoing hypnosis?"

Eyes averted, Danielle Falk shook her head. "I only hope it helps."

Lauren closed the blinds and dimmed the lights. The thick carpet muffled her footsteps as she crossed the office and returned to her chair. "Now. Danielle, I want you to sit back and relax. Close your eyes and listen only to the sound of my voice."

At her instruction, Danielle had moved to the leather recliner, away from the window and the street noise below. She sat quite still, her hands forming tight fists at her sides.

"Relax and take a deep breath, hold it for a count of five— " Lauren counted it off "— and as you exhale, imagine that all of your fear is leaving with it."

Danielle complied, but her hands remained clenched and there was a worry crease between her eyes.

"Relax and breathe, slowly and evenly. Slowly and evenly. Slow, deep breaths, and you feel good, very good, calm and relaxed."

Gradually, the young woman's breathing slowed.

"Relax, Danielle, that's good. With every breath, you feel lighter and calmer. Your muscles are relaxing, you can feel the tension leaving your body, and in its place is a soothing warmth."

Danielle's hands began to uncurl.

"Very good," Lauren said approvingly, "and now you can feel the warmth spreading through your body.

The tension is easing, you feel the glow of warmth, a wonderful feeling as you drift into sleep, and your muscles are very heavy now, as you relax and breathe."

A sigh, and the worry line had disappeared.

"You are warm and relaxed, drifting gently into sleep. I'm going to count from five to zero, Danielle, and with each number, you will drift deeper and deeper . . . and you will not awaken until I tell you to. Five . . ."

Counting backwards slowly, Lauren watched closely for indications that Danielle had achieved an appropriate level of relaxation, the hypnotic state. Deep enough in, the eyes stopped moving behind their lids, and the breathing slowed to near hypoventilation.

". . . one . . . and zero." She fell silent, watching for signs of restlessness, but there were none. "Danielle, can you hear me?"

"Yes."

Lauren noted with satisfaction the calm serenity in Danielle's voice. "All right. I want you to think back, to yesterday."

"Yes?"

"I want you to remember for me how the day started, how you felt, who you saw, and what you did." It was her practice to begin with nonthreatening aspects of the subject's life, since doing so allowed each individual to find a comfortable rhythm of divulgence. "Tell me about yesterday, Danielle."

"Yesterday?"

Somewhat hesitant, even now. "It's Friday," Lauren prompted. "Today is Friday, and it's a beautiful morning in May."

"It *is* a beautiful day . . ."

And they were off. Lauren settled back to listen, content to follow where Danielle might lead. She hadn't liked the Big Brother intrusiveness of the camera when it was first installed five or six years ago, but she had since come to appreciate the fact that she needn't divide her attention by taking exhaustive written notes.

Technology undeniably had its advantages. The downside was that on occasion her mind wandered.

But not today.

With so very much at stake, even the most mundane details were potentially significant. To save a little girl's life, she needed to try and slip into Danielle Falk's skin.

Patience was its own virtue.

An hour and fifteen minutes into the session, while talking about giving the weekly spelling test, Danielle stopped for no apparent reason, and shifted uneasily in the recliner. Eyes closed, she reached out tentatively with her right hand, fingers splayed, and then withdrew it quickly, as if burned.

"What's happening?" Lauren asked.

"The van is there."

That was odd. Danielle had mentioned the van in passing last night, but it didn't make sense for her to be anxious about it under hypnosis, at least not until she relived the actual kidnapping.

It was, subconsciously speaking, putting the apple cart before the horse.

"What time is it, Danielle?" She needed to determine if her patient had skipped forward in the day. Stranger things had happened.

"Ah . . . I don't know."

"You can look at your watch," Lauren suggested.

Danielle glanced at her wrist without opening her eyes. "Eleven thirty-three."

"Are you in the classroom?"

"Yes, by the window."

So much for that. "All right, that's good. What's the next word on the spelling list?" she asked, hoping to focus Danielle in time and place.

"Misgivings," Danielle said softly, and, every inch a teacher added, "Suzy had misgivings about going on the Ferris wheel ride. Misgivings."

Lauren smiled at the sense of nostalgia that evoked; she could almost smell the chalk dust in the air. "Okay, that's good. You're in your classroom, standing near the window, giving a spelling test. Look out the window, and tell me what you see."

"David's there."

That was a new wrinkle. "David who?" When Danielle didn't answer, she revised the question. "Who is David? What's his last name?"

"Nguyen, David Nguyen. He's the vice principal at Northcliffe."

"What is David doing?"

"Oh, he's just walking the grounds. He does that before every Angel's Night."

Lauren jotted down the name, intending to pass it on to Matt Price so he could check it out. You just never knew what might be important in cracking the case; Nguyen might have noticed something Danielle had missed. "Is there anyone else around?"

"No, no one else."

"All right. David is walking the grounds, and you're at the window looking out. What else do you see?"

Danielle made a sound in her throat, not unlike a whimper. "The van."

Back to that again. "Describe it for me."

"It's . . . dark. Forest green, maybe. Maybe even black, I can't tell."

Years ago, a private investigator she was dating had suggested that the vehicle identification number found on automobiles included a coded reference to color. True or not, she wasn't certain the Department of Motor Vehicles categorized cars that way. Even if it did, tracking the van by its color would require a massive effort on the part of the police, one that started with the assumption that the van in question had never been painted.

Regardless, she printed BLACK on her notepad and drew a box around the word to remind her to mention it to Price. If he was even speaking to her after their chilly encounter last night.

"I don't know what you call them," Danielle was saying, "but it's . . . closed in, one of those vans without the extra windows on the side— "

"A panel van?"

"— and it has regular doors instead of the kind that slide shut."

Thinking it pertinent, Lauren wrote that down, too. In the brief silence that ensued, she heard loud footsteps— someone running?— outside in the hall. Glancing up a moment later, she was startled to find Danielle Falk sitting forward in the recliner, her body trembling, her hands gripping the armrests as if holding on for dear life.

More disturbing was the rapidity of the young woman's breathing and the fine sheen of perspiration on her deathly pale face. It was difficult to tell whether or not she was still in a hypnotic trance.

"Danielle," Lauren said, "what's wrong?"

"Don't you hear that?"

Had she heard whoever it was running in the hall? If so, the trance wasn't deep enough. Hoping to salvage the session, she said firmly, "I want you to listen only to my voice, Danielle."

But it was already too late; Danielle stood abruptly, opened her eyes, and without warning, slumped to the floor in a dead faint.

Eleven

Billy Gaetke squeezed his way between the automatic doors, which were in the process of closing, and skipped down the front steps of the police station. He scanned the lot for Price's Taurus— not the easiest task in a fleet of light-colored Fords— but didn't find it.

The creak of leather behind him warned him of the desk sergeant's more leisurely approach. "He's gone?"

"Just missed him."

"Always in a hurry," the sergeant said, shaking his head. "Rushes around so fast, his own shadow can't hope to keep up with him."

Gaetke turned to squint up at Cavello on the top step, just as the sergeant took a huge bite of a sugar-cinnamon doughnut and began to chew contentedly, jowls flapping, his eyelids at half-mast. Gaetke repressed a shudder, patting his own flat stomach for reassurance. "I'll try to raise him on the radio— "

"Wouldn't count on it. Dispatch is having trouble with the damned signal. Keeps fading in and out, never mind the static. It's those sunspots, mark my word."

He'd heard the sergeant's sunspot theory many times. "Listen, I gotta go."

"Sure thing." Cavello crammed the remainder of the doughnut into his mouth, then brushed the crumbs off his uniform shirt. Talking with his mouth full, he said, "Be careful out there."

"Count on it."

The call had come in on the 911 line less than five minutes before, a report of a suspicious vehicle, described as a brown truck, parked or abandoned in an overgrown apple orchard off Cider Drive. The caller, an elderly female judging by the quaver in her voice, had refused to give her name to the 911 operator.

"I can't be getting drawn into police business," she'd said on the tape. "No, sir, not me."

Evidently the woman didn't know that by calling the emergency line, the system automatically displayed both her phone number and address. Lucky for him, no one had informed her of that particular fact, which probably would have scared her off.

In his experience, citizens were a schizophrenic bunch. They'd clamor for more protection, while simultaneously belly-aching about tough police tactics. Then for good measure, they'd turn ostrich, burying their heads in the sand to keep from having to get involved.

Gaetke loved the job, regardless. From the first day, it had been an E ticket ride.

And still was. There were patrol units en route to Cider Drive, but that area had been on his beat when he was in uniform, and he knew a shortcut or two. Backing out of his space, he stuck the portable cherry on the dashboard and turned it on.

No sirens on this run, but what the hell, you couldn't have everything.

After straightening the wheel, he floored it with just enough emphasis to lay a little patch of rubber, and hauled ass out of there.

* * *

Gaetke was gratified to be the first on the scene, even if by less than a minute. The black-and-white placing second pulled up in a whirling cloud of dust.

Some guys didn't know how to be discreet.

"Hey, Billy Boy," Officer Holliday said. "How's life treating you up at MCU?"

Gaetke ignored the use of his old nickname, which he hated, and smiled. "Can't complain. At least I'm not papering windshields these days."

"Ain't it the truth? Traffic's a bitch." Holliday leaned against the front fender of his car, arms folded across his barrel chest. "Twenty years as a patrol jockey, I should know."

"You'll get no argument from me."

The second unit arrived then, manned by one of the department's two female officers, who, intentionally or not, parked at an angle on the dirt shoulder, effectively boxing both other vehicles in.

"Jesus, O'Keefe," the patrol cop groused, "learn to fucking drive, will ya?"

O'Keefe smiled sweetly, flipped him off, and got out of the car. "What's the story here?"

Holliday snorted. "Too busy checking your mascara to listen to the call, sweetheart?"

"Drop dead, honey-bun."

"Knock it off," Gaetke said—and was totally surprised when they did. Encouraged by that, he quickly related the particulars, treating them to a condensed version of what might be in the works. "Of course, it's anybody's guess whether this abandoned vehicle is even remotely connected to our case. Odds are we're chasing smoke, but maybe we'll get lucky."

"I don't know," Holliday scratched his head. "A brown truck ain't my idea of a green van."

Gaetke nodded to acknowledge his point. "But . . .
the caller is an old woman— "

"Watch it," O'Keefe warned.

"— and she might not know the two are different
things. For that matter, maybe we'll get *real* lucky and
it'll turn out she's color-blind."

Holliday snickered. "If you say so."

They walked in silence down the wide dirt path that
led into the orchard. The apple scent was predomi-
nant, but mingled in was a kind of curious burnt
smell, he guessed from the dried-out underbrush, a
consequence of California's persistent drought.

It was warm again this morning, the air hardly stir-
ring. Gaetke could feel himself begin to sweat, a trickle
running down his spine.

Holliday, a few steps ahead, was perspiring profusely, his dark blue uniform shirt clinging to his
broad back like a long-lost lover. And this was the
summer issue, short-sleeved cotton shirt, no less.
O'Keefe, by contrast, looked cool and collected, if
slightly dangerous, carrying her riot gun.

The deeper they moved into the orchard, the more
the trees seemed to close in on them. As they approached a deep curve in the footpath, Gaetke glanced
back over his shoulder, gauging the distance they'd
come. Quarter of a mile, he estimated.

"There it is," O'Keefe said quietly.

He practically gave himself whiplash, turning to
look. Sandwiched between two trees and shaded by a
canopy of thickly leaved branches, was a decrepit Volks-
wagen bus, a relic of the hippie era. Not a truck, then,
but also not green. Rust-red primer could be mistaken
for brown from a distance, he supposed.

Like a lot of VWs from the sixties, this one had

curtains which could be— and were— drawn across the cab for privacy. These were breathtakingly ugly paisley curtains, splotches of psychedelic color, redeemed only in that they had faded from years of exposure to the sun. "Well, shit," Gaetke said.

Holliday continued on. When he was eight or so feet from the VW, the rear window popped open, and what appeared to be a bushy-haired, nearly nude male in combat boots rolled out and took off into the trees.

"Check the bus," Gaetke shouted at O'Keefe, and joined Holliday in the chase.

It wasn't easy. The ground was littered with apples in various stages of decay, which made the footing difficult, and there were soggy spots and actual mud from what had to be the world's leakiest irrigation system.

Gaetke slipped a couple of times, once falling on his right knee so hard that his mouth snapped shut and he barely avoided biting through the tip of his tongue. Still, he kept the suspect in view. Holliday was to his left, huffing and puffing.

Up ahead, their suspect was making like a gazelle, weaving his way through the rows of trees, darting this way and that, high-stepping effortlessly.

Or so it seemed from behind. Gaetke had a rather unflattering view of the bastard's derriere, through boxers so threadbare they were . . . what was the word Price would use? Superfluous, that was it.

The foot chase went on forever. He was filtering bugs through his teeth, for crying out loud, and if that weren't bad enough, he got a killer stitch in his side roughly at the same time Holliday began to fall back.

"Let me shoot him," Holliday gasped.

"Hey, the bastard's ours." In fact, they were no closer than they'd been at the start, and he strongly suspected this guy was getting his jollies running them in circles. In which case, shooting was too good for him.

Then the suspect began scrambling up an incline— where had *that* come from?— showering them with dirt as they played follow the leader. A second later, Gaetke heard a startled yell, and the snap, crackle, pop of branches being broken . . . and possibly, a few bones as well.

He crested the rise and saw their suspect lying faceup and spread-eagled on the ground below. Evidently the gazelle had leapt off a low cliff.

Officer O'Keefe was standing a yard from the suspect's head, aiming the riot gun between his eyes in classic make-my-day style. "Don't move," O'Keefe said, "don't even think about it."

"I'm cool," the suspect said.

Holliday finally wheezed his way to the top of the rise. Red-faced and breathless, he bent over at the waist, bracing himself with his hands on his knees. "Please tell me . . . he broke his fucking neck."

"No such luck."

"What's . . . she . . . doing here?" Holliday gasped irritably, noticing O'Keefe.

"Nailing bad guys, looks like." Gaetke started down the cliff at an angle, causing a minor avalanche of dirt and rocks, and managed to jar his sore knee again. At the bottom, he limped over to O'Keefe and the gazelle, who grinned up at them as if delighted with his impromptu game of catch-me-if-you-can.

"Almost got away," the suspect said with a wink, and actually laughed.

This close, Gaetke could see that his pupils were huge, all but eclipsing the iris. The whites of his eyes were horribly bloodshot. "Never happen, pal. And you know what? I think maybe you're under the influence of an illegal substance . . . or ten."

His smile was blissful. "Only thing I'm under the influence of, officer, is the joy of life and the wonder of God everlasting."

"Then why'd you run?"

"Exercise, man."

"Tell it to the judge." Realizing he hadn't any cuffs with him, he bummed a set from O'Keefe.

"You okay?" O'Keefe asked, handing them across. "You're limping pretty badly."

"Oh yeah, I'm dandy." He ordered the gazelle to turn over and place his hands on the back of his bushy head. With some difficulty— he couldn't bend his knee well enough to squat— Gaetke handcuffed him, and then assisted him to his feet.

In short order, they determined that their suspect, one Raymond Charles Bugalossi, was a garden-variety pothead with a penchant for Acapulco Gold, but who'd apparently never met a pharmaceutical he didn't like well enough to abuse. He willingly admitted to having a history of drug arrests, but only one conviction, up in Medford, Oregon, circa 1979, for which he'd served six months in the county jail.

Whenever and whatever Bugalossi scored, his pattern was to quickly make himself scarce, so he wouldn't have to share his stash with his friends. He had, Bugalossi said, a dozen or so "hidey-holes" in which he would take cover, the better to work his way through the inventory.

A waste of a life, yes, but also a monumental waste of their time.

O'Keefe had the honor of selecting an ensemble for Bugalossi from a pile of wrinkled and none-too-clean clothing overflowing the passenger seat, and Holliday more or less dressed him, trading the combat boots for sandals, a little less lethal in a jail environment.

They locked the VW and sealed the doors with orange evidence tape. A city tow truck would arrive at some point— Holliday had volunteered to wait for it— and haul the bus to the police impound lot. There the VW would be thoroughly searched, assuming they were able to convince a judge to sign a search warrant.

Which wasn't bloody likely, he knew.

Frustrated, Gaetke stuck Bugalossi in the back of O'Keefe's squad and slammed the door. O'Keefe raised her eyebrows at him, but said nothing. A moment later, she drove away.

Holliday ambled to his patrol car chuckling, his good humor inexplicably restored. "Look on the bright side, Billy Boy. At least we didn't go and make fools of ourselves by requesting backup on this."

Which in all honesty, he *would* have done, were it not for the radio transmission problems. Talk about being saved by the bell. Or Cavello's sunspots.

"Imagine trying to live that down," Holliday continued. "Having to call in reinforcements to nab a fucking mope like Bugalossi."

"Imagine," Gaetke said, flinching at the thought . . . and the throbbing pain in his now-swollen knee.

By the time he got back to the Major Crimes Unit, his knee had stiffened, further limiting his range of motion. He limped into the office as unobtrusively as possible, heading directly for his desk.

"What happened to you?" another detective asked.

"Not a damned thing." Gaetke pawed through the drawer in search of aspirin. He found the bottle and swallowed three tablets with cold, somewhat murky coffee, left over from the morning. He sat down, carefully stretched his leg out straight, and sighed in blessed relief. "Anything going on?"

"Not really, except Price was in here looking for you a little while ago."

He located Price in the hall near the department's Community Relations Office, deep in hushed conversation with Captain Salcedo. Price acknowledged him with a nod, but didn't indicate by look or gesture that he should join them, so he didn't.

Instead he leaned against the wall, watched and waited. Salcedo looked gloomier than usual, and Gaetke wondered idly if his sour expression was attributable to the noon press conference. The editorial page in this morning's paper had been highly critical of the department in general, and Salcedo personally for "not having taken adequate measures to protect the children of La Campana."

How Many Children Must Die? the headline read. The photographs of Lucy Marie Bosworth, Rachel Elise Kraft, and Cassandra Dawn Wilson were potent reminders that more than a rise in crime statistics was at stake.

Short of assigning an officer to every kid in town, Gaetke doubted anything would work.

"What's with your leg?" Matt Price asked, coming over to him.

"Oh, I whacked my knee," he said, waving it off. "It'll be all right. You were looking for me?"

Price nodded. "I'm flying up to San Francisco. We found a current address on Alyssa Reid in Monterey. The lady likes to drive fast, according to the DMV. And since I'll be in the neighborhood, I plan to stop by and talk to Cassie's father at San Quentin. With any luck, this'll be a quick two-for-one deal."

"You're going tonight?"

"My flight's at six. I'll be back Sunday night, barring complications."

Gaetke glanced at his watch and saw it was just shy of a quarter to one. "And?"

"And while I'm gone, I'll need you to follow up on a couple of things for me."

"No problem," he said.

Twelve

"Wouldn't you rather wait in the Green Room?" one of the production assistants asked.

"No thanks, I'm fine," Zeke Wilson said, his attention focused solely on his mother, only now being introduced to the blond anchor who would be interviewing her on tape for broadcast on the six o'clock news.

"It'll be much more comfortable," the young woman persisted. "And less of a distraction."

"I want her to be able to *see* me."

"But that's just it; she won't see you, standing in the dark. The lights will be in her eyes."

Zeke shrugged. "She'll know I'm here."

The look the assistant gave him suggested she thought he was either irrational or simply being difficult. She gave a disgusted little "Hmmph," then turned abruptly and walked away.

He didn't really care; he wasn't out to win a popularity contest.

On the set, the makeup person was applying last-minute blush to the blonde's flawless face. The blonde took a final peek in the mirror, touched a hand to her stylishly short golden hair, and nodded her approval.

"Ten seconds," someone said.

Like magic, the set cleared, leaving only his mother and the blonde, who surprised him by smiling warmly as she reached across and patted Evangeline's hand. The set was designed to foster such intimacy: there were two plush chairs, mere inches apart, in front of a soothing blue-gray background.

Except for the glare and heat of the lights, it might have been someone's front parlor. If anyone had front parlors anymore.

"Five seconds, four . . ."

The segment director held up three fingers, two, and then one. A few seconds of the Channel 7 news theme, which built to a minicrescendo before fading out, and the middle camera of three glided forward.

"Good evening, I'm Stormy Landon— "

Stormy Landon? So *that* was where he'd seen her before; she used to be the station's weather girl. In the old days— when he was in high school— Lewis could always break him up with his wicked, dead-on imitation of her forecasts, complete with helpless fits of giggling, and suggestively mangled meteorological terms.

Today, however, the ex-weather girl was all business, her demeanor appropriately solemn. "Yesterday morning, every parent's worst nightmare became a terrible reality for the mother and father of Lucy Marie Bosworth, whose body was found nine weeks and five days after she disappeared, in broad daylight, from the quiet Orchard Heights neighborhood where she lived— "

Zeke tuned her out, not from lack of interest, but because his mother had closed her eyes and appeared to be whispering to herself. He was familiar with the practice; growing up, he had seen her do the very same thing perhaps hundreds of times, as a way of bracing herself mentally and steadying her nerves.

"I'm thinking it through," was how she'd explained it to him the one time he'd asked.

A moment later, she gave a slight nod, lifted her chin, squared her shoulders, and opened her eyes. He was relieved to see the calm expression he knew so well . . . and in fact had depended on, all of his life.

"— the most recent abduction," Stormy Landon was saying, "which also occurred yesterday, of Cassandra Dawn Wilson. The seven-year-old disappeared from the playground of the private school she attended."

On a monitor, Zeke saw taped footage of Northcliffe Academy. The day Cassie had been accepted, on scholarship, his mother had called him in Boston, and they had toasted his niece's success. He in Boston with a lukewarm Corona— the ancient refrigerator in his apartment was temperamental to say the least— and they in La Campana with Cassie's favorite Hawaiian Punch, spiked with 7-Up for some "fizzle" as Cassie called it.

He smiled at that.

"I have with me this evening Evangeline Wilson, little Cassandra's grandmother. Mrs. Wilson, thank you for joining us. I'm sure I speak for our viewers when I say our hearts go out to you and your family."

"Thank you."

"And, of course, to Cassandra, wherever she is." Ms. Landon frowned prettily. "But I understand that you're here tonight for another reason, a very special reason, to ask the person who took her to return your granddaughter unharmed."

"Yes."

His mother looked directly into the camera; in the monitor, he saw that she was in close-up.

"I want you to send my baby home," she said, her voice husky with unshed tears. "Cassie's life is pre-

cious to us. We love her very much, and we miss her.
I ask you, I beg you . . . please let her go."

There was a hint of a quiver about her generous
mouth, a mouth meant for smiles and laughter, and
he felt something akin to rage that she should suffer
like this. And, too, that her pain be made public.

He knew his mother thought differently, but he
couldn't shake his belief that even the most genuine,
heartfelt grief was trivialized at the hands of television
news. It was hard not to be cynical at the way the
media spoon-fed a family's private anguish to the viewers.

"You're the only one who can bring her back to us,"
Evangeline went on quietly. "She's known a lot of pain
for a young girl. Please don't hurt her. Please, if you
would, just . . . send her home."

Blessedly, a minute or so later, the interview was
over. The P.A. closest to him wiped her eyes.

"Everyone stay put for a sec, if you would," the
segment director said briskly. "Let me check if we've
got coverage on all cameras, before you scatter to the
winds."

Stormy Landon either didn't hear or didn't care.
With a whispered word to his mother, she stepped off
the set and hurried down a darkened back hallway.

The director's request obviously didn't apply to
him, so Zeke followed her, fully expecting to be chal-
lenged by one of the crew.

He didn't draw so much as a glance.

The reason the hall was so dark, he discovered, was
that the walls were painted a dull, flat black. The lighting was recessed in the ceiling, casting a pale, milky
glow that hadn't a chance of overcoming the gloom.

That sense of gloom was further enhanced by the

thick carpet which absorbed the sound of his footsteps, culminating in a claustrophobic silence.

Ahead of him, he heard a door opening. Quickening his pace, he reached a corner in time to see the door in question partially close. Slivers of light from within enticed him onward.

As he neared, he could hear a one-sided conversation, from which he gathered Ms. Landon was on the phone.

". . . don't know why I'm always left hanging out there without a net. Listen, I'm the talent, *you're* the brains, do me a favor and give me something reasonably intelligent to say."

Standing outside, Zeke raised his hand to knock, but didn't. He could see Stormy Landon sitting on the corner of a granite-slab desk, one shapely leg swinging furiously back and forth.

"Don't give me that altruistic shit" she said. "It's voyeurism, plain and simple. You know it, I know it, so cut the crap. What pulls the ratings is wallowing in someone else's misery."

She turned then, reaching for a glass cigarette box, and saw him.

"Murray, I can't talk now. Just do what I asked for a change, and we'll be fine. Okay?" Without waiting for a reply, she dropped the receiver into its cradle. She took a slim brown cigarette out of the box, lit it with the matching glass lighter, and blew smoke in his direction. "You're not supposed to be back here."

Zeke nudged the door open. "Sorry."

"Sure you are." She gave him a deliberate once-over, no doubt calculating his age, marital status, and quite possibly his net worth. "I saw you come in with Evangeline. You're the brother, right?"

"I'm Zeke Wilson, Cassie's uncle."

"Your mother told me. Harvard Law School, top

ten ranking. Destined for glory on the Supreme Court, and all that jazz."

"Not to mention— " he finished for her "— a credit to my race."

"That, too. So, is there truth in advertising?"

"Not really, but I've been called worse."

"I doubt it." She came to the door. "I assume you're here for a reason?"

The problem was, he wasn't completely clear on what had compelled him to follow her. He'd acted on an irresistible impulse, which in itself was more than a little unusual for him. But he did his best to punt, saying, "I wanted to thank you for the kindness you showed my mother. She's a very private person, and it wasn't easy for her to do what she did."

Her finely arched eyebrows raised. "I'm sure it wasn't."

Zeke wondered if the passage of time had put the keen skepticism in Stormy Landon's gaze, or if the ditzy weather girl thing had been an act. Whichever was the case, he could tell she wasn't buying *his* act. "All right, to be honest, I haven't a clue."

"Really," she murmured.

"I guess I thought you might know more about what's been going on— "

"And I'd tell you?"

"The police don't have a lot to say— "

"Now there's a news flash." Her smile was all style and no substance. "In the interests of saving time— by which I mean mine— let's cut to the chase. What is it, exactly, that you want to know?"

"Do they have a suspect?"

Ms. Landon regarded him for a moment before shaking her head. "Not that I've heard of. Not that I necessarily would know."

He didn't believe her. "You must have sources in the police department . . ."

"Of course."

"Is there a description of this guy floating around somewhere?"

"If there is, I haven't heard it." She walked back to the desk, took a last drag on her cigarette, and ground it out before glancing at him with undisguised amusement. "Why do you ask, Zeke? You think you could find him if the police can't?"

"That isn't it."

"But if you did . . ." She left the thought unfinished, leaned against the desk with a contemplative look, and said, "I'd be very interested in having an exclusive on the story. 'Vengeance is mine,' that kind of thing."

He got the impression she was talking more to herself than to him. "This isn't about vengeance."

"If you say so." She selected another cigarette and tapped it, filter side down, on the polished granite surface of the desk.

"All I want, Ms. Landon, is to know what the police aren't telling us. If they have a suspect or suspects, or maybe there's a witness— "

She paused in the act of lighting her cigarette. "They didn't tell you about the teacher?"

"What teacher?"

"The one on the playground yesterday. Rumor is, she might have seen the guy."

No one had said a word to him about any of this. He wondered, did his mother know? He remembered what she'd told him about yesterday, of arriving at the school late, of finding a swarm of police there, of being taken to an office and waiting there alone, of someone— she didn't recall who— finally telling her what had happened, of her many calls to Boston before he came home to a ringing phone. But nothing about a teacher, he was certain of that.

His headache, dormant for hours as a result of Doc Bigelow's ministering, returned full force. "Excuse me, but I don't believe you mentioned a witness when you were interviewing my mother."

"You're right, I didn't, because it's really only a rumor, and—"

"Wait a minute, how does that qualify as a rumor? She was there or she wasn't. It can't be both."

"Oh, she definitely was there; the question is, did she see the guy or not? Nobody knows, from what I've heard, and that includes her."

It didn't seem logical to him. "Do you know her name? How can I reach her?"

Again that pretty, practiced frown. "The police have asked that we not release her name for the time being. I'm sorry."

"I just want to talk to her."

"I'm sorry, I really am, but I can't help you. I mean, for all I know you might decide *she's* to blame. Hmm? Or you could be laying the legal groundwork for a negligence suit or—"

"I'm not that devious."

"Whatever." She straightened, extinguished the cigarette, and smoothed the fit of her rose-colored blazer. "In a nutshell, what it comes down to is this: a journalist flat out can't function without a network of confidential sources."

"I understand that—"

She waved him off. "It takes years to put all the pieces together, but one false step and those sources dry up and blow away."

"What about Cassie?"

That brought her up short. She stalled for a moment, adjusting the cuffs of her silk blouse, and then met his eyes fully for the first time. "I don't think you know what you're asking me to do."

"She's seven years old," he said.

"I worked my tail off to get where I am today." This time her frown was bitter, fine lines bracketing her mouth. "I'll have to think about it."

"That's all I'm asking."

"Sure it is."

Thirteen

Dakota Smith stepped from the darkness of the stairwell into the late afternoon sunshine.

Technically, as of this minute, she was off work until Monday. She'd just turned the station's Sony over to Freddy, who needed it to tape his bizarre "Neanderthal On The Street" series, which aired every Sunday opposite her own favorite, "Murder, She Wrote."

Weekend programming at KOUT was an acquired taste, at best, tailored to fit the station's outlaw image— hence the call letters— and slightly twisted to accommodate their loyal viewers.

All three of them.

Her own assessment was that weekends were strictly amateur hour, imparting little or nothing to the cultural consciousness, and registering a whopping double negative for redeeming social value. With the exception of *her* taped two-minute news brief, which would be broadcast tonight at eleven o'clock, KOUT's Saturday slate was totally lame.

Sundays were even worse, without a millisecond of scheduled news.

Oh, they might spot her a minute for a quickie, if something truly sensational came down, especially one of those slice 'em, dice 'em, serve 'em on toast, Jeffrey

Dahmer kinds of deals, but otherwise weekends were strictly all flash and no substance, thank you very much, targeting the elusive six-pack guzzling, tractor-pull devotee demographic that advertisers had yet to crack.

Nevertheless, the station paid her bills— sort of— and although she was off the clock, she never really stopped working. She had her Pentax 35mm with auto focus and power zoom, and while still shots lacked the raw energy of tape, in a pinch she could slum a little, maybe peddle her pictures to the local newspaper.

Solely for front page, above-the-fold placement, of course; she had no desire to see her hard work show up as filler in the Metro section. In this case, she didn't think there would be a problem, since the Wilson kidnapping was prime-time, Grade A material.

And if everything went as planned, she might just add this story to her demo tape. Maybe *that* would make CNN sit up and take notice.

If everything went as planned.

She'd wrangled the use of her cousin Sam's sixty-something Buick Skylark by promising to babysit his precious eight-month-old son over the horrendously *long* Memorial Day weekend. A major sacrifice, since she wasn't fond of kids in general and His Highness, Samuel Junior, the Crown Prince of Drooling in particular, but she had too much ground to cover tonight to be forced to rely on the city's quixotic mass transit system.

Of course, a hot pink Skylark convertible with lavender upholstery and a horn that played "Little Latin Lupe Lu" was a shade more conspicuous than she would have preferred for working undercover, but this was another one of those annoying beggar situations. Meaning, she knew damned well she had no choice.

Not an infrequent occurrence in her life.

Still, the cover of night couldn't arrive soon enough, Dakota thought, swatting Sam's fuzzy dice out of the way to turn the key in the ignition.

She parked across the street from Northcliffe Academy, in the small private lot behind the insurance office, which was conveniently closed. Walking at a leisurely pace towards the school, she surveyed her surroundings, noting that, with the exception of the old fossil who owned the antique store, there was no one else nearby.

So far, so good.

A habitual jaywalker, today she crossed obediently at the marked intersection. The way she had it figured, that was one less infraction to count against her if she was wrong and the police were hiding in the bushes, watching her every move from afar.

This way they'd only get her on the big stuff, like breaking and entering.

"Make that entering," she said under her breath. "No breaking required."

Dakota continued on, doing her utmost to appear nonchalant, like any law-abiding citizen out for an afternoon stroll. At the border of the Northcliffe property, she stopped, shading her eyes as she scanned the grounds. When no one sprung from the shrubbery to confront her, she made a beeline for the far side of the school, out of sight from the street.

One advantage of having attended good old Northcliffe, she knew every chink in its armor. In this case, a certain window in the music room that fit so poorly in the frame that it could not be locked.

In sixth grade, she and her best-friend-for-life,
Kandi, who she hadn't spoken to in years, had snuck
into the school through that very window. Giggling
and shushing each other, making enough noise to
wake the dead, they'd tiptoed through the empty hallways, intent on mischief. At twelve years old, however,
they had a limited repertoire of tricks— none of which
were in the least original— and settled for switching
salt for sugar in the cafeteria and teachers' lounge,
leaving a trail of thumbtacks on chairs, and squirting
liquid soap on a few doorknobs.

Kid stuff.

Now she wanted simply to get in, flip through Principal Rifkin's Rolodex for Danielle Falk's address
and/or phone number, take a peek at Cassandra Wilson's confidential student file, make a note of whatever seemed relevant, and get out. If all went well, no
one would ever know that she'd been here.

Dakota turned the corner at the back of the school
and approached the music room window. Even at a
distance, she could tell it was indeed unlocked, al
though it looked smaller than she recalled. Of course,
she'd grown hippier in the last ten years.

"Great," she said, "I'm gonna get stuck in the
damned window. The fire department's gonna have
to grease me down with Crisco to get me out."

With her luck, today would be the slowest news day
in television history, sending her desperate peers into
a bloody feeding frenzy over what few tidbits there
were, and the story of her humiliation would go national. Her tush would be infamous.

Reporter Gets To The Bottom Of It All.

CNN would *not* be calling.

Resigned to her fate, she opened the window and
hitched herself up on the sill. Some vigorous wrig-
gling, and she was inside.

She wasn't even breathing hard. "Piece of cake," she said, dusting her hands on her jeans.

Dakota headed directly for the principal's office, her Reeboks squeaking faintly on the polished wood floor. There was no other sound, which was kind of unsettling. Somehow, without the laughter of children, the school didn't seem familiar to her.

It was only the second time she'd been back since she "graduated" from the sixth grade. The first was a couple of years ago, back in her glory days at Channel 2— where she lasted all of three months— when she covered an explosion in the chemistry lab.

Not much of a story, as stories went, but she got a date with a hazardous material specialist out of it. He turned out to be as toxic as any chemical spill, but *c'est la vie*. Win some, lose some.

She reached the school office and found that door closed, but unlocked. Inside, the principal and vice principal's doors stood wide open.

As she saw it, that amounted to an engraved invitation; she RSVPed by going in.

The Rolodex was first on her agenda. She sat at the desk and flipped through it. Evidently alphabetizing was not one of the qualifications necessary for the job of principal, and it took her a moment to locate Falk between Foster and Ferrari. She copied down an address on Brighton Way and the phone number, and deduced that the red letters UNL next to the number meant it was unlisted.

She was, after all, a skilled investigative reporter.

"We're halfway home," she said gleefully. Force of

habit made her give the Rolodex a couple of full spins to disguise the area of interest.

The file cabinets were next. These were locked, naturally, but this was hardly her maiden effort in picking locks, nor would the gray metal cabinet ever be mistaken for the vault at Fort Knox. She straightened a paper clip, hooked one end, and set to work.

Two minutes later, she pulled the desired drawer open with a satisfied smile. The files were more orderly than the Rolodex, and she found Cassie Wilson's student records in nothing flat.

She had just begun to page through the contents of the manila folder, when she heard a door *clang* open somewhere in the building. Dakota froze, holding her breath as she listened to footsteps echo in the hallway. A man, she thought, by the sound of the stride.

Coming her way.

She took the face sheet before slipping the file back in place, and ever so carefully slid the drawer shut, wincing at the metallic *whunk* it made. She debated whether or not to lock the drawer, recalled it as making an inordinately loud sound, and decided not to chance it.

She folded the face sheet and tucked it in the back pocket of her jeans.

As quietly as she could, she crossed to the desk and turned off the green-shaded banker's lamp. The soft shadows of late afternoon reclaimed the room.

She ducked into the kneehole of the desk, and thought longingly of the open window down the back hall. In the movies, a plucky heroine such as herself would make a daring escape at this point, sprinting down the hallway and plunging headfirst out that window— never mind that she'd closed it— tucking her lithe body into an acrobatic roll while airborne, before landing gracefully on her feet.

In real life she was more likely to break her damned fool neck.

And get caught in the bargain.

So much for that idea. Instead she huddled like a bunny in a hutch. Whoever was out there was very close now, in the outer office. She braced herself, expecting to be discovered any minute.

He went into the vice principal's office, next door, instead.

Dakota strained to hear what he was doing in there, but other than his footsteps, none of the assorted squeaks and creaks coming from the room were identifiable. She had an insane thought— that it was another reporter snooping around after *her* exclusive lead— but decided that was unlikely, since he'd come in through what should have been a locked door.

Scrunched up in such tight quarters, she felt her toes begin to tingle, threatening to go numb from the lack of circulation. She sank down to a sitting position, her back against the modesty panel, and tried to stretch out without sticking out.

Then she heard a sound she recognized, the dialing of an old-fashioned rotary phone.

Shortly thereafter, a voice said, "May I speak to Gladys Adams, please? Oh, Mrs. Adams, how are you today? This is David Nguyen, at Northcliffe Academy. I'm so sorry, but under the circumstances, our board of directors has decided that we'll have to cancel Angel's Night on Monday. Yes, yes, it is a shame . . ."

Dakota relaxed, relieved that Nguyen's presence had nothing to do with her. Angel's Night was the school's way of showing appreciation for the generous financial support of supposedly anonymous donors who provided scholarships for approximately half of the students. The Academy was prohibitively expensive, costing nearly as much as some Ivy League schools.

Were it not for the Angels, a lot of bright kids would be unable to afford the tuition.

She'd had an Angel of her own, back then, none other than Judge Aloysius Booth. The students weren't supposed to know who was paying their way through school, but Principal "We'll have none of that" Rifkin had left her alone in the office one day with her file, and who could blame her for looking?

It wasn't like she'd harbored intentions of showing up on the Judge's doorstep and asking the man for more money. As sweet and shy as she'd been at that age? Perish the thought.

Of course, *now* it didn't seem like a bad idea . . .

Dakota shook her head at the direction her thoughts were taking. Early senility, that's what it was. Frigging Alzheimer's Disease.

In the other office, Nguyen cleared his throat. "May I speak to Thomas Addison? Is this Mrs. Addison? David Nguyen at Northcliffe Academy here . . ."

Trapped where she was, Dakota settled in to wait. A catnap might be in order, she thought, considering she'd gotten up at dawn in a vain attempt to beat Detective Matt Price to the morgue. Then there was the news conference with Captain Salcedo, after which she'd chased leads for the rest of the day.

Plus, who knew how late she'd be out tonight?

She yawned. Listening to the vice principal's voice drone on and on, she closed her eyes, and soon was feeling pleasantly drowsy.

"May I speak to Simon Avery?" Nguyen was saying, as she drifted off to sleep.

Some time later, she awoke to find the room in total darkness. The silence was deafening.

Nguyen had gone, evidently.

She pressed the tiny button on her digital watch, which made the face light up. Dakota blinked in disbelief: somehow it had gotten to be eight-thirty.

"Wonderful," she muttered, and crawled out from her hiding place on her hands and knees, then got to her feet. Without turning on the light, she felt her way to the door and out of the office.

She left the way she came, through the music room window. As her feet touched the ground, she remembered the unlocked cabinet.

Dakota considered going back in, but she'd already lost a couple of hours of surveillance time. Add to that, she didn't want to push her luck; she'd had a close call in there with Nguyen. What if he had been the type who got a perverse kick out of sitting in the boss's chair?

She'd be getting strip-searched and deloused down at the city jail right now, if he had.

No, she'd dodged one bullet already. No sense painting a bull's-eye on her chest.

Besides, she thought as she skirted the building, what kind of anal-retentive, detail freak would it take to notice an unlocked cabinet?

Twenty minutes later, she killed the engine and cut the lights on the Skylark. She had parked on Dartmouth, in sight of Danielle Falk's residence on Brighton Way. The house was California stucco, on the small side, the kind of house that she'd heard referred to as a Widow's Cottage or Spinster's Bungalow.

The curtains were drawn, but there were lights on inside, which she took to mean that someone was home.

Dakota reached for her binoculars.

Fourteen

In the living room, the grandfather clock chimed the hour in its rather portentous fashion. Danielle stood at the kitchen sink, debating whether or not to take the Valium that her doctor had given her when she refused his offer of a sedative.

"Anxiety is a normal response to stress, but a little goes a long way," the doctor had said. "You need something to calm you."

Danielle couldn't deny that she needed calming; today was the first time in her life that she'd ever fainted. The episode this morning was unnerving and slightly embarrassing, fainting like someone's maiden aunt! She considered herself tougher than that.

Even so, she couldn't dispute that she felt restless and distracted. It reminded her of finals week back in college, when she would stay up all night cramming for tests, fighting exhaustion with cold caffeine by drinking enormous quantities of Pepsi.

Right up until the moment of the inevitable crash, she'd felt overstimulated and edgy, extraordinarily tactile, aware of the slightest touch . . . or glance for that matter. It wasn't a pleasant feeling, but she'd endured it then, because she knew it would pass.

She wasn't sure *this* would pass.

There were an alarming number of child abductions with no resolution. Children disappeared and their families waited, in the beginning hoping desperately— and quite often illogically— for a happy ending. Eventually, as the days turned into weeks and months and years, that futile hope was transformed into an absolute need for closure.

The day would come when any ending, happy or not, would suffice.

Danielle knew that to be true for the simplest of reasons; growing up in Northern California, she'd gone to school with a girl named Tara, whose ten-year-old brother vanished while delivering newspapers early one Sunday morning, in the fall of 1980.

Thirteen at the time, she hadn't really been friends with Kevin— or Tara, for that matter— but she knew him in the way children of different ages in any school were familiar with each other. Of course, she had been somewhat isolated from the rest of the kids by her responsibilities at home, which included caring for her mother, by then an invalid due to chronic heart disease.

Even so, she had witnessed the gradual devastation of Kevin's family. At first, there was a kind of frantic energy that fueled the day-long searches and all-night vigils. Kevin would be found, everyone assumed, and when he came home they would all do whatever was necessary to help him deal with the experience.

In time that guarded optimism gave way to the ugly realization that if Kevin was found alive, he probably would have suffered extreme psychological damage as a result of his abduction. There was talk in the neighborhood of the Stockholm Syndrome, by which hostages came to identify with their captors.

Everyone knew what had happened to Patty Hearst, among others, but at least she had been a young adult when she was kidnapped in 1974. It was horrible to imagine how a child's mind might be warped or shattered by that kind of continual abuse.

Unspoken except in whispers was the assumption that the abuse was sexual in nature.

In the third year after Kevin's disappearance, his parents divorced. The father moved to Florida, where he died a few months later in a fiery car accident that killed three other people. He'd been driving while intoxicated, and although it was never proven, his death was widely assumed to be a consequence of the family tragedy.

Like dominoes, Kevin's older brother and sister fell over in line. Tara, searching for security or a father substitute, married a year later at seventeen to a used car salesman some twenty years her senior.

As in many small towns, there weren't many diversions to be had, and people often drank for recreation. When Tara's husband drank, he found it entertaining to beat her black and blue. It was rumored that he'd kicked her in the stomach while she was pregnant, but whatever the cause, her baby boy was born hydrocephalic, and had to be institutionalized soon after birth.

The middle brother enlisted in the Navy that same year. Bitter at the family's long-standing preoccupation with Kevin, he promptly pulled his own disappearing act by going AWOL. The Military Police caught up to him at a tattoo parlor in Oakland, where he was having a skull pierced into his skin, and he was thrown in the brig. There he upped the ante by assaulting a guard and doing his best to incite a riot. In the end he was discharged from the service; no one had heard from him since.

To this day, the mother lived alone in Kevin's house. She spent her days stuffing fliers into envelopes, seemingly oblivious to the fact that if her youngest son was alive, he had aged in the past fifteen years.

She stored his beloved bicycle under a heavy shroud like a priceless artifact, and reportedly kept his room exactly the way he'd left it, right down to the dirty socks on the floor.

Last summer, Danielle had visited her hometown for the first time in years. Walking by Kevin's house, she noticed that tatters of what had once been scores of yellow ribbons were still visible in the walnut tree in the front yard. Later that night, she had seen a light shining in what would forever be Kevin's room.

No, a tragedy of this kind would never simply pass. And however bad the uncertainty might be for the family, she had no doubt that the terror and fear the child went through was many times worse.

And poor Cassie, that sweet, sad child, might already be—

Danielle couldn't stand to finish the thought. She spilled the yellow Valium tablets from the bottle into the palm of her hand, selected one, and swallowed it with a sip of water.

She turned off all the lights in the house on the way to her room.

Later, she curled up in her favorite place, a rattan cocoon lined with down cushions, suspended from the ceiling in a corner of her bedroom. From here, she could look out into her small, private patio through the open French doors, and feel the evening breeze caress her bare legs.

Fresh from a shower, her hair damp, and dressed only in an oversized T-shirt, she welcomed the sensation of cool air on her skin.

The cocoon swung gently in the wind.

A neighbor's wind chimes tinkled, its delicate tones

coupled with the rustling of the leaves to produce an oddly soothing sound.

Or maybe it was the Valium.

Whatever the source, Danielle began to relax. Through the branches of the avocado tree, she could see the full moon rising in the east. The moon was dazzling, big and bright enough to cast shadows. It had a faint reddish hue . . . a blood moon.

Danielle shivered. She stretched the T-shirt over her knees and hugged her legs to her.

Don't think about it, the voice in her head advised.

How could she not?

Later. Tomorrow you can savage yourself with guilt and blame, but for tonight—

From somewhere nearby, she heard a noise like glass shattering. Startled, she listened for a moment— was someone trying to break in?— and when she heard nothing else, she got reluctantly out of her cocoon.

And stood there, uncertain of what to do.

She was hesitant for a reason: there had been *nine* hang-ups on her answering machine when she'd returned from the police department late this morning. All but one were more or less silent, with the only sound the quiet *click* of the switchhook being pressed to cut the connection. The ninth call— the last of them— was different, in that she could hear the caller's labored breathing, followed by his parting shot, a single whispered word, "Bitch."

Detective Price had warned her that she might receive a few crank calls, when and if her name and involvement in the case was made public. To the best of her knowledge, however, the police were withholding that information. Furthermore, the detective had promised to advise her before her name was released to the press.

It didn't make sense, then, that someone would be

calling her, but neither was it likely to be coincidence. More alarming was the possibility that someone had been able to get her unlisted number.

Or her address.

Another muffled sound from the front of the house. She went to the bedside table for her cordless phone. With phone in hand, she left the bedroom.

The house was dark, save for the dim light from the aquarium, and she preferred it that way. She'd lived here long enough to be able to get around without bumping into the furniture.

Danielle walked the periphery of the living and dining rooms, checking the windows, looking for broken glass. She found nothing out of order; all of the windows were intact and locked. The kitchen window had wrought-iron lattice-work across it, with ivy entwined among the bars. It, too, was closed.

The bathroom "window" was actually a wall constructed of glass blocks, which would make one hell of a racket if someone were foolish enough to try and break the glass to get in, never mind that they'd be sliced to ribbons.

And the window in the second bedroom was obstructed by a ten-foot-tall prickly pear cactus. Foolish wouldn't even begin to describe anyone attempting entry through that spiny route.

Which left the doors. There were three of those, including the French doors in her bedroom. The side door, which opened into the kitchen, was only accessible through the garage. Anyone using that avenue would have to get past her recently installed automatic garage door, which had its own security code. The front door was equipped with a dead bolt, safety bar, and chain.

As a woman living alone, she didn't care to take chances.

Danielle completed her sweep in the foyer. She opened the two-inch-square peephole— set at eye level in the middle panel of the front door— and looked outside.

If anyone was out there, they were being quiet about it. After a minute had passed, she slipped the safety bar back, unlocked the dead bolt, and opened the door as far as the chain would allow.

The fresh air cooled her flushed skin.

The street seemed darker than usual, full moon or not. And then she realized why: the light on the pole across the street from her house was out. Either the bulb had exploded, or someone had deliberately broken it.

That was what she'd heard, that first sound. And the second?

She'd wait until morning to check that out.

Danielle flicked on her front porch light to act as a deterrent. Pulling the door towards her, she glanced down and saw a dark *wetness* on her porch.

It was, she thought, a gelatinous mass of some kind, purplish red in color. She sat on her heels and stared at it, her heart pounding.

There were *flies* swarming all over whatever it was, attracted no doubt by the ripe smell.

Somehow she found the nerve to reach her hand through the crack in the door and touch it. As soon as she did— amid a buzzing cloud of flies— she knew what it was.

A liver. Judging by the size, it was probably a cow's liver.

Or that of a young child?

"Oh god," she said aloud.

And then her legs gave out and she sat abruptly,

dropping the phone, which slid noisily across the wood floor. She scrambled to her knees and yanked the door closed, then engaged the locks with trembling hands.

Fifteen

Simon Avery walked towards the house from the gate. A quick glance over his shoulder at the taillights of Sharon's car as she drove away reassured him that finally, the woman was going, going, and . . . gone.

His weekend transcriber, usually the most reliable of the lot, hadn't shown up for work until noon. Some sort of baby-sitter problem, he gathered, not that he really gave a damn.

Whatever the cause, the effect was that she hung around all evening. Every time he suggested to her that it would be fine with him if she knocked off early and went home, she declined.

"I'll never catch up, if I get any further behind," Sharon had said. "Heaven help me, if I left an extra tape for the Monday crew. I'd never hear the end of it, you can be sure."

Impatient as he was to be left alone with his little treasure, he surrendered at that point. Of course, he'd ground a layer of enamel off his molars throughout the day and into the evening, exasperated in spite of himself by the woman's good-intentioned dallying.

It was all he could do to keep from dancing a jig, when she announced she was calling it a day. Finally!

Heading for the house as fast as his stubby legs would

take him, he hummed a tune from "West Side Story,"
the one with the refrain, "Tonight, tonight . . ."

Avery showered and shaved, although with his
sparse facial hair, he hardly needed the second.

Regardless, he'd scraped his skin enough going
through the motions that it stung when he splashed
on his Fahrenheit after-shave. He had a low tolerance
for pain— his own, at any rate— and normally wouldn't
have bothered, but he wanted to present a good appearance. A favorable first impression was essential in
any relationship, and tonight was their first . . . ren-
dezvous.

Yesterday, what with the ether and all of the fuss,
really didn't count.

And he wanted the child to like him. It would be
better for them both if she did.

Failing that, he hoped she wasn't a screamer like
the last one, Rachel, the little blond girl. That had
been more of a sticky wicket than he ever would have
anticipated. The guest room was soundproof, of
course, but his eardrums simply couldn't take the
abuse of her piercing, high-pitched shriek.

It was a shame to have gone through the trouble of
finding a suitable subject, only to have to dispose of
her so soon, because she just wouldn't shut up.

Avery studied his face for a moment in the mirror,
wondering at what had repulsed Rachel. Not a bad
face, he thought, although certainly no one would ever
call him handsome.

His features were unremarkable, he knew, if a trifle
pudgy. His eyes were mud brown in color—

Shit brown, the Good Simon said.

— and closely set under heavy eyebrows that strained
to meet each other over the bridge of his nose.

And his nose! It was the Avery ancestral nose, more the pity, and not the patrician, slender nose of his mother's family. Not quite pug, but with a bulbous tip and the suggestion of a hook.

Add to that a score of tiny spider veins, and it begged for a plastic surgeon's scalpel. Not that he was convinced that rhinoplasty would solve his problem.

There was also the matter of his fleshy lips—

The Good Simon snickered with delight. *Fish-belly lips*, he said.

— and the jowls that aged him prematurely. Plus the jagged scar on his chin from his mother's casket; leave it to her to mark him for life.

"Ugh," he said in disgust, and turned from the abomination of his own reflection. He must be crazy, thinking his face wasn't so bad. The question wasn't why had Rachel screamed, but why on god's green earth didn't everyone?

Avery grabbed his burgundy velvet smoking jacket from the hook on the door, and fled.

Regaining his composure, Avery went to the kitchen for the picnic basket he'd packed earlier. From the refrigerator he took a six-pack of boxed fruit juices, each with its own tiny straw.

As far as he could determine, there wasn't a kid alive who could resist a *box* of juice.

In the wee hours of the morning, he'd used one of his mother's disposable insulin syringes to inject the juice with a homemade concoction of sleeping pills, which he crushed and dissolved in sweet wine.

An ice-breaker was how he thought of it.

To fortify himself, he took a couple of swallows of Blue Nun straight from the bottle. He corked the wine and returned the bottle to the fridge without bothering to wipe the top of germs.

His mother would be aghast.

Such was life.

The door creaked when he opened it. The girl sat up on the narrow bed and scooted away from him until her back was against the wall, hugging her knees to her in a defensive posture. Her overalls hitched up a bit, exposing the tawny skin of her slim legs between the denim pant cuffs and her white anklets.

God, but he loved little girl's socks! Especially those with a hint of lace.

"Hello, Cassandra," he said. He pulled the door securely shut behind him.

The child looked at him with her expressive dark eyes, but said nothing.

"I brought your dinner." He held out the picnic basket. "I'm sorry about lunch, but with the day I've had . . . well, I won't bore you with the details."

When he sat on the foot of the bed, she brought her right hand up to her mouth. Expecting a scream, he flinched, but she didn't make a sound. He smiled, unable to disguise his relief, and saw that she was playing with a loose tooth. A wave of nostalgia washed over him; he remembered exactly what that felt like.

"Oops, you won't be able to eat the apple, I'll bet," he said, opening the basket. "But I've got a peanut butter and jelly sandwich for you, and potato chips, and Twinkies. And grape juice."

Her expression remained wary.

Trying not to appear overeager, he punched the straw into the box of juice and offered it to her. "You must be thirsty."

At least a minute passed before she reached out

with her left hand to take the juice. But she didn't drink it.

Avery unfolded a linen napkin and spread it on the bed. Humming "When I'm Sixty-four," he removed the wrappers from the food and arranged it on a paper plate, which he placed on the napkin.

"You know, when I was your age, I used to put my potato chips inside the sandwich. You have to eat fast, naturally, or the jelly makes the chips soggy, but if you do it right, it's the best."

Cassandra sighed. In a quiet voice, she said, "I want to go home."

He was somewhat taken aback by her directness. As he saw it, he had no choice but to lie. "You *will* go home, in a few days. I— "

"How many days?"

Avery forced a smile. "It isn't polite to interrupt your elders, Cassandra."

"I want to go home," she repeated.

He detected fear in her voice, and it angered him. As nice as he was being, what did she have to be afraid about? "One more word, and you *won't*— "

The child scrunched up, pulling as far away from him as she could. Her hand returned to her mouth. Her dark eyes brimmed with tears.

Avery took a deep breath; this wasn't going as planned. "Look, Cassandra, I'm sorry if I sound mean, but you have to understand that I can't take you home."

She didn't ask why not, but the question was very much in the air.

"*Yet*," he amended, aware that his apology hadn't helped. "I can't take you home *yet*."

Cassandra looked away from him.

His glance strayed again to her creamy brown skin. Such a tender morsel, this one. He knew things would go more smoothly if she was drugged first, but it was pure agony not to touch her.

"Come on, don't be that way," he cajoled. "Eat your dinner and, uh, we'll play a game."

The child ignored him.

Simon Avery had to fight the urge to slap the insolence from her pretty little face. His eyes narrowed and his breathing quickened. After all of the trouble he'd gone to, trying to make things nice for her, and this was how she treated him?

He lashed out, sweeping her dinner off the bed and onto the floor. He stood and flung the picnic basket across the room. It bounced off the wall, disgorged its contents— the apple and the rest of the doctored juice— and skittered back towards him, so he gave it a brutal kick.

Unfortunately, his foot got caught between the handle and the basket, and he had to take a few hopping steps before he freed himself.

Furious at how absurd he must look, he slammed the basket into the wall, again and again, until it came apart in his hands. Panting from exertion and shaking with rage, he turned to the girl. "See what you made me do?"

Eyes wide, she stared at him.

He took a step towards her and then saw the blood on her mouth. And on the front of her overalls. And on her fingers, which were holding a tooth.

Avery hated the sight of blood. No, much more than hated; it frightened him silly, with all the diseases it carried. A single drop of contaminated blood could kill, and how was he to know if she were clean?

That was the reason he suffocated them, to keep them from bleeding all over the place. All over *him*.

But they do bleed, don't they? the Good Simon asked.

He dare not think of that. All that mattered was

that in the interests of self-preservation, there was no way he could touch her now.

His evening was ruined.

"If you're hungry," he said with barely contained fury, "your dinner's on the floor."

And stalked out.

Later, mellowed by the Blue Nun, he turned on the TV to catch a few minutes of the news.

"— refused to confirm that the police have an eye-witness in the Wilson kidnapping," the anchor said. "But a source close to the investigation indicated that the police are aggressively pursuing all leads."

Avery snorted derisively. The cops were a joke; those guys couldn't catch a cold in the dead of winter, if their *own* lives depended on it.

"— has been speculation that the witness, whose identity is being withheld, is undergoing hypnosis."

That caught his attention.

The screen blanked for a split second before changing to a taped interview with an intense-looking, bearded male, who was standing in front of the very recognizable Medical Arts building, near downtown. The caption under the man's hirsute chin identified him as Richard Valle, Ph.D., M.D., and J.D., the proverbial triple threat.

"Hypnosis is a tool," Valle said, "and like any tool, its effectiveness is determined by the skill of the practitioner. But yes, under hypnosis it is certainly possible to recover details which are lost to conscious memory."

Avery frowned, considering the possibilities. He aimed the remote at the set and switched it off.

So the police had a witness. How clever of them. Except he was twice as clever as they could ever hope to be. Too bad for them, he knew damned well who their precious witness was, because *he* had seen *her*, supervising the kids on the playground yesterday.

He even knew her name; he'd been introduced to her any number of times, including at last year's Angel's Night. And while *she* never seemed to remember *him*, he had a facility for recalling the faces and names of people he met.

It was a talent, really.

"Ms. Falk," he said to empty room, "didn't anyone ever warn you never to tell secrets out of school?"

Sixteen

Sitting at the head of the bed, hugging her knees close, Cassie could smell the peanut butter. She was very hungry. All she'd had to eat since she'd been brought here was a ripe, mushy banana and a package of powdered sugar minidonuts that she'd found by the door earlier, but that had been a long time ago.

It was hard to tell what time it was without a window to look out of, but she guessed it was late. It felt late, somehow. Plus what the man had said about being sorry about lunch . . .

And her dinner was on the floor.

The sandwich had survived, from what she could see, partially hidden under the overturned paper plate, but the potato chips had scattered, only to be stomped to pieces during the man's tantrum. As for the Twinkies, one of them stuck to the man's shoe when he'd stepped on it on his way out. The other had disappeared under the bamboo screen that shielded the portable toilet.

Lost for good, but then, her grandmother had never bought Twinkies for her anyway.

Boxes of juice were all over the place, amid the ruins of the picnic basket.

She still had the juice he'd given her, and she took a cautious sip. It wasn't as cold as she liked it, and grape wasn't her favorite flavor, but after having had nothing but lukewarm water to drink, the juice wasn't bad.

Her thirst took over, and in a minute she was sucking the last drops from the box, moving the straw from corner to corner to get it all. With a glance at the door to reassure herself the man hadn't come back, she moved quickly off the bed and retrieved the sandwich and a second container of juice.

There was so little light in the room, she couldn't really tell if the bread was dirty from the floor, but as hungry as she was— her mouth was watering at the thought of food— it didn't matter. She sat at the foot of the bed and ate.

It was so good! Crunchy peanut butter and strawberry jelly on white bread, but it was gone too soon.

Cassie unwrapped the juice, poked the straw into the box, and drank greedily. Halfway through, she had to stop and take a breath.

Her stomach was aching and she remembered her grandmother's warnings about eating too fast, but her hunger was more of a discomfort than a tummyache. She saw a couple of uncrushed chips under the wash table with the apple, which she'd eat, missing tooth or not.

But as she stood, she got a woozy feeling. All of a sudden, her legs felt weak and kind of shaky, the way they'd felt that time her Uncle Zeke had taken her to the San Diego Zoo, and she'd climbed about a hundred million very steep stairs . . .

And there was a bad taste in her mouth.

Cassie sat back down. The weakness had spread to her arms; it took all of her strength to bring the straw to her mouth for another drink.

By the time she finished the second box of juice, she had to lie on the bed. She crawled up to where the pillows were and hugged one of them to her, burying her face in the cool softness.

Her ears were numb. The tip of her nose had no feeling either.

A little scared, Cassie closed her eyes. She'd never been a crybaby, but she couldn't stop a whimper from escaping from her throat.

"Grandma," *she said into the pillowcase,* "please come find me."

Grandma always told her she was a brave little girl, but she didn't feel brave right this minute. Right this minute she was so very, very scared.

"Please, Grandma," *Cassie whispered,* "I want to go home."

SUNDAY

Seventeen

Billy Gaetke watched the Emergency Room nurse paint his knee orange. Not that it was recognizable as his knee; it was bruised and swollen, and tender enough so that even the fleeting touch of the sponge the nurse was using to apply the antiseptic made him wince.

The nurse offered a sympathetic smile. "Sorry, I'm trying to be gentle."

"Don't worry about it, I can take it," he said: "I'm a cop, I'm tough."

"Wait'll you see the needle." She draped a blue linen cloth with a cutout in the center over his knee. "You're sterile now, so don't touch anything."

Right on cue, his knee began to itch.

The nurse took the stainless steel basin with the antiseptic wash and headed for the opening in the curtain. "The doctor will be right in."

"I can hardly wait," he said.

Nor did he have to: the doctor showed up a minute later with an older nurse in tow.

"Okay," the doctor said, "let's relieve some of the pressure on that knee. Ready?"

Gaetke nodded. He watched the nurse open the folds of the sterile-wrapped procedure tray, hoping for a glimpse of the aforementioned needle.

The doctor donned a second pair of thin latex gloves. "Just relax," he said in that breezy, I-won't-feel-a-thing way doctors had.

"Right."

"This will be over before you know it." The doctor held out his hand, into which the nurse placed a blue-capped disposable syringe.

It was of average size, for which he was grateful . . . until he caught sight of the second syringe on the tray. That one—the serious one—was gleaming metal and glass, with a needle at least a couple of inches long.

"Oh boy," Gaetke breathed.

Half an hour later, the fluid had been drained, and his knee was now snugly bound in an Ace elastic bandage. The nurse had fitted him with a lightweight, flexible brace.

"I suggest you take the medication before the pain becomes intolerable," the nurse said, her tone as brisk as her manner. "And you'll need to stay off your feet for a day or two—"

"I can't take any time off."

She made a minor adjustment to the bottom strap of the brace before looking at him. "Doctor's orders," she said, as if that were that.

"Well, he'll have to change his orders," Gaetke said, and stood up gingerly, "because there's no way in hell that I'm sitting this one out."

In the back of his mind, he'd harbored the thought that he might actually go home to catch a couple hours of sleep—and a shower—but Dispatch had a call waiting for him when he checked in.

". . . 821 Brighton Way," the dispatcher said through the static. "See the officer."

Gaetke acknowledged, and then focused his attention on getting his right leg positioned so he could drive. The knee brace complicated matters considerably— it did not allow much lateral movement— but he finally managed to find a workable placement.

Backing out of the parking space, it occurred to him that he had to hope that any suspects he might have to pursue were old and feeble . . . or better yet, lame.

There were two squads parked in front of the house on Brighton Way. The lights were on, the front door open, and he could see both officers inside. Their backs were to him, apparently oblivious of the clear target they offered to anyone inclined to take a shot at a cop.

"This is Victor Eight," he said, keying the mike, "I'm 10-23 on Brighton."

Without waiting for a response, he struggled out of the car and limped up the walk. He had reached the porch before one of the officers turned around and saw him.

"Bang," Gaetke said, and pantomimed pulling the trigger. "You're dead."

The cop offered a sheepish grin and stood aside, making room for him to pass.

He saw at once what was distracting them: Danielle Falk, wearing a large navy-blue T-shirt over white denim shorts, was sitting bare-legged on the couch. He had, of course, noticed prior to tonight that their witness was attractive, but his main concern was the missing girls, Rachel Kraft and Cassandra Wilson.

"What's the problem?" he asked, all business.

The second cop held up a plastic bag with a brownish red blob inside. "Somebody left this by the door."

Gaetke frowned. "What is it?"

"Evidence," the first cop said, adding with a straight face, "or else someone *really* didn't want liver for dinner tonight."

"Liver?"

"Liver, no onions. And now it's yours."

"Shit." He accepted the evidence bag. "Anything else I should know?"

"The house is secure. We walked the perimeter and found nothing to indicate an attempted break-in, but— " the patrolman shrugged "— that isn't exactly a bouquet of roses."

Danielle Falk, who had been silent since he arrived, met his gaze. "I think someone deliberately broke the light across the street."

"You mean tonight?"

"Yes." She lifted her chin, as if she didn't expect to be believed. "I didn't see who did it, but I heard it, and someone *was* out there."

Gaetke considered that possibility and its potential consequences, none of which were good. Something in her eyes told him there was more. "Go on."

She got up and walked to a small table on which sat a phone answering machine. Without comment, she played the messages— or lack thereof— which culminated in an epithet, "Bitch."

Definite hostility there.

"You have Call Return?" Gaetke inquired. The service was one of Ma Bell's more useful inventions, which listed the phone number of a given incoming call.

"No."

"Then I'd advise you to get it." Technology was making it more and more difficult to be anonymous these days; when word got around to the heavy-breathers,

there would no doubt be fewer nuisance calls. "Or
change your phone number, or both."

It was pretty much standard advice, but he doubted
it would be effective against any asshole who was that
skewed mentally . . . assuming that the jerk on the
phone had followed up by flinging liver at the door,
and there weren't two creeps at play here.

"In the meantime—"

The second uniform's radio interrupted him, sput-
tering out the one call guaranteed to turn any cop's
blood to ice: Officer Needs Assistance.

The others were out the door before Gaetke had a
chance to blink. The street cop in him wanted to go
with them, but he couldn't very well leave Ms. Falk to
her own devices. And realistically, he knew he was in
no condition to be out in the trenches, reinforcing the
thin blue line.

"It's the moon," he said when the patrol units had
sped off into the night. He shut the door. "Science
hasn't figured out the genetics of it, but sewer rats
and criminals have a lot in common, and they dearly
love to come out when the moon's full."

"Do they really?" she asked, and laughed.

It surprised him, that laugh, but he liked her for it.
He searched her eyes and saw a determined young
woman in way over her head, but striving as best she
could not to give in to her fears.

He might be jumping the gun, but he believed she
had a legitimate reason to be afraid. The broken
streetlight, the implied threat in that strident, whispered message, and even the damned liver, which he
construed as a crude and heavy-handed form of intimidation.

"Listen," Gaetke said, "I think maybe you need to
get out of here."

"And go where?"

"The city has a safe house—"

Already wan, her color further paled. "Is that necessary?"

"In my opinion, yes. I'm not sure what's going on, but someone's trying to get your attention—"

"He has it," Danielle murmured.

"— *and* ours. The bad guys get a thrill out of taunting the police. They like to rub our noses in it, that they're too smart for us. We'll never catch them . . . or so they think."

"But you will, won't you?"

Gaetke heard the desperation in her voice. And even though she hadn't asked if they'd find Cassie, he answered that question, too:

"Count on it," he said.

Eighteen

Lauren Harper got down on her hands and knees to look under the bed for her Nikes. She wasn't really the sport shoe-type, regardless of her sporadic and halfhearted participation in aerobics class, but she'd be doing a lot of walking today, and anything less comfortable would be a foolish choice.

Perhaps even a clinical sign of borderline masochism.

She saw something that could be a shoe and reached for it, stretching out on her belly on her prized imported Oriental rug. Her fingertips brushed against whatever was under there—

"I hate to ask," a voice said from behind her, "but what are you doing?"

"Chasing dust bunnies." She snagged a lace and pulled out her quarry, a scuffed but still presentable left shoe. Then she glanced over her shoulder at her seventeen-year-old daughter, Brandy, standing in the doorway. "I thought you'd sleep till noon."

"Hmm, couldn't." Yawning, Brandy came in and sat Indian-style on the cedar chest at the end of the bed. "Don't forget I'm on the decorating committee—which you suggested, if I'm not mistaken— and we're supposed to drape crepe this morning."

"That's today?"

"Yes ma'am."

Lauren sighed and peered again into the darkness under the bed. "Seems like only yesterday was your first day at school . . ."

"And now graduation is upon us. I know, Mom."

She detected an anomalous object just out of reach, and squeezed her shoulder under the metal bedframe. Reaching blindly, she made contact with the patterned sole of the second shoe, and batted it hard enough so that it exited on the other side of the bed.

"Anyway," Brandy said, "may I please, pretty please use the Cherokee?"

"I suppose." She wriggled free and flopped over onto her back. Tempted to stay where she was, she made herself ask, "Do you want breakfast this morning?"

"God, no, I'm as fat as a pig."

Lauren laughed. In her thin cotton pajama shorts set, with her flat tummy and that gorgeous strawberry blond hair flowing in a mass of silken ringlets to the middle of her back, Brandy was a willowy vision of youth.

"Mom," her daughter said, disapproving. "It isn't funny."

"You're right about that; it's hysterical." She got to her feet and circled the bed to retrieve the other shoe, then sat down to put them on. "That and all else aside, my beautiful piglet, I'm going to be out most of the day, so if you need to reach me, call the Department and they'll track me down."

"Where are you going?"

In spite of her resolve to maintain an emotional distance about today, she got a sinking sensation in her stomach, as if she were in free-fall from ten thousand feet. "I'm going to help put posters on doors and in windows around town."

"Oh." Brandy's eyes widened, and she bit her lower lip. "The missing girls."

Lauren nodded, and tied an emphatic knot in the first lace. "I'm not sure a poster has ever helped find anyone, but I want to do something."

"Maybe I could beg off at school?"

Lauren smiled and shook her head. "I love you for offering, honey, but that's really not necessary. You go on and have fun with your friends."

"That's the point," Brandy said, twirling a strand of red blond hair. "I mean, having fun, while those poor little girls . . ."

"I know." Lauren reached over to hug her daughter, and found it hard to let go.

Waving to Brandy as her daughter carefully backed the Cherokee out of the driveway a short time later, Lauren sent a prayer heavenward that her not-such-a-child would stay safe.

Was there a parent of a teenager in town, she wondered, who didn't feel they'd dodged a bullet with their own kids? Brandy was an only child, who she'd raised by her lonesome after Gary died, eleven years ago this July. As difficult as that had been, she was profoundly grateful not to have faced what the families of Lucy, Rachel, and now Cassandra were going through.

More insidious was the relentless climate of fear that this current generation of children were growing up in: just yesterday, she'd noticed a full-color advertisement in the newspaper for an identification kit designed specifically for young children. The kit included a do-it-yourself fingerprint ink strip and re-cord card, as well as a laminated photo ID card.

Peace of mind for $3.99, plus tax.

And a few weeks back, at a so-called Kid's Health Fair— which obviously wasn't referring to *mental* health— there'd been a booth at which parents could have a dental technician take wax impressions of their children's teeth.

As the big, bad wolf might say: "All the better to identify your skeletal remains, my dear."

According to the TV coverage of the event, business had been brisk.

On an intellectual level, she could understand the anxiety that would lead a parent into taking such extreme measures; not knowing if a missing child was alive or dead had to be the ultimate torture. But she had to wonder, what kind of emotional trauma were they putting their kids through? And what kind of paranoia were parents instilling in those youngsters by readily anticipating and preparing for the worst possible outcome?

Nickelodeon had Linda Ellerbee offering tips on child safety in a program called, frighteningly, "Stranger Danger," and that was only one of many like-themed specials.

Girl Scouts didn't sell their cookies door-to-door these days. Parents hovered watchfully in the background on Halloween, as their little ones played Trick or Treat. Kids carried personal alarms that, sadly, didn't always bring a hero running.

Life had gotten scarier.

Death, behind a mask of presumed civility, was inching ever closer.

"The wolf," Lauren mused, "is at the door."

* * *

The volunteers gathered in the Department's Community Room. Some kind soul had supplied coffee, tea, juice, donuts, and an assortment of muffins. After resisting temptation for perhaps five minutes, she gave in to the simple pleasure of dunking a plain cake donut into hot, sweet coffee.

Conversation, already subdued, stopped altogether when Evangeline Wilson entered.

Lauren had spoken with her briefly Friday evening, and was heartened by how well the woman looked. Tall and regal, she was dressed in a peach-colored linen dress with a crisp white collar, and wore a small white hat beaded with seed pearls and a hint of lace.

It was Sunday best, Lauren realized.

The young man with her seemed a little worse for wear, with a bandage angled above his left eye and assorted facial bruises, but even so, the resemblance of son to mother was striking.

She'd heard talk in the halls about Zeke Wilson, who some station wit had nicknamed The Zone Ranger, because he took a swing at a shakedown artist despite being outnumbered, three to one. His Harvard Law School status didn't give him any cover with the police; they'd taken one look and figured him for a budding defense lawyer.

None of which concerned her.

She had started to wend her way towards them when Captain Salcedo came into the room, trailed by a tangle of reporters.

"—at least finished checking out the registered sex offenders?" a reporter asked, thrusting the microphone at Salcedo.

Salcedo looked at the man as if he were certifiable, but spoke calmly: "As you probably know, there are sixty-five *thousand* registered sex offenders in California, and tracking their whereabouts is next to impossible— "

"Why is it impossible?"

Lauren recognized the young woman who'd asked that question as a former television reporter whose firing a few months ago had caused quite a stir. Dakota Smith, that was her name. She'd been dismissed after she suggested that her coanchor engage in an explicit, anatomically challenging act after he'd pulled rank to take over a live interview with the mayor.

Presumably Ms. Smith thought they were off the air when she cussed him out. For a day or two, she had been quite the *cause célèbre,* but the public's attention wandered, as it often did, and she'd faded from view.

The frown on the captain's face indicated he was not thrilled to see her. "I'm sorry?"

"Why is it impossible?" Ms. Smith repeated. "We're in the computer age, aren't we, Captain? It shouldn't *be* impossible."

Lauren was close enough to see that the young reporter was not equipped with either a camera or tape recorder, but held a small wire-bound notebook and a stubby, tooth-marked pencil with the eraser chewed off.

"Because," Salcedo said, "we live in a society in which people are free to move around without government restriction or police scrutiny."

"But not criminals— "

"That's all I have time for now," the captain said, raising his hand to ward off further questions. "There'll be Q and A later."

Ms. Smith did not appear pleased, but neither did she protest, instead following her fellow reporters as they swarmed the refreshment table. Lauren watched her for a moment, intrigued by the latent anger in the young lady's demeanor.

Then again, Dakota Smith had had a tough year.

Lauren turned and scanned the crowd, looking for Evangeline Wilson, to whom she wanted to offer assistance in her capacity as a psychologist. Soon after Lucy had been taken, she'd counseled the Bosworths in concert with their minister, and liked to think she'd helped. The Krafts had refused any help from anyone, and remained in nearly total seclusion.

She spotted Cassandra's grandmother and headed in her direction. Along the way, someone handed her a flimsy box overflowing with posters— so fresh that the paper was still warm from the copier— along with a staple gun and a monstrous roll of tape.

Hands full and distracted by the logistics, she wasn't watching where she was going and literally bumped into Zeke Wilson. "Oh, I'm sorry," she said, and promptly dropped the tape.

Wilson bent to pick it up for her.

She rewarded him by raining posters upon him when the box shifted in her arms. Meeting his startled glance, Lauren could only smile. "Would it help if I promise not to staple you?"

"It might." He collected the posters scattered around him on the floor and straightened them into a neat stack. There were laugh lines at his eyes, and a smile tugging at the corners of his mouth.

"I *am* sorry."

"Don't give it a thought. You're here this morning, and the work you're doing . . . that's what counts."

Contrary to what she'd heard, Evangeline Wilson's youngest son appeared soft-spoken and sincere. Lauren accepted the posters back, noting that Zeke's gaze lingered briefly on Cassandra's photograph.

On impulse, she reached out to touch his hand, but his attention had already turned elsewhere, and she saw why: Dakota Smith was approaching.

The two of them might have been alone in the room, Lauren thought, for the intensity of the look that passed between them.

"I saw you last night," Dakota Smith said in a low voice, enunciating each word in a clear and deliberate way, "Okay? I want you to know that."

Zeke Wilson said nothing.

What, Lauren wondered, was going on here?

Nineteen

Matt Price stood at the balcony window, looking out at the spectacular ocean view. It was raining still, and the storm had turned the Pacific steel gray and choppy, sending a flurry of white-peaked waves crashing to the shore. Dark, ominous clouds boiled overhead.

The foul weather fit his mood.

He'd been cooling his heels since he'd arrived in Monterey yesterday evening. He'd paid a courtesy call to the local P.D. to inform them he would be operating in their bailiwick— and had an enlightening conversation with the duty officer. Afterwards, he'd made his way here, to Alyssa Reid's cliffside apartment.

Only no one had been home. Which, on a Saturday night, probably wouldn't qualify as front page news.

Nonetheless, he'd sat in his rental car for hours in the drizzling rain, before giving up around one o'clock and returning to his hotel room. By then he was thoroughly disgusted with himself for not calling ahead to arrange an appointment with Cassie Wilson's runaway mother.

Truth was, he hadn't wanted to surrender the element of surprise.

On the way over again this morning— trying to be philosophical about it— he'd reminded himself that

Sunday mornings were usually prime time for catching people at home and off guard. Unless, of course, by some twist of fate they had *maids* who answered the door and politely insisted upon announcing all visitors.

Which Alyssa Reid did.

Surprise, surprise.

Price heard footsteps behind him, and turned. The former Mrs. Lewis Natchez Wilson didn't look like anyone's mother, in a clinging satin negligee the color of the angry sea. Slender and petite, she was fair-skinned, a honey blond with eyes a deep shade of blue that he had never encountered before.

The fact that she hadn't bothered with a robe told him a thing or two about her.

"Will you be wanting coffee, Miss?" the maid asked from the doorway.

Alyssa Reid studied him for a moment before shaking her head. "Don't bother. This won't take long."

The maid closed the double doors.

Ms. Reid held his card in her hand, and she glanced at it— and then at him again— with mild amusement. "Detective Price?" she asked in a husky, fuck-me voice. "My, but aren't you a long way from home?"

He knew better than to react in any way, shape, or form. Instead he came right out with it: "You are Cassandra Dawn Wilson's mother."

A flicker of annoyance on that perfect face. "I was, in another life."

"I see. Are you aware that Cassie is missing?" Watching her intently, he added, "That she has presumably been kidnapped?"

"No, obviously not."

He detected not the slightest glimmer of concern for her daughter; they might have been talking about a neighbor's lost cat. Which was consistent with what he knew of her past *and* present. "Why obviously?"

"I've had no contact with my ex-husband or his family in several years."

By his definition, Cassie was *her* family, but he let it pass. "And that was by choice?"

"It certainly was and is my choice. I'm entitled to live my own life, Detective Price. Or have they passed a law against that, too?" She arranged herself decoratively on the plush, eggplant-colored couch. On the table beside it sat a huge brandy snifter, full of Tootsie Roll Pops. Alyssa took a red one, unwrapped it, and looked at him with a sly smile. "Want a lick?"

He ignored the invitation. "Are you aware that Lewis is in prison?"

"No. But it's not a shock to hear he's inside. Lewis had little use for the law."

"He killed someone."

"Well," she shrugged a bare shoulder, "he also had a quick temper. He could be incredibly vindictive, if things weren't going his way."

Price considered that. "Did he ever hit you? Is that why you left him?"

"Hardly." She ran her tongue over the candy. "He might be a sociopath, but the man isn't stupid. He knew I'd have cut his heart out in his sleep, if he ever raised a hand to me."

Price thought her capable of that. "I gather it was irreconcilable differences."

"Very much so. As you might imagine, we had many, many differences. It was hot as hell while it lasted, but . . ." she paused as though remembering, if not entirely fondly, "it didn't last long."

"And he hasn't been in contact . . ."

"No. The decision to get divorced was mutual. But just in case Lewis someday were to change his mind about it and conclude I've done him wrong— the man is pathological about settling old scores— I thought it prudent to make a clean, total break."

"And a clean break with your daughter as well, from what I've been told."

"If you know so much about it," Alyssa Reid said archly, "why bother asking me?"

"I like to be thorough."

"How admirable," she murmured. "Are you done being thorough? Because I do have plans this morning."

Price shook his head. "Not quite. You haven't heard from your ex-husband or— "

"I just said no," she interrupted, sounding edgy. "Have I failed to make myself clear?"

"Or," he persisted, "the Wilson family since Cassie was a baby?"

"Once again, the answer is no. Shall I summarize? I walked away from an early marriage that should have never taken place, and abandoned my only child without a second thought."

He believed that.

"I'll admit I'm a self-absorbed, self-centered bitch, but it suits me. Beyond that, I think you're wasting my time and yours."

"Possibly," he acceded.

"Then why are you still here?"

"Because a little girl is missing. I wanted to see for myself if you might have had a change of heart and grabbed her. A long shot, maybe, but stranger things have happened, although— "

"I don't have a heart," Alyssa Reid said, and then laughed. "That *is* what you were going to say, isn't it? You want to hurt me, don't you?"

"I'll leave that for your paying customers." He flashed a caustic smile and started for the door, but couldn't resist a parting shot: "I didn't realize until now how lucky Cassie was that you ran out on her."

Her laughter followed him out into the storm.

It was a fair distance to San Quentin, but traffic was relatively light. Perhaps the Sunday drivers of common lore didn't care for rain-slicked roads.

He'd already checked out of the hotel, so he took the 156 to historic Highway 101, and headed north towards Marin County.

More or less on autopilot, he allowed his mind to wander over the details of this case. He did some of his best thinking while driving, and if ever a case had required critical thinking, this was it.

Why, he wondered, did he have a nagging suspicion that he was overlooking something obvious?

The problem was, with three separate abductions to consider, there was a tendency for the investigation to be scattershot instead of focused. Add to that, they didn't have the luxury of time to dot all the *i*'s and cross every *t*. Inevitably, some things were missed or, heaven forbid, dismissed in the rush.

It was difficult to know what might be important among the thousands of pieces of information they had to deal with along the way. If they set out to treat each lead as though it might break the case, and investigated accordingly, they'd be bogged down in seconds flat. On the other hand, if they skimmed over the intelligence gathered, it was almost certain that someone would disregard the one legitimate clue to be had in the case.

Neither result was acceptable.

Rain beat down on the car, and the temperature differential between inside and out made the windshield fog up. Price turned on the defroster and bumped the wipers up to full speed.

"Okay," he said, catching his own eyes in the rearview mirror. "The girls didn't know the guy who grabbed them, and he probably didn't know them. But he was *ready*. He was out there, looking for an easy opportunity, and when it came, he was prepared . . ."

A moving van passed to his right, splashing grimy, oily water on his windshield. The bastard was really booking, bad weather be damned, and Price regretted not having a siren to shiver the SOB's timbers.

"Another time, another place, pal," he muttered, switching lanes, and resumed his train of thought. "But . . . what does that tell us?"

What it told him was that their perp lived alone. The kidnapper obviously didn't have to worry about the little woman finding incriminating evidence in his car after he'd been out cruising. And he could bring the girls home, where he felt safe and in control.

Not a shock, there. He figured to be a loner. Had he recently moved to town?

Not likely. None of the abduction sites had good freeway access. In fact, the opposite was true, which seemed to suggest that their bad guy was a local who could find his way around town on secondary streets without having to worry about getting lost.

That implied a comfort level which would be incompatible with the just-passing-through predator theory.

Okay then, a local who lived alone. The third question that occurred to him was what in the world had set this guy off? In his experience, sex offenders usually began their criminal careers with relatively minor offenses, like peeping or flashing; this guy seemed to have skipped straight to the big time. Often that signalled a trigger mechanism at work, but what?

A divorce maybe.

As tragic as it was, sometimes a father abused his own children sexually. When and if the mother found out what was going on, she often— but sadly, not always— fled with the kids. With their relatively low risk, in-house victims thus out of reach, a certain percentage of such men felt driven to look elsewhere for gratification.

The little girl or boy who stayed late at the playground or wandered off alone in a mall became unwitting prey. It was a sordid and ugly business their kidnapper-killer had undertaken.

His job was to make it stop.

Somehow, he would.

Even on a sunny day, San Quentin was a forbidding place. Today, beneath dark gray clouds and lashed by a stinging wind coming off San Francisco Bay, it was bleak to the point of melancholy.

And that was appropriate for a facility in which one hundred and ninety-five lives had been taken in the name of the People of California. The apple green gas chamber, installed in 1938 as a humane alternative to hanging, had sat idle for twenty-five years before the execution of Robert Alton Harris in 1992.

The chamber had remained idle since then, however, as the courts argued over whether cyanide gas constituted cruel and unusual punishment. Lethal injection was next at bat, but the day might come when the only way to kill 'em was with kindness.

Their victims had no such luck.

As a law enforcement officer, Price was summarily granted permission to talk to Lewis Wilson, even on such short notice. After showing his police I.D. and driver's license, and handing over his weapon, he was taken to one of the small, private meeting rooms usually used by attorneys visiting their clients.

He sat and drummed his fingers on the scarred wood table, trying not to let the institutionalized gloom get to him. He rather thought he'd prefer the death penalty to spending life in a place like this.

Which might be the point.

Five minutes passed, and then ten. He got up and paced the narrow, windowless room. Price often felt claustrophobic in tight quarters like this, and the sweat began to trickle down his spine.

Then the door opened and Lewis Natchez Wilson was ushered in, dressed in prison blues.

Price had seen a couple of booking photographs of Wilson, but would not have recognized this prisoner as the same man. His hair was close-cut to his head, and he was clean-shaven. More than that, he wore glasses now, which gave him a mild, bookish look.

Except that there was an air of malevolence about him that his changed appearance could not disguise. Menace emanated from the man, little psychic waves of intimidation backed up by the dead nothingness in his eyes.

"I know why you're here." Wilson sat down and took off his glasses, directing his cold stare at Price. "My brother called. You come to tell me what happened to my kid?"

Price heard the raw anger in Wilson's carefully modulated voice, and it raised the hair on his arms. "We're doing everything we can— "

"So am I," Wilson interrupted, "and when I find out who's responsible, who the shit-head is, fucking with my family, I'll see to it the police know where to look for the pieces." Eyes narrowing, Wilson grinned and added: "You'll be needing tweezers to pick the bastard up."

Twenty

Sitting on his heels, Simon Avery used a glass cutter to trace the outline of a square next to the right handle of the French doors. He took his time, scoring the glass deeply to ensure an even edge.

When he was satisfied, he used a triangular rubber mallet he'd stolen from his mother's doctor to tap along the perimeter of the cut, separating the inner section. Humming "Maxwell's Silver Hammer," he wrapped his gloved hand in a dish towel, and with one quick blow, knocked out the piece of glass.

It fell to the hardwood floor inside and broke into shards. The sound wasn't terribly loud, nor was it readily distinguishable from a neighbor's chimes tinkling restlessly in the wind.

Avery looked around himself. The patio at the rear of Danielle Falk's house was quite private within its six-foot adobe walls. And quite pleasant, he thought, shaded as it was by an enormous avocado tree that effectively obstructed the view of anyone glancing his way.

He put the dish towel aside and reached through the glass to unlock the doors.

Like taking candy from a baby.

He stepped over the broken glass into the sanctity of the young teacher's bedroom. It was cool inside, and silent as a tomb. The bed was turned down, although it didn't appear to have been slept in. He sniffed the air delicately, but couldn't catch a scent. Of course, she'd been gone for a while . . .

He would do this room last, he decided.

In the kitchen, Avery looked through the cabinets and drawers, searching for something to take. He had it in mind to leave a memento of some kind for the police to find with Cassandra, when that day came.

Whatever he took needed to be distinctive enough that, *one*, the police would notice it in the first place, and *two*, that Danielle Falk would recognize it as hers when the child's body was found . . . and belatedly realize it had been stolen from her house.

A pleasurable tingle passed through him at the thought. He imagined Danielle's dismay at knowing that the killer had been in her house and touched her belongings, her most private possessions.

The tricky part would be getting the police to confront her with the item, so that she knew what he'd done. That required a degree of cleverness from him, that he select something relatively rare and specific. Something with her initials, perhaps.

An engraved key chain would do, or a sterling silver serving tray, some kind of heirloom. Although maybe not every family went to the extreme his own mother had by having her name etched on each piece.

You think it should be your *name on the silver?* the Good Simon asked.

Just what he didn't need.

If it was, no one would have the stomach to eat. Why would anyone ever want to put your filthy, disgusting name in their mouth?

Avery closed his eyes tight. His mind had gone blank

all of a sudden, and he couldn't remember any of his songs. He felt so vulnerable, so weak, and even *naked* without the protection of his music.

The Good Simon, like a shark in chummed waters, circled his bloodied psyche. *You're the one who ought to be smothered, not those little girls.*

"You don't understand, I have to kill them."

Have to? You mean, want to.

Avery placed a hand on either temple and pressed hard. His brain was squirming inside his skull. "I don't want to, I don't."

Liar.

"I'm not lying, damn you—"

You're the one who's damned.

Holding his head, he sank to the floor. "If you saw them, you wouldn't say that. If you saw the look in their eyes—"

What about their eyes?

Avery wanted to scream.

What is it in their eyes?

"Leave me alone, leave me alone." He pounded on the sides of his head with his fists, fighting pain with pain. "A song, damn it. Think of a song!"

Tell me about their eyes.

"I can't," he cried, in excruciating pain. There was such incredible pressure within the confines of his cranium, that he prayed the bone would crack like a walnut under God's heel.

What makes you think He would spare you? Tell me about their eyes.

"They're dead," Avery whispered hoarsely, in surrender. "Their eyes are dead. After a few days, what's been done to them—"

What you did to them.

"Yes, yes, what *I* did! The light goes out of their

eyes sooner or later, and . . . I can't bear to look at them, or have them look at me, with dead eyes."

So you kill them.

"I kill them as a kindness."

Liar.

"As a kindness," Avery insisted. "When the light leaves them, it's better if they die."

Better for you, you mean. The only kindness in that is to yourself.

It was the only way to end this, so he stopped resisting and gave in the rest of the way. "Yes," he sighed, "better for me."

Shame. the Good Simon said, and was gone.

After several minutes had passed, Avery dared to open his eyes, blinking at the sunlight streaming in through the ivy-covered lattice at the window. A little woozy, he thought it best to remain where he was, and sat huddled on the kitchen floor, his head resting on his knees. Physically exhausted and emotionally drained, he allowed himself the luxury of total relaxation.

He could spare the time: Danielle Falk wasn't here and hadn't been since approximately three o'clock this morning, when she'd been spirited away by a cop who limped like Chester on "Gunsmoke."

Avery had secured her address quite easily. She'd sent him a sympathy card in February after his mother's death; the staff at Northcliffe had impeccable manners. He'd been lax in responding to her condolences— he had too many things on his mind— but thankfully so. He'd simply thumbed through the stack of cards and letters that had piled up until he came to hers.

Thus he'd been standing across the street in the shadows this morning when she left.

Sometimes his luck was absolutely phenomenal.

He'd followed the two of them, naturally, and was relieved to find it a less complicated process than he'd imagined. There was hardly any traffic to contend with in the wee hours, and he'd been able to hang back a safe distance without having to worry about losing sight of their taillights.

Neither had he needed to concern himself about *being* tailed, thank God.

For some reason, Dakota Smith had been doing a little freelance surveillance of the Falk house on her own. He'd spotted her within seconds of his arrival, of course, which left him confident that she hadn't seen him.

Not that she'd hung around long. In point of fact, Ms. Smith had pooped out rather quickly— not everyone had his stamina— and took off at one-thirty, leaving the field open for him.

It was only fitting that he had been rewarded for his patience and perseverance, in that *he* knew where Danielle Falk had been taken. Which was, oddly enough, to a five-story commercial building in the very center of the downtown district.

Clearly, the woman was in hiding, although he wasn't sure from what.

Or rather whom, except it couldn't be him. He hadn't done anything other than check out the neighborhood . . . and now break into her house.

Avery shook his head. Life in the midsized city, he guessed. There were kooks everywhere.

Whatever, it was good to know where she was, just in case he changed his mind about letting her live. He thought it best to keep all of his options open.

And if she were to remember having seen him that day . . . he'd always been curious about garroting.

For now he mustn't allow himself to be distracted by inconsequentials, he thought, and returned his attention to the task at hand.

When he found the memento, its simplicity and utter perfection for his purpose was dazzling.

He found it in a leather attaché on the desk in the second bedroom: Danielle Falk's attendance notebook from Northcliffe Academy.

In her neat handwriting, she'd listed each child's name, including that of Cassandra Wilson. Next to Cassandra's name were dozens of small blue check marks, indicating the child's presence in school on a given day.

Avery ran a shaking finger down the line, and shivered with delight: Cassandra had been in class on Friday, but wouldn't be on Monday.

Or ever again.

This went *beyond* perfection, far beyond. He fumbled through the attaché and found a blue Flair pen. He tested it on a scrap of paper to verify that it matched those check marks. Then he drew a heavy bold line through the empty boxes indicating the re maining days of the academic year. In the last box, he sketched a tiny cross.

So *apropos!*

There were times he amazed himself.

Before he left, Avery made a quick tour of the house, looking for signs of intrusion. There was nothing he could do about the broken glass, but other than that, he wanted the place to appear undisturbed.

He exited the way he came in, through the French doors in the bedroom. Outside, after closing the doors, he stood and listened for indications that anyone was nearby. The good thing about a daylight break-in, was that people expected a certain amount of noise this time of day.

Hearing nothing, he wrapped his prize in the dish towel and tucked it inside his shirt.

A moment later, he was on the street, walking casually in the direction of Dartmouth, where he'd parked the car in the shade of an old elm tree.

After a false start or two, he began to hum "Getting Better."

Yes indeed.

Twenty-one

Zeke was standing at the kitchen sink eating a cold chicken leg, when the phone rang. He'd been avoiding answering the phone of late, but Evangeline had gone to church after the walkabout this morning—their minister had offered to hold a prayer session for Cassie following the noon service—and she'd promised to call him when she was ready to come home.

He'd thrown caution to the wind by renting a car at thirty-plus bucks a day, after a review of his finances convinced him that there was virtually nothing left to salvage of his credit rating. He was bound and determined to get every dime's worth of his money.

He crossed to the wall phone and, still chewing, picked up the receiver. " 'Lo?"

"This is the long distance operator," a bored voice informed him. "Will you accept a collect call from Lewis Wilson?"

Not again, Zeke thought, and swallowed hard, his appetite gone. "Yes ma'am."

"Thank you," the operator said, "Go ahead."

"Lewis?" He tossed the chicken into the garbage, and wiped his fingers on a paper towel. "I didn't expect to hear from you this soon."

"No kidding."

Zeke stretched the phone cord so he could stand by the kitchen window, from where he was able to see the front yard. "What's up?"

"I had a visitor this morning," Lewis said, sounding a trifle put out. "A cop from home."

"Did you catch the name?"

"Name *and* badge number, little brother. Hell, if I had a roll of Scotch tape, I could lift the son of a bitch's fingerprints off my fucking case. Price, Lt. Matthew. Number Seven One Six, La Campana Police Department. You know him?"

"He's the detective handling the kidnapping—"

"Mishandling, you mean."

"That I couldn't tell you." He coughed to clear his throat. "What'd he have to say?"

"Not a lot, considering he came all this way to see me. He wanted to know if I had any enemies who were stupid enough to try and get at me through my kid—"

"Shit."

"—but what the fucker was really getting at was whether or not *I* did it. Or had it done by one of my minions on the outside."

Zeke hesitated, remembering what his mother had said about Price considering everyone a suspect. It was a concept he understood to be valid in theory, but nonetheless despised in practice.

On the other hand, Lewis still had buddies in town who were willing to do his bidding as a means of securing a bad rep in the streets. To Evangeline's deep sorrow— and his chagrin— three years in San Quentin hadn't kept his brother from being named in a criminal complaint for conspiracy to commit arson.

Lewis still had *reach*. Prison bars couldn't change that.

In the interests of preserving family harmony he refrained from comment, asking instead, "What makes you think that?"

"Why else would he come up here?"

"I don't know," he admitted. "Price strikes me as the kind of guy who trusts his instincts— "

"You think he wanted to look into my baby blues and probe the depths of my soul?"

"Something like that."

Lewis laughed. "Either you're delusional, or you been hanging with the wrong crowd, Ezekial."

"Not as much as you have."

"Don't go getting uppity on me," his brother said with a snort. "I told Mama wasn't any good gonna come from you going to *law* school."

This was familiar ground; every time they spoke, Lewis needled him about his "high-tone education" and belittled his accomplishments. He refused, at least this once, to get drawn into an argument.

"Speaking of Mom, she's going to be calling for a ride soon; I'd better get off the line. You want me to have her call you, or— "

"Hold on, little brother. I ain't through. Did you get that address?"

Zeke detected an undercurrent of hostility in his brother's voice. "Lewis, do you think it's a good idea to discuss this— "

"I'm not *discussing* anything, baby brother. Just answer, yes or no?"

"No," he lied, "I haven't."

"What's the problem?"

"No problem, I just haven't gotten around to it." Outside, what was beyond question an unmarked police car pulled to the curb in front of the house. Irrational or not, his first thought was that the phone line was tapped, and someone had been listening in on his conversations with his brother.

It would be easy to misinterpret his brother's request . . . and his response.

"Haven't gotten around to it?" Lewis breathed noisily in his ear. "A simple little thing like *that,* and you can't handle it in three fucking days?"

"It hasn't *been* three days. And if it's so simple, why don't you have one of your toadies do it?"

"Hey, I'm covering the bases, okay? But you owe me, you piss ant punk."

"Look, I can't talk now." The young detective, Gaetke, had gotten out of the car and was standing inside the open car door, arms resting on the roof, staring at the house. "I'll tell Mom you called."

"Zeke, don't fuck with me— "

He'd heard enough trash talk; he pushed off from the counter and walked over to hang up the phone. When he returned to the window, he saw a second car pull in behind the first. The police captain, Salcedo, got out, and the two of them started up the walk.

Zeke met them at the door, looking from one face to the other, trying to read in their eyes what this unannounced visit meant.

Had they found Cassie?

Both men appeared grave, ill at ease. His heart was jolted by a sudden rush of adrenaline, followed by a numbing sense of dread at the prospect of terrible news . . . and having to be the one to tell his mother. His mouth went dry. "What is it?"

Gaetke seemed to recognize the conclusion he'd jumped to. "It isn't your niece."

"Then what?"

"May we come in?" Salcedo asked.

Zeke didn't answer, but stood aside and allowed them to enter. He noticed Gaetke wince as he walked past, and knew the feeling; a little more than thirty-six hours since he'd gotten his clock cleaned, and his back muscles were increasingly stiff and sore. He'd been warned it would get worse before it got better.

Since he wasn't physically up to playing host— nor frankly, in the mood— he followed them into the living room, sat down, and waited for an explanation of why they were here. He didn't have long to wait.

"I wonder if you'd care to tell us, Mr. Wilson," Salcedo said, "what you were doing outside Danielle Falk's house last night."

Zeke didn't even blink; the mock trials in law school had taught him never to express any emotion that could be misconstrued by the opposition. The stakes were higher here, and under the circumstances, he knew, a denial would do more harm than good. Since the first rule in dealing with the police was to keep any answers short and sweet, he said only, "I wanted to talk to her."

"Why is that?"

The second was never to volunteer information or overexplain. "I was told she was the teacher on the playground the day Cassie disappeared."

"Who told you?"

"A reporter."

Salcedo and Gaetke exchanged a look. "Which reporter would that be?" the captain asked.

Zeke couldn't fathom what difference it made, but the very fact they wanted to know made him instantly cautious. "I've talked to at least a dozen reporters in the past few days . . . I couldn't say for sure who said what. Why, is it important?"

"Probably not— " Salcedo began.

"Was it Dakota Smith?" Gaetke interrupted.

Evidently his encounter with Dakota Smith this morning had not gone unnoticed or unreported. Determined as he was not to mention Stormy Landon, neither did he care to get anyone else in hot water with the police. "Sorry, I really can't recall."

"But it was a female reporter?"

"It might have been." There was no lack of female reporters in this town, both television and print, and he assumed it safe to answer that much. "Come to think of it, I believe it was. A woman, I mean."

Gaetke leaned back, an Aha! look in his eyes.

"Did this reporter, whose name has slipped your mind, also give you Danielle Falk's address?"

He knew damned well that Cassie's teacher wasn't listed in the phone book. "I don't want to get anyone in trouble," he said carefully. "I'd rather not say."

Salcedo's brow furrowed. "That's your privilege. But you did in fact go to the house to talk to Danielle Falk late last night."

"It was relatively late, but— " he showed them his bare wrist, "I couldn't say what time exactly, because my watch was stolen. I filed a police report, naturally."

As soon as the words were out of his mouth, he regretted them. The third rule, perhaps the golden rule, was never to be a wiseass.

Salcedo definitely was not amused. "And yet you didn't speak to her, did you?"

"No."

"Why not?"

Something was wrong here: the questions didn't track. Zeke sensed he was about to take a step off into the deep end, but he couldn't see how to avoid the plunge. "I thought better of it."

"Really?"

"Really."

"That's interesting." Salcedo scratched his ear. "Why don't I tell you what I think."

"By all means."

"I think, Mr. Wilson, that you've been harassing Danielle Falk."

Incredulous, Zeke started to protest, and then didn't. He wanted to hear what the police department's brain trust had dreamed up. He listened silently as Salcedo listed several incidents of alleged harassment, which ranged from innocuous to truly bizarre.

Hey, I'm covering the bases, okay? Lewis had said.

"— and I don't believe that you got her address and phone number from a reporter," Salcedo concluded, raising a hand to silence Gaetke, who was frowning and shaking his head as if to disagree.

For a moment, he thought they were going to trot out the old good cop, bad cop routine.

"I think that you got Ms. Falk's address by breaking into the school—"

"What?"

"— and jimmying a locked cabinet, in which you located and possibly removed confidential personnel information from Ms. Falk's file."

"That is the most blatantly ridiculous thing I've ever heard," Zeke said. "Why would I—"

"That, coincidentally, is the same question we've been asking. Why would a smart guy like you do something so stupid?"

"I didn't."

The captain's smile was sardonic. "I'm sure you'll understand, if I find that hard to believe."

Zeke stood up. "I'm sure you'll understand that I'd like to see you prove I did anything. And that's all I've got to say."

Standing at the door, he watched them drive away A scant five seconds later, he heard their sirens begin to wail. Troubled, Zeke stepped out onto the porch to listen, and in the distance, he could hear a chorus of faraway sirens joining in.

In the house, the phone rang.

Twenty-two

Dakota knew better than to try and park close to the crime scene, press pass or not. Instead she pulled off Blue Canyon onto a dirt road that probably accessed some recluse's private property. Fifty yards in, she parked the Skylark by a graying tree stump.

No shade, but in the cosmic scheme of things, maybe the air molecules were still being cooled by phantom tree limbs. It was worth a try, she figured.

She grabbed her notebook and hung the Pentax around her neck, then waited until the dust cloud she'd raised blew by before getting out of the car. After locking up and pocketing the keys, she hurried towards the line of police cars and other emergency vehicles, many with lights still flashing, parked on the other side of the road.

There was an ambulance among the litter, its back doors wide open with the stretcher removed, but she'd heard on the scanner that there'd been human remains found out here, as in beyond resuscitation. The EMTs were on site strictly as a formality.

Or out of morbid interest.

Morbid interest, of course, was the bread and butter of KOUT and every other station in town. There was nothing to compare with the grim titillation of a glimpse of a body under a bloodstained sheet.

The air was dry and dusty, redolent with sagebrush and jimson weed, and she sneezed half a dozen times before she reached the yellow-taped perimeter. She'd never mastered a ladylike sneeze, which meant everyone in a five-mile radius knew she was coming. She even thought she heard an echo off the canyon walls.

The first cop she saw was standing by himself near the trunk of a squad car, red-faced and gulping air like a landed trout.

This was a bad one, then.

Her own stomach turned in anticipation, threatening mutiny, but she ventured on. She noticed several other reporters, clustered in a group near a formation of boulders, and was struck by how subdued they seemed. No one was doing any talking, a rarity in her profession.

Very bad.

None of the camera jockeys were shouldering their equipment, which told her she hadn't missed anything. Dakota shaded her eyes and surveyed the area, trying to locate the actual crime scene.

Of course, it could be back in among the rolling hills, far from the road and prying eyes. Dumping a body was an indelicate transaction, most often done in private, although there were plenty of exceptions to that rule. Cops were partial to black humor, and she remembered a disgusting joke she'd heard about a serial killer who specialized in curbside service—

She saw them, then.

They were standing in a staggered semicircle around a broad, flat rock at least a quarter of a mile from where she was. There had to be at least thirty cops, but the way they were spaced imparted a sense of isolation as though none of them could tolerate human contact.

Even at this distance, she could feel the anger in the way they stood.

Something was laid out on the rock, but she couldn't tell what . . . except that it had to be a who.

Dakota removed the lens cap from the Pentax and peered through the viewfinder. The camera's telescopic lens wasn't as good as binoculars would be in this situation, but hers were dangling on a doorknob in her apartment where she'd left them in a rush this morning, and the zoom would have to do.

She adjusted the focus and zeroed in on the rock.

At first her mind refused to register what her eyes were seeing, and then she gasped. If not for the strap around her neck, she would have dropped the camera.

Or thrown it.

She closed her eyes and turned away, but the images were seared into her brain. Torn flesh and exposed bone, loops of intestine . . . bile rose in her throat.

"Get your shot?"

Dakota recognized the voice as belonging to Bud, the KRAH crime reporter, who had a well-deserved reputation as a hard case. He was one of the few who didn't treat her as if she were the Typhoid Mary of television journalism. Even so, a little of Bud went a long way. She looked at him with a certain trepidation. "Is that . . ."

"What's left of her."

"Oh god, the poor kid." Her knees felt weak, and she hugged herself. It was small comfort, considering, but would have to suffice. "Who could do that to a child? What kind of animal . . ."

"It wasn't the killer who did *that*. But," Bud sighed, "he left her for said animals to find."

"That's just as bad, isn't it?"

"If it makes you feel better, the word is she was already dead when they got to her, tore her up that way." Bud scratched his beard as if in deep thought. "Coyote, more than likely, although a pack of dogs could do it. Death pretty much rattles the links in the food chain."

"You're not helping."

"Sorry 'bout that."

"Who found her?"

Bud startled her by chuckling. "Funny you should ask. You know what's on the other side of that hill?" He gestured with his chin.

"Can't say that I do." She hated twenty questions, unless she were the one asking them.

"The police department's shooting range."

"You're not serious . . ." No wonder the cops looked mad, a body dumped virtually under their noses.

"As a heart attack. Yes, I am. A couple of off-duty officers were out practicing the old quick-draw, wiling away a lazy Sunday afternoon. The way I heard it, they noticed all these scavenger birds circling in the air and figured there must be something dead nearby. Something with some *size* to it."

Dakota felt her stomach churning and took a couple of deep breaths.

"Now they're not admitting to this part, but I was in the Army my own self, and I figure cops are every bit as bloodthirsty as your average grunt. They decided, what the heck, they wouldn't mind pumping a few rounds into something more substantial than a paper target, if only for the sound of the bullets striking flesh."

Her mind, ever accommodating, supplied the appropriate sound effects, and she flinched.

"And lo and behold, our marksmen stumble across what's left of Rachel Kraft."

"No offense," Dakota said, covering her mouth with her hand, "but I think I'm going to be sick."

"None taken," Bud called after her.

She found a place to sit down afterwards, and rinsed the bad taste from her mouth with sips from a can of tepid Coca-Cola given to her by a sympathetic paramedic. He'd offered her a whiff of pure oxygen to clear her head, but she had to work in this town, and knew she'd never live it down if she accepted.

Tossing her cookies was bad enough.

Fuzzy-headed or not, she meant to do her job. For the moment, she settled for making notes describing the scene and drawing a rough map of the terrain. She sorely missed the station's Sony, but figured she could con Bud into giving her a minute or so of generic footage to use in lieu of taping her own stuff.

He owed her, after grossing her out.

Frowning in concentration, she didn't notice Billy Gaetke until he was standing directly in front of her. She looked up at him, but didn't say anything for the simple reason that there was nothing to say.

Gaetke made a face and sat down next to her, stretching his right leg out straight. A moment later he handed her a packet of Kleenex.

"What's this for?"

He glanced at her briefly and looked away. "You're crying."

"I am?" She raised a hand to her cheek and felt the wetness of her tears. "Wonderful. Always the last to know." She took a tissue out of the pack and wiped her eyes. "Thanks."

"Anytime." Gaetke shook his head. "Days like this, I wish I'd been a fireman . . . no, that isn't true. I want to catch this guy."

"Somebody damn well better catch him." She wadded up the Kleenex and stuffed it in the Coke can. "That reminds me, I haven't seen the honcho in awhile."

"The who?"

"Detective Price," she clarified. "He's still in charge of the task force, isn't he?"

"Why wouldn't he be?"

"Obviously no one ever told you it's not polite to answer a question with a question."

"They told me," Gaetke grinned engagingly, "but I don't give a rat's ass about being polite. I repeat: why wouldn't Matt be in charge of the task force?"

"There's been talk— " she shrugged. "The investigation is going nowhere fast, and the mayor is pressuring Salcedo to assign someone new, someone with a fresh perspective on the kidnappings."

"If that's true, the mayor's a bigger fool than even I thought he was."

"And that Gennaro thing simply won't go away— " Dakota stopped short; the look he was giving her was cold enough to flash-freeze buttercups in a mastodon's mouth.

"There are some questions that aren't worth answering," was all he said.

"Maybe, but my mother always taught me, try try again. Let's change the subject . . . it might be insensitive, but can you tell how long the body's been out here?"

"No comment— "

"— pending autopsy. Right." Dakota noticed Gaetke rubbing his knee and resisted the impulse to offer to help. "Hurt yourself?"

"What?"

"Your knee."

"Yeah, I banged it up pretty bad. The Emergency

Room doctor gave me a brace, but it limits my mobility, so I haven't been wearing it."

"Typical," she said under her breath. Men could be such nincompoops.

"Listen, turnabout's fair play, so I want to ask you a question . . . about Zeke Wilson."

She glanced sideways at him, intrigued. "Ask whatever you want."

"Did you give him Danielle Falk's address?"

Dakota feigned an innocent look. "Who, me? How could I? I don't have it."

Gaetke laughed. "Bullshit. You were parked on Dartmouth last night in a 1965 Buick Skylark, license number Zebra Ocean Ida— "

"I don't own a car."

"The same Buick which is parked a couple of hundred yards from here."

"Okay, okay, I was there." She ran a hand through her hair, brushing it back from her face. "I knew that car was too damned *pink*. Who saw me? No, don't tell me, I know, everybody."

"Everybody," Gaetke agreed. "The first call came in about a quarter after nine."

And she'd gotten there at eight-fifty. "Didn't waste any time, did they?"

"It's a nice quiet neighborhood. They notice strange vehicles that park on their streets, particularly when no one gets out of the car."

No question that she'd have to work on her surveillance technique. Or else stick to noisy neighborhoods, where nobody could be bothered to call the police if the devil himself showed up packing an Uzi.

"And you did honk the horn."

"Don't remind me. Besides, what does any of that have to do with Zeke Wilson?"

"Someone overheard you say to him that you'd seen him last night— "

Dakota narrowed her eyes. "It's getting so a person can't have a private conversation."

"— and since we know you were in the neighborhood between nine and one last night, the assumption is *that* was where you saw him."

"Hmm." None of what she'd done yesterday was against the law . . . except, of course, for that little escapade at Northcliffe. Considering that, she thought it wise to give Wilson up.

This was her comeuppance for trying to persuade the guy to talk to her. Okay, she'd been a mite heavy-handed with the I-saw-you-last-night routine, but no one was anxious to be interviewed by a reporter for an outlaw station, and she had to be inventive.

"All right," she sighed, *"mea culpa*, I saw the man. He walked by Danielle Falk's house, twice."

"What time was that?"

"Shit, I don't know. Early. I'd just gotten there myself. What is this, anyway? Me, the neighbors saw, but this guy's invisible?"

Gaetke waved that off, as if it were unimportant. "Did he go up to the door?"

"Not that I saw."

"You're sure?"

"I'm sure. He looked at the house when he walked by, nothing more. And pardon me, but so what?"

"This isn't for release," Gaetke said.

"No, it never is," she murmured, and listened as he detailed a bizarre series of events which, evidently, the police were inclined to attribute to Zeke Wilson. When he'd finished, she nudged his leg with hers. "You're working too hard, Gaetke."

"I'm sure you can appreciate the department's concern for the well-being of a witness."

After Gennaro, she thought, they'd better be. But for once, she didn't blurt out what she was thinking. Instead, she nodded solemnly. "The thing is, why would Zeke Wilson want to harass Danielle Falk?"

"Word on the street," Gaetke said, lowering his voice, "is that Cassie's father wants to send a message to Danielle that he holds her personally responsible for his daughter's disappearance."

"But that's crazy— "

"And who better to deliver it than a clean-cut Harvard law student?"

Looking past him, Dakota noticed a stretcher being carried over the rough terrain. The black body bag strapped onto the stretcher was much too large for the small form within.

"A child killer?" she suggested.

Twenty-three

Danielle heard the soft *ding* of the elevator in the apartment's private foyer and turned in that direction. A stone-faced cop had been sitting guard in the hall all day— and still was, as far as she knew— but otherwise no one had ventured up to the penthouse.

The penthouse sat atop a five-story building which also housed the city's personnel department, located on the fourth and fifth floors. The third floor was vacant, she'd been told, and was undergoing renovation to the specifications of the future tenant, while the first and second floors had been made over into a mini-mall of small boutiques and specialty shops. There was also a bakery and a hole-in-the-wall cappuccino bar.

All of the shops in the building were closed on Sunday, as was most of downtown. When she'd looked out a few minutes ago from the glass-walled terrace, the surrounding streets were nearly deserted. The only person she'd seen was a heavy-set woman wearing a red coat and a checkered scarf, who was waiting at the bus stop on the corner.

The object in being here was to stay out of sight, but somehow the very quiet made her edgy and restless. Moreover, in retrospect, she had serious doubts that it was necessary for her to hide.

The more she thought about it—and she'd had plenty of time to think—the more convinced she became that bringing her to this safe house represented a major overreaction on the part of the police. At best it implied a kind of knee-jerk response to an imagined or grossly exaggerated danger; at worst it hinted at hysteria.

But any hope she had for liberation faded when the door opened and detectives Price and Gaetke walked in, their expressions grim.

"I'll be going, then," the uniformed officer said with a nod to her from the doorway, as though more than two words had passed between them all day. "I'll see you in the morning."

When the door closed behind him, Danielle asked, "What is it? What's happened?"

Price looked at her, his eyes conveying both outrage and pain. "We found Rachel this afternoon."

There was no mistaking what that meant. Danielle took a step back from him, a dull ache in her heart, wanting to turn away and not have to hear any more . . . but then stopped. She couldn't run from this.

"There hasn't been an autopsy yet, but the coroner's preliminary findings would seem to indicate that she hasn't been dead long. They figure four days at a minimum, but no more than a week."

"That poor child . . ."

"Which means if the bastard killed Rachel as late as Thursday, he kept her less than three weeks. That isn't much time."

"For Cassie, you mean."

"To find her . . . if we can."

Danielle searched his eyes. "If you find him, the man who's doing this, you'll find her."

"That's one big if. Beginning the day Lucy was taken, we've been tracking the usual suspects, eliminating them one by one, but it's a slow, tedious process. Without a partial tag on the van, we're at a total dead end there. In all honesty, we don't have much to go on."

"I was out there today," Gaetke added, "where they found Rachel, and I can tell you, the crime scene techs weren't very optimistic about developing any physical evidence at the scene."

Price nodded in agreement. "We've been hampered all along by the way this guy operates. We're either going to have to get lucky— "

"—or his luck will have to change."

Was that what it all came down to, then? Danielle had a theory that people made their own luck, good or bad, by the choices they made. Sometimes it was those choices that had to change . . .

All at once the obvious hit her, and she knew beyond question what she had to do. "What if he were to come after me?"

"That's not gonna happen," Price said, reassuringly. "You're safe here."

"You don't understand . . . I *want* him to come looking for me."

"What?"

"I want to be the bait."

Behind Detective Price, Gaetke was already shaking his head. Price merely looked at her as if he believed her certifiably insane.

"If the killer thinks I saw him," Danielle reasoned, "and I can identify him, he'll have to come after me, won't he?"

"Not necessarily," Price said. "I hate to say it, but grabbing a kid is easy. It's the ultimate crime of opportunity; if the circumstances don't feel right to him, he can always walk away. There'll be another kid to-morrow, or the day after that."

"Yes, but— "

"Let me finish. Targeting one specific person is a different matter entirely. It's a question of control, and he won't like that he can't choose the time or place that suits him."

"But we can choose," Danielle said, "to make it easy for him to find me."

Gaetke grinned. "Maybe leave a trail of bread crumbs, like in Hansel and Gretel?"

"The trouble with that is, even if we served you up on a silver platter, an adult is more dangerous to him than a child."

She considered that argument specious, since it was how dangerous *he* was to Cassie and other children that concerned her. "Look, I want to do this. I have to at least try, or I won't be able to live with myself."

"Too many things could go wrong," Price said. "I'd never get it past the captain."

"There has to be a way."

"Well," Gaetke said thoughtfully, "we could always use a decoy. I mean, it's been done before. Let this guy think she's home, alone at night, but have a police officer stand in for her."

Now Price was the one shaking his head. "No."

"Come on, Matt, it could work."

Slightly stunned to find Detective Gaetke on her side, Danielle was content for the moment to let the two of them argue it out, and remained silent.

"That kind of setup is too damned complicated, not to mention labor- and time-intensive. Don't forget the captain's motto: Keep it simple."

"But it *would* be simple— "

"We'd have to leak the story that she's an actual

eyewitness, get the right kind of press coverage, *and* enough air time to make sure he'd hear about it— "

"No sweat. I've got half the reporters in town eating out of my hand."

Price's laugh was mirthless. "I'd get a rabies booster, if I were you. But there are always risks, whether you use a decoy or not."

"It's worth a try."

"It isn't an effective use of manpower. We'd be pulling guys off the streets to watch the house, and in the meantime ignoring leads— "

Gaetke held his arms out as if beseeching the heavens. *"What* leads? We haven't got any leads."

"And we won't get any, sitting in the dark waiting for our prince to come— "

"Excuse me," Danielle said quietly, "but I don't need permission from the police department or anyone else to do this."

Judging by their expressions, they'd forgotten she was there. Price scowled at her. "What the hell are you talking about?"

"I can get press coverage on my own, simply by agreeing to an interview. I can say that I saw someone who I believe to be the kidnapper— "

"Who happens to be a killer," Price said.

"I can go to work tomorrow, sleep in my own bed, and otherwise make myself visible. The odds are, he'll come looking for me."

"Odds are you could wind up dead."

Danielle lifted her chin. "I can protect myself, if I have to." That was an outright lie, but she needed them to understand she was willing to take a risk.

"Shit." Price ran a hand through his hair. "Talk some sense into her, will you?"

Gaetke hesitated, and then said, "I would . . . except I think it's a good idea. And it might be the only real chance we've got to get this guy."

The silence was absolute.

"Wonderful. Okay, fine. I'll talk to Salcedo first thing in the morning." Price took two steps towards the door, then snapped his fingers, stopped and turned, pointing at his partner. "Tell you what, Billy, in the meantime, I'm assigning you to guard her. You shouldn't be on the street with that bum knee, and I'm sure the two of you can come up with a nifty little plan, preferably something that doesn't get her killed."

"What was that all about?"

Detective Gaetke sighed, took his jacket off, and sat down on the couch. "He's been working twenty-hour days, the man's got to be tired. And he's kind of touchy, when it comes to the care and feeding of witnesses."

"Why?"

"It's a long story."

She sat in the chair opposite him. "I think I can spare the time. I'd like to know what set him off."

Gaetke looked at her wearily. "It's not a pretty story, but I guess not many of them are. You heard of a guy named Salvatore Gennaro?"

"No, I don't think so. Should I have?"

"Maybe not. It was in the papers, but didn't get a lot of play. The family objected, maybe, I don't know."

There were weeks during the school year when she never got around to taking the rubber band off the newspaper, when her life was too hectic to do more than glance at the weather forecast.

"This guy, Gennaro, had seen a gang shooting, teenage punks fighting over a lack of respect." Gaetke made a sound of disgust. "That's what these kids kill for, disrespect. Nobody ever told 'em no one has to *give* you respect, you got to earn it.

"Anyway, Gennaro saw the shooting and did the stand-up thing by reporting it to the police. He gave a statement and identified the shooter."

"And?"

"Naturally, the bad boys didn't like that idea at all. They set out to cause Gennaro some grief. They broke windows, slashed his tires, the obvious things. Of course, there were threats: testify and die. We're gonna rape your daughter and your wife, and while we're at it, maybe your white-haired mother, too. We'll burn your house down with you and your family in it."

"Wasn't there anything—"

"The police could do? Yes and no. He was here for a while, but he had a business to run, a mom-and-pop grocery over on Chestnut, and if the store didn't open six days a week, the family would go bankrupt before the case ever went to trial."

It seemed to her that the only person who had rights was the criminal, and that was an injustice on its own.

"But Matt did what he could," Gaetke went on. "The safe house, patrol units cruising the neighborhood, and he even got Gennaro a permit to carry a concealed weapon.

"What he couldn't do was relieve the pressure. A month went by and Gennaro was a basket case. I was on patrol then, and I had never seen anyone look as bad as he did. His *skin* turned gray, his hands were shaking so bad he couldn't make change."

Danielle noticed Gaetke's hands had tightened into fists, and she wondered if that were intentional or involuntary.

"No one knows what the guy was thinking, but the day comes when he calls Matt and says he can't take it anymore. He's scared shitless and he wants out. His wife has taken to her bed and won't eat. His twelve-year-old daughter is chewing her fingernails down to the bloody quick, and his sainted mother is having palpitations. Sal thinks he's developing amnesia all of a sudden. What does it matter if these kids kill each other, anyway? What business is it of his?

"Matt hurries over to the grocery, and they go across the street to this little park to talk in private." Gaetke frowned and looked away from her. "If Gennaro dummies up, it's over, the shooter walks. Any cop would hate to see that happen, and Matt had been after this shooter for a couple of years. Plus the D.A. was rabid that they get the guy at any cost."

"Even so . . ."

"Yeah, I know, sometimes the cost paid exceeds value received. In the end, Matt did the human thing and let Gennaro off the hook. He told Sal to go home, close the store, and lay low until the word got out that he wasn't gonna testify."

"This isn't a happily-ever-after story, I take it."

"You could say that." His glance still averted, Gaetke squinted, as though trying to make out some distant object. "Gennaro got shot crossing the street, not two minutes later. Never knew what hit him."

"But Matt did . . ."

"He was standing maybe ten feet away when Gennaro got wasted."

"For which he blames himself," Danielle said, softly.

"Exactly. Although what else he could have done, I don't know."

She met his eyes briefly, and it was her turn to look away. "He doesn't want it to happen again."

"Neither do I."

Danielle felt his hand on her shoulder and shivered in spite of herself.

Twenty-four

Cassie struggled to open her eyes. She felt so bad, her head hurt and her tummy ached from being sick.

The man had left a paper sack inside the door while she slept, in which she'd found another peanut butter sandwich, a bag of corn chips, and three boxes of fruit juice. She was so very thirsty, she drank two of the juices— today it was Rockadile Red— but had only eaten half of the sandwich, when she needed to throw up.

Her throat was sore, and it hurt to swallow.

Worse than that, she was getting weaker. Her legs were kind of quivery, and when she sat up in bed or tried to walk, she got dizzy, the way she did after dancing in circles on the front lawn at home. She would fall to the grass and watch the sky above her spin . . .

That was a better kind of dizzy, because she was home. More than ever, Cassie wanted to go home now.

And she was scared the man wouldn't let her.

Somehow she had to get away from here. Somehow she had to convince the man that she wouldn't tell on him and get him in trouble. She was good at keeping secrets. She'd learned to keep stuff private when she was real little, because she hated the looks people gave her when they discovered her father was in prison.

She would promise never to tell anyone about the way the man tricked her with the toy cat in the box, or say anything

*about being kept in this terrible place. She would swear on
her mother's eyes, cross her heart, and hope to die.*

The problem was, adults didn't always believe kids.

*In her experience, adults were quick to decide a kid was
fibbing, although more often as not, it was the grown-ups
who were telling lies.*

Cassie had heard a lot of adult lies:

*A nurse saying, "This won't hurt" before giving her a
booster shot.*

*The social worker who told her "Of course, your daddy
loves you . . ."*

*And anyone who ever said to her, "This is for your own
good . . ."*

*The only person she absolutely trusted not to lie to her
was her grandmother. Grandma had a way of looking at a
person that let them know there was no need for an untruth,
that she might hate the deed, but never the person.*

*Uncle Zeke lied sometimes. She'd heard him on the phone
once, telling a friend that he couldn't go to a party because
he had to babysit with her, when the fact was he had a date
with the friend's ex-girlfriend.*

A white lie, her uncle called it.

*Her father lied, she knew. She had seen it on the news,
that he went to court, swore an oath on the Bible, and said
somebody else did it. Somebody else shot Isiah Washington,
although he admitted to having been there, and having
brought his gun.*

*Grandma told her later, in private, that it wasn't the
truth, that her father had to say what he did to save his own
life. The lawyer, who told Grandma he preferred not to know
if her daddy was guilty, had warned that the jury would
give him the death penalty if they weren't able to raise the
least little doubt.*

*Still, if she could convince the man to let her go, she
would keep her promise not to tell. No matter who asked*

*her, no matter how many times they asked, she would lock
her lips and throw away the key.*

*Cassie turned over on the bed, so that she could see the
door. It was dark in the room; the night-light wasn't as bright
as it had been at first.*

*She wondered when the man would be back, and if he
would believe her promises. She wondered, too, if he meant
to keep his promise to let her go home . . . and when?*

How many days had she been here already?

How many days were there in Forever?

MONDAY

Twenty-five

The full moon all but filled the night sky, its pale light casting odd shadows through the maple trees that lined the street.

The screen door squeaked behind him, and Zeke glanced over his shoulder. "What are you doing up?" he asked his mother. "I thought you took a little pink pill and went to bed."

"I did," Evangeline smiled as she sat next to him on the steps, moving with a younger woman's grace. "I'm guessing it hasn't kicked in yet. And I could ask you the same question, young man; you've hardly slept a wink since you've been home. Where is it you go in the middle of the night? And what in heaven's name are you up to?"

"Nowhere and nothing," he said, which was at least half-true; he was doing an inordinate amount of nothing. "It relaxes me to wander."

"If it relaxes you, why can't you sleep?"

"Too much to think about." Zeke took his mother's hand in both of his, and kissed it. "Don't be fussing about me, Mom. You're the one who needs to rest. How are you doing, really?"

"I'm getting by."

He ran his thumb over the work calluses on her palm,

acutely conscious of the fact that his own hands bore no such evidence of manual labor. "Do you ever think about why this happened to our family?"

"Never."

"How do you keep from it? I mean, first my father with his troubles, then Lewis, and now Cassie. And don't tell me the Lord never gives us burdens greater than we can bear, because I don't believe that."

"It isn't that," Evangeline sighed. "I know He would never allow a child's life to be taken for the sole purpose of strengthening a parent's character."

"Even so— "

"It's simply the way life is. Terrible things happen all the time, no rhyme or reason to it. Why bad things happen to a specific person is a question that has no single answer."

"But enough is enough."

"Who's to say what's enough? You could argue, for example, that if I hadn't so many lofty ambitions for my granddaughter, she would have been going to the neighborhood school three blocks over, and this man would have kidnapped someone else's child. How is that better?"

"Cassie would be home now."

"I would willingly give my own life to save Cassie, but I could never trade another child's life for hers. It isn't mine to do. Am I being punished, then, for wanting a better future for my grandchild?"

"Do you accept that you might never see her again?" He paused and took a breath before adding, "That she's . . . that she might already be dead?"

In the dim light, Evangeline's eyes seemed to shine, and she gripped his hand tightly. "Cassandra isn't dead. I feel that in the marrow of my bones."

"Mom . . ."

"In my heart I know, the child is alive."

It hit him, then, that in his own heart he'd been every bit as certain that Cassie *was* dead, that her life had ended long before he'd ever boarded the plane in Boston. The numbness he'd felt, the emotional distance he'd kept, both were a result of that certainty. He'd been operating on the premise that all of the energy being expended was directed at recovering a body . . . and he could afford to play along with his brother's game.

And if he was wrong?

"We have to have faith that Cassie will come through this," his mother said, as though reading his mind, "and pray for her safe return."

"I can do more than that," he said quietly.

The only cloud in the sky drifted in front of the moon, which illuminated it with an otherworldly light.

At the police station, he sat in the parking lot for a good while, going over everything in his mind. He needed to convince himself that he wouldn't be making a mistake by talking to the police, because once he did, there would be no turning back.

He hadn't broken the law, but neither had he been entirely forthcoming with Captain Salcedo or Detective Gaetke yesterday afternoon.

With any luck, it wasn't too late.

When Lewis found out, there would be hell to pay, but he would deal with his brother when the time came.

The desk officer listened to his story without comment, glanced at the wall clock, shook his head, and picked up the phone. "I don't know if anyone's here at this ungodly hour, but I'll try to find a warm body for you to— wait a second." He held a hand up as if stopping traffic. "Lutz, yeah, this is Hastings. Is there anyone from the task force hanging around?"

Restless, Zeke crossed the lobby to a glass-enclosed bulletin board. Posted inside were announcements of a bike safety class and an upcoming police auction of unclaimed stolen property. There were, as well, grim listings for the Domestic Abuse Hotline, Rape Crisis Center, and the city's Drug Intervention Program.

Testimony to the inherent cruelty of humankind, or testament to the will to survive and persevere in the face of all odds? His mother, the eternal optimist, would believe the latter.

"Mr. Wilson," the desk officer called to him, "you can go on back now."

For some reason, Zeke wasn't in the least surprised to find Matthew Price still at his desk, working at one in the morning. A phone at his ear, Price motioned for him to pull up a chair, which he did.

A second later, without having said a word, Price dropped the phone into its cradle. "What can I do for you?" the detective asked.

"Actually, I think I can do something for you," Zeke said. He reached into his inside jacket pocket, withdrew his Olympus— a palm-sized, voice-activated tape recorder— and placed it on the desk. "This was a Christmas present from my mother and my niece."

Price smiled faintly. "No one mentioned today was show-and-tell."

"I think you need to listen to the tape."

"Okay." The detective picked up the recorder. "Do you want to tell me what I'm going to hear?"

Zeke shook his head. "Afterwards."

"Whatever you say." Price pushed Play and set the

recorder down again, drumming his fingers on the desk without making a sound.

"— tell you what to do," Lewis said on the tape. "Get me whatever you can. Address, phone number, the kind of car she drives, all of that— "

"Why? What's the point?" His own voice sounded distant and unfamiliar.

"The point is, I asked you to do it and you owe me, *mi hermano.*"

"Tell me what you're going to do."

"What the fuck can I do from here?" Lewis never bothered to try and disguise his irritation. "Nothing, am I right? So don't bust a gut over it . . . no one has to know the Boy Wonder sunk to my level. You should know by now I won't rat you out— "

Price stopped the tape with a glance at him. "Your brother's been in prison too long; he's starting to talk like Jimmy Cagney in *White Heat.*"

Startled, Zeke could not hold back a nervous laugh. "Why'd you turn it off?"

"We're not amateurs at this, we already know." Price shuffled through a small stack of files, selected one and handed it to him. "In fact, I've been waiting for you to come in and do the right thing."

He read his own name on the file label: Wilson, Zeke Juarez. When he opened the folder, it was empty. "What does this mean?"

"It means you don't have an arrest record, per se. But an empty jacket always piques my interest, so I made a few discreet inquiries and found out you were picked up when you were fifteen with your brother for questioning on a burglary charge."

Zeke blinked, but said nothing.

"Lewis swore you weren't involved and that kept your name off the criminal complaint, which I assume is why he thinks you owe him. A burglary rap would

very likely have kept you out of law school, so maybe
you do."

"I didn't do anything wrong."

"Glad to hear it." Price took the folder back, got
up, and walked over to a paper shredder. He fed the
empty file into the shredder, which reduced it in quick
order to manila confetti. "Since you stayed out of
trouble, when you turned twenty-one, your juvy sheet
was destroyed."

"That's reassuring."

"Isn't it, though?" Price sat on a corner of the desk.
"Which brings us to today. We've heard through other
sources that Lewis isn't behaving himself. Salcedo
thinks you were helping him harass Danielle Falk, doing the leg work. Were you?"

"No, I . . . no."

"Then why go by her house? Enlighten me."

"I went there to stop them, if I could." It was the
truth, but it sounded improbable, even to him. "I
know what my brother is capable of, and it isn't pretty.
If he decided to harm Danielle Falk, he'd order it
done with no hesitation whatsoever."

Price frowned and shook his head. "I can't see how
that would help Cassie."

"His mind doesn't work that way," Zeke said. "This
isn't even about Cassie anymore, it's about *him*, period. The way my brother sees it, Danielle Falk com-
mitted a crime against him personally, and he's gonna
be the judge, jury, and executioner."

"Shit."

"I feel responsible, because I slipped and mentioned
her name to him on Saturday after a reporter— " he
hesitated momentarily, but then decided to trust Price's
discretion. "After Stormy Landon told me that
Danielle Falk was a witness. Lewis was after me to get
more information about Ms. Falk, but I thought from

the outset that it was a diversionary tactic. He admitted to me later that he had someone else working on it."

"And instead of calling to inform us, you enlisted in the cavalry."

"What?"

"Inside joke, never mind. What exactly were you going to do, if someone showed up to do the lady harm?"

"Warn them off somehow, or reason with them."

The slightest hint of sarcasm entered the detective's voice. "That would work."

"But what I did was watch," Zeke said, reaching for the tape recorder. "And dictate the license plate numbers of any cars that drove through that neighborhood, that night, just in case."

Price looked intrigued. "How many cars are we talking about?"

"Eight, maybe nine." He ejected the tape and handed it over. "I was there when Detective Gaetke and Ms. Falk left. And I wasn't the only one; there was a guy watching from across the street."

"A guy. Could you describe him?"

"Not well enough to stand up in court. I didn't recognize him, but I don't know all of my brother's friends. He was standing in the shadows, I couldn't see his face, but when he walked away, he looked to be about five foot ten or thereabouts, a medium build."

Price nodded thoughtfully. "Anything else?"

"The guy got in his car and followed the detective and Ms. Falk. A light-colored sedan. I got all but the last two numbers on his plate when he drove by. It's on the tape."

"Nice work," Detective Price said, then stood up and extended his hand. "Welcome to the cavalry."

Twenty-six

Ill at ease standing in the deserted foyer, Lauren Harper pushed the buzzer again. She had expected to find a guard at the door, which was standard operating procedure, but found the small desk unattended.

If she let her imagination run wild, she could visualize a hulking figure overpowering the guard and taking the keys, while inside—

Detective Gaetke opened the door. His dark brown hair was slightly damp and mussed, a thick lock of it falling over his left eye. His black shirt was unbuttoned, revealing a white sleeveless undershirt that fit him like the proverbial glove.

He had a nice body, slender but assertively masculine. The fact that she noticed made her blush; she was old enough to be his . . . psychologist.

It was, she thought, symptomatic of spending too much time with teenaged girls. Of late she'd noticed in herself a disturbing tendency to behave almost like her daughter, who clearly thought nothing of ogling an attractive young man. Sometimes, to her motherly horror, Brandy actually whistled at one.

Times had changed since she was Brandy's age, but she hadn't. And never, not for one fleeting moment, had she ever thought of herself as the May-December type, lusting after a younger man.

"Am I early?" she asked, determinedly turning her attention to business.

He stood aside to let her in, and locked the door behind her. "No, if anything, the others are late. Which is fine with me, since I overslept."

Lauren noticed he wasn't wearing shoes. "Overslept? You spent the night here?"

"Uh-huh." Gaetke led the way into the spacious living room. There was a pillow on the couch and a blanket on the floor, which he picked up as he walked by. "Matt is ticked off at me, so I'm playing bodyguard."

"And the body that you're guarding," she said, arching an eyebrow at the cozy implications of this arrangement, "where is she?"

"In the shower, I think."

In fact, Lauren could hear water running in a distant corner of the apartment. "Do you mind if I ask what you did that ticked Matt off?"

"This time, you mean." Gaetke ran a hand through his hair, brushing it out of his eyes.

An endearingly boyish gesture, which she scolded herself for noticing. If this kept up, she'd have to consult her doctor for an antidote.

"I thought," he said, "we should give Danielle's plan a try."

She'd had an early morning conversation with Captain Salcedo, during which he'd outlined a plan to attempt to lure the kidnapper into a trap, but he'd neglected to mention whose idea it was. "I gather you think it'll work and Matt doesn't."

"I figure it's worth a try." Gaetke sat on the arm of the couch to put on his shoes, wincing as he bent his right knee. "Another rookie mistake, which I'll undoubtedly live to regret."

"Maybe you won't. Regret it, that is." Based on the sketchy details the captain had given her, she thought the plan had potential. "About Matt—"

The buzzer sounded just then.

It didn't take a trained professional to comprehend the relief on Billy Gaetke's face. Without question, he thought he'd been saved by the bell.

"The only problem I have with this is that we have no proof the killer is remotely aware of Ms. Falk's existence," Captain Salcedo said. "I know the press has been nibbling around the edges of the witness story, but it could be that he's oblivious to the news."

"We'll get his attention, count on it." Gaetke sounded confident and looked intent. "A couple of headlines in the paper, breaking stories on TV and radio. We'll give him an eyewitness to worry about."

Danielle, standing alone by the window, turned to look at them. "Don't you think he's the one making the phone calls and . . . the rest of it?"

"I'm not totally convinced of that," Salcedo admitted. "We know there are other players in the mix. Then, too, like Matt says, the bedbugs seem to crawl out of the woodwork on a case like this."

Lauren glanced at her watch. It was nine-thirty; if Detective Price was coming, he was now thirty minutes late, which was definitely unlike the man. "Speaking of Matt, shouldn't we wait for him?"

"He's working on another aspect of the investigation," Gaetke said.

That was classic police-speak, and a nonanswer only marginally more informative than No comment, which she interpreted to mean that Matt was *still* ticked off, and holding. "I see."

"Getting back to the matter at hand," Salcedo

segued smoothly. "As high as the stakes are, I'm willing to commit the resources and manpower to pull this thing off. But it's your baby—" he nodded at Gaetke "—and you'll be the point man this afternoon."

To his credit, Billy Gaetke added: "Along with Matt, of course."

The meeting lasted precisely an hour to the minute. Lauren listened to the intricate plan and after taking all possibilities into consideration, concluded that it might actually work.

If they were lucky.

Her own contribution would be far from easy, in that she was assigned to coach Danielle Falk on how to pretend to recover a memory on camera. It was up to her to choreograph the subtle facial expressions and body language that would accompany that complex act.

Confusion at the outset, certainly, followed by growing awareness as the young teacher searched inward through her mind, and ending in startled recall.

Preferably in sixty seconds or less.

Danielle had to sound right, too, with the appropriate inflections in her voice. And she had to say more or less what they'd scripted her to say, since they would only get one shot at— as Gaetke so aptly put it— selling it to the reporters.

"How much time do I have?" was her only question as Salcedo stood up to leave.

The captain adjusted the cuffs of his pearl gray Armani suit. "I've already scheduled the news conference for one o'clock sharp."

"That's probably cutting it a little close to make the afternoon edition of the paper," Gaetke said, his expression pensive, "but we should get plenty of play on the evening news. And if this son of a bitch works for a living, he can maybe catch a sound bite on the radio in prime drive-time on the way home."

Danielle's smile appeared a trifle shaky. "I can't think of what more we could do, other than having me walk down the middle of Main Street yelling, 'I saw you, come and get me.' "

"Hold that thought," Gaetke said with a wink, "we might need a backup plan."

Salcedo and Gaetke took off a few minutes later, leaving them in the stoic care of the uniformed cop stationed outside the door.

"Well," Lauren said, "we've only got a couple of hours, we'd better get to it."

"I'm not much of an actress; I was never any good in drama."

"Join the club." Hoping to ease Danielle's fears, she went on: "I played a wooden soldier in 'Babes In Toyland' at our community theater, and the reviewer said that he'd once been paddled with a hickory stick— and I'm assuming he meant as a child, although I have no proof of that— which showed a more vibrant personality than I did."

Danielle laughed.

Even so, Lauren recognized the underlying sadness in those expressive brown eyes. And something more, a kind of *stillness*. A heightened sense of awareness, perhaps. As if she were . . . listening?

Might it be that since Danielle blamed herself for not having heard Cassie cry, she now was attuned to the slightest sound? That would explain why she'd snapped out of the trance the other day, when she heard someone running in the hall.

An intriguing possibility, Lauren thought, one she

would like to explore after all of this was over. But first things first, she told herself, and said: "You know what might work . . . instead of trying to fake it?"

"What?"

"I could hypnotize you again, and leave you with a posthypnotic suggestion— "

"To remember?"

"Exactly, to remember *someone*. It's the perfect solution." Her mind raced at the thought, and she felt a tingle of anticipation, the way she often did when she had a promising idea. "Then you wouldn't be acting at all. It would be real to you."

And absolutely convincing to anyone watching.

Twenty-seven

Dakota's eyes were fixed on the monitor, but she was nonetheless distracted by Freddy, who stood behind her in the editing room, devouring a raw carrot at a decibel level approaching that of a commercial trash compactor. "Do you mind?" she asked without turning around.

"This Bud," Freddy said, wagging his carrot at the screen, "is supposed to be such a hot-shit cameraman, but from the looks of that, he couldn't frame a shot if his life depended on it."

"We're damned lucky we got anything," she muttered. "We could have been stuck with a hokey graphic as background, one of those lame chalk outlines every station manager in the country trots out when the crime scene footage self-destructs in editing. So don't bitch."

Freddy snorted. "Look who's talking, the goddess of the foaming mouth. You— "

"Knock it off." Through clenched teeth, she added, "I'm not in the mood, okay? I've got to be downtown by one o'clock for a news conference at the police department, and this . . . this . . ."

"The word you're looking for is crap," Freddy suggested, ever helpful.

DARK INTENT

"This *segment* is nowhere near ready."

"Whose fault is that?" He reached over her and grabbed a handful of used videotapes that the station insisted they recycle, then leaned in to breathe in her ear. "If I was the last one in the pool with the week's top story, I'd be in a fucking bad mood, too."

Dakota put her padded headphones on and plugged into the board, effectively blocking any further commentary. A moment later she sensed, rather than heard, Freddy leave. She leaned forward, elbows on the control board, her hands covering her face. Infuriating as he could be, Freddy was right for a change; the footage Bud had sent her sucked big time.

It occurred to her that it wasn't coincidence, but by design that Bud had given her this washed-out, incoherent mess.

They were competitors, after all. Why shouldn't he keep the good stuff for himself? She would, if their situations were reversed.

This entire kidnapping story was turning out to be a disaster of epic proportions. She had yet to break a single significant development in the case. She hadn't been first to air the discovery of either girl's body, nor had staking out the rumored witness brought her anything but the unwanted attentions of the neighbors.

Not to mention the police. It remained to be seen if she'd gotten away with the B & E at Northcliffe. Whatever the outcome, the net result in news value so far was zero, zilch, *nada*.

All that hustle with nothing to show for it.

Going in, her intention was simply to make the most of a once-in-a-lifetime opportunity and prove herself as a top-notch investigative reporter, as well as distinguish herself from the crowd . . . again.

Only this time for the right reasons.

There was also the tantalizing prospect of professional redemption in La Campana, and beyond. The town's proximity to the lucrative major markets of Southern California made it worth her while to try.

But if she didn't get a break soon, it all could slip through her fingers . . .

If she failed here, she might as well pack it in and go home to Bakersfield. Marry one of her old high school beaus and have a couple of kids, freckles optional. She could use her TV experience to get a part-time job introducing the old movies— duly censored to satisfy rural sensibilities and then butchered by commercial interruptions until unrecognizable— on Night Owl Theater.

Change her name to Debbie Sue and learn to shuck corn with a baby balanced on her hip.

Take up square dancing, maybe, or succumb to the siren song of league bowling.

"Like hell I will," Dakota said.

Five minutes later, after scrapping Bud's charity footage and writing a note to the station manager promising tape from the afternoon news conference in its place, she hurried down to the street corner, Sony in hand, and waited for the crosstown bus.

The scene at police headquarters fell under the heading of organized chaos. There were at least a hundred reporters, including a fair showing of the foreign press, perpetually eager to report on American crime as proof positive of the country's moral decline . . . and thereby prove *their* intrinsic superiority. There were, as well, a healthy smattering of "journalists" from the tabloid shows and papers, presumably with checkbooks at the ready.

Dakota felt a tingle of electricity in the air; this was her kind of crowd.

"Gonna stand there all day, love?" someone with an Aussie accent asked, edging by her.

"I just might, mate," she retorted, even as she scanned the room for a vantage point. There was a media caste system in play, with the chairs at the front taken by the national network drones. Next came the local affiliates, the Fox almost-news crew, and so on down the line.

Her outlaw peers had been relegated to the standing-room-only spots along the back wall. With a sigh, she joined them. Of course, she couldn't see a damned thing, but she found an empty metal trash basket which she upended to stand on.

Suddenly tall, Dakota had a clear view of the speaker's table. She checked the battery on the Sony, and brought the viewfinder up to her face.

"Any time now," she said under her breath, eager for the show to begin.

"There has been speculation," Capt. Rudy Salcedo said in his trademark gruff voice, "that there's an eye-witness in the abduction of Cassandra Wilson. We're here today to put those rumors to rest."

The reporters reacted nonverbally, with a rustle of notebook pages turning and the soft clicking of 35mm camera shutters, followed by the distinctive *whir* of film advance motors.

"Danielle Falk is the teacher who was supervising the children at the school Friday afternoon." Salcedo cleared his throat, took a sip of water, and glanced at his notes. "At the time Cassandra disappeared, Ms. Falk was inside the school tending to a child with a superficial injury. She did *not* see the Wilson girl being taken."

Dakota panned from Salcedo to Danielle Falk, whom

she'd caught only a glimpse of before, briefly, from across the street late Saturday night. The station manager at KOUT wasn't a fan of zoom close-ups, which he claimed were way too theatrical, too Hollywood for their purpose, but she couldn't resist.

She could imagine every male in the room grousing that teachers weren't as young and pretty as Ms. Falk back when they were schoolboys, or they would never have missed a day in class.

Men were so predictable. Pitiful, really.

"Ms. Falk has agreed to answer your questions here today, in the hope that by doing so, your attention will be redirected back to the real issues."

"Fat chance," Dakota said under her breath, which earned her an "Amen" from the guy on her right. Panning again while Salcedo pontificated on the responsibility of the media or lack thereof, she located Billy Gaetke standing in the far corner, but was unable to spot Matt Price anywhere.

She knew very well of Price's aversion to the press—and who could blame him?— but even so thought it curious that the head of the task force wasn't here. Unless . . . unless maybe something major was going down, and all of this was an elaborate diversion?

"Hold on, Sherlock," she cautioned herself out loud, drawing a stereo *shush* from the reporters on either side of her. Ignoring them, she turned the camera on Gaetke again, this time watching for what her journalism professor had called giveaways, subtle mannerisms and expressions that suggested deception.

She looked for rapid blinking or darting eyes, an inability to be still, frequent glances at his watch, that kind of thing, but there was nothing. Detective Gaetke, although he appeared tired, seemed to be maintaining his cool.

Secret service-style cool. She was impressed, if reluctantly, in that it blew her theory.

". . . but when I got to the street," Danielle Falk was saying, "no one was there."

"How long were you inside the building?" the Aussie asked.

There was a slight hesitation, and then she said, "I can't be absolutely certain, but I think it was no more than three to five minutes."

In deference to her station manager, Dakota drew back from the close-up in a reverse zoom, and turned once again to the front of the room. She didn't bother checking out old Salcedo for giveaways; the captain was as inscrutable as Mao had ever been.

"Can you tell us whether the other children saw anyone?" a CNN reporter asked. "Captain?"

"To the best of our knowledge, no."

Stormy Landon stood, raising her voice to be heard over the clamor of questions. "Is it true that you underwent hypnosis, Danielle?"

Through the viewfinder, Dakota saw the teacher take a quick breath before nodding.

"Yes, I did."

"And what was the purpose of being hypnotized?" Landon asked in follow-up before anyone else had a chance to interrupt.

This time Danielle Falk glanced down ever so fleetingly before she answered.

"To find out if I could recall seeing anyone on the street that day, that is, earlier that day, who might have been the kidnapper."

"And did you?"

Danielle Falk blinked. A worry crease appeared between her eyebrows, and she frowned prettily. All at once, a hush fell over the room, until it was as silent, if not as reverent, as a church. "Do I recall seeing anyone? I . . . I think . . . there was a man."

"Yes," Dakota whispered.

Her fingers fumbled for the zoom. Wanting to get even closer, she very nearly stepped forward, before she remembered that she was standing two feet off the ground on her trash can perch . . . and wouldn't that be lovely, taking a header in front of an international audience?

Not that anyone would notice. Not with a potential payoff so close at hand.

Cassandra Wilson's teacher stood perfectly still, a distant look in her eyes. Confusion and doubt flickered over her features like time-lapse photography of clouds racing across the sky.

Dakota shivered as a chill ran along her spine, and felt goose bumps begin to rise.

Through the camera lens, she saw Danielle's lips part in a delicate, inaudible gasp, as the color drained from her face.

"I saw him." Her eyes widened and she blinked again, several times. "I did see him. He has brown hair, but it's thinning, I think. And brown eyes?"

Definitely a question mark on that last one. Dakota wondered who it was being asked the question, since she had an overwhelming feeling that Danielle was *not* talking to herself.

Or to them, for that matter; she almost appeared to be in a trance.

"He's of average height, I guess," the teacher went on haltingly, "and average build, except for a . . . he's got a pot belly."

"Is he white?" one of the reporters in the front row inquired. "How old is he?"

A quiet groan rippled through the room at the audac-

ity of the network anchor-in-waiting, daring to put
questions to her and risk blowing it for all of them.

Danielle closed her eyes and gasped again, this time
out loud. She looked startled, if still somewhat confused. "I know him," she said. "I know that face, that
profile. I've seen him before, at the school, but . . . I
don't remember his name."

Then, with the finality of a marionette whose strings
were clipped, she sat down.

For a heartbeat, there was silence, and then the
room erupted in bedlam. No one had been allowed
to broadcast live from within the conference, because
the signal might interfere with the emergency radio
frequencies, but any station with a satellite truck had
the capacity to go on the air once outside the police
station.

A stampede ensued.

Dakota lowered the Sony and leaned against the wall
to wait it out. She had to be smart, now more than
ever. The way she saw it, she was but a hitchhiker on
the information superhighway. A hand-held camcorder was no competition for a satellite feed.

Technologically speaking, she was outclassed. As for
intellectually, hell, she'd take them all on with one
hand tied behind her back—

She noticed, then, a woman she recognized as the
police department psychologist walk over to Danielle
Falk and begin to talk to her. Gaetke followed a few
seconds later, a smile playing at the corners of his
mouth.

"What's this?" she asked softly, and out of instinct
raised the camera again to resume filming. They were
too far away for her to hear what they were saying
without benefit of a microphone, but her skill as a
lip-reader, honed to a fine art through years of snooping, prevailed.

The psychologist asked, *Are you okay?*

I'm fine, Danielle said.

Detective Gaetke placed a hand on the teacher's shoulder. *You did great. Better than we planned. I almost believed it myself.*

It went well, the psychologist agreed.

Now let's get you out of here, Gaetke said, and extended his hand to her.

Danielle took his hand and gave it a little pull, the way a child does to get someone's attention. *Listen, I have to tell you—*

What?

It wasn't an act. I remember.

Dakota was afraid to blink and risk missing a single word. Her heart was pounding, and the release of adrenaline sent liquid ice through her veins.

What? Gaetke said. *You saw the guy?*

The teacher nodded. *There was a man who walked past the school several times that day. Back and forth, back and forth. It struck me as odd at the time, but I'd completely forgotten until just now. He looked familiar to me, someone I've seen before . . . someone I should remember . . .*

Gaetke was still holding her hand in both of his, and he looked searchingly into her eyes. *But you don't know who he is?*

Not yet, but it'll come to me, Danielle Falk said. *I know it will.*

Abruptly, Gaetke turned and led Danielle Falk out through a back door, the psychologist a step behind. Only when the door closed did Dakota lower the Sony.

"My god," she said to the empty room.

Twenty-eight

The summer she was five, Cassie had been enrolled in swimming lessons, held five mornings a week for a total of six weeks at the indoor Municipal Plunge.

That was the first time in her life she'd been in anything other than a kiddie wading pool. Standing by the side of the Plunge, looking down into the clear, deep water at the pretty aqua tiles on the bottom, she'd been scared and excited at the same time.

She had taken to swimming, her grandma said, like a baby duck to water. While the other kids puddled in the shallow end, she had learned to swim underwater, gliding silently and gracefully along the bottom, propelled by the rapid kicking of her feet.

Sometimes, she would hold her breath and sit in a corner on the aqua tiles, looking at the others as they splashed and shouted at the other end of the pool.

She had never forgotten the muffled sound of voices in the water, and how it seemed the kids were so very far away from her. And there was also the memory of the rhythm of her heart, beating softly in her ears.

And the sensation she had of floating, like an astronaut in liquid space.

That was the way she felt now. When she'd woken this morning— at least she thought it was morning— her head felt as if it were stuffed with cotton candy. The ceiling fan *turned above her, but although she knew it was making noise, she couldn't hear it.*

When she whispered to herself— her hand on her throat so she could feel the vibrations that assured her she was indeed speaking— her voice sounded distant and unfamiliar . . . as though it were coming from the far end of a long, dark tunnel.

Cassie remembered one particular tunnel that she'd seen on TV, that people passed through towards a beautiful bright light at the end of their lives.

It made her wonder if she were dying.

She felt sick enough to die. Sick and very weak. She couldn't even sit up without getting dizzy and light-headed. And if she somehow managed to stand, her legs were shaky and kind of numb, not at all strong enough for her to walk.

Her throat was dry, and it hurt terribly to swallow. She hadn't been able to keep any food in her stomach for what seemed like a day or two. She'd gotten sick several times, which she hated doing because throwing up made her throat itch afterwards, and she couldn't rinse her mouth of the bad taste.

All she could do was take tiny, tiny sips of lukewarm juice, and even that made her tummy ache. Ache or not, she was worried that the juice would soon be gone.

She wanted a drink of cool water, but there was none to be had, since the man hadn't come by yet today. The pitcher that held the water she was supposed to use for washing up was empty. The washcloth she'd used to clean her face that first morning had long since dried out, so she couldn't even moisten her dry, cracked lips.

She craved the feel of water on her skin almost as much as she thirsted to drink.

"Don't think about it," she whispered hoarsely.

To distract herself, Cassie watched the fan blades turn, until her eyelids grew heavy and closed.

* * *

She felt and smelled the cooler air even in her sleep, and fought to wake up. It was still dark in the room, but there was a lighter darkness coming through the open door . . .

The door was open? Or was this a dream?

Cassie turned her head to stare at the doorway, and struggled to sit up. The way out. That was the way out, the way home—

"*Awake, are you?*" *the man asked.*

She hadn't noticed him, standing in the shadows by the foot of the bed. Startled by his nearness, she gave a little cry.

"*We have a problem, you and me,*" *he said.*

Cassie swallowed and tried her voice: "*Can I . . . have a drink . . . of water?*"

"*Is that how you ask?*"

"*Please?*" *The word echoed in her head.*

"*In a minute. First things first.*"

He took a step closer, and she realized that he was dressed in dark clothing, which was probably why she hadn't noticed him at first.

Even in the dim light, she could tell that he was mad, his eyes narrowed, his mouth contorted into a tight-lipped sneer. He was breathing in a strange way, kind of panting like a dog.

"*More trouble than you're worth,*" *he said, glaring at her.* "*All the fuss, and for what?*"

It didn't seem to Cassie that he expected an answer from her, so she stayed silent, watching him wide-eyed.

"*What makes you so precious?*" *he snarled.* "*You'd think there weren't enough fucking children on the planet the way they're taking on. The truth of it is, the way people are breeding, there's an inexhaustible supply.*"

Cassie desperately wished for the strength to return to her legs. In her mind, she saw herself running from him, up the stairs beyond the open door, and away. If she wasn't so weak . . .

The man kicked at an empty juice box. "I should kill you now and be done with it."

She closed her eyes and prayed without moving her lips, not wanting him to know what she was doing, afraid to anger him any further. She understood that he was working himself up to do something bad.

"Damn that bitch for interfering!"

As frightened as she was, she didn't think she could cry. Her tears had dried up.

A hand closed around her bare ankle and held it tight. "You're going to help me, you hear?" He yanked hard on her leg. "Answer me when I talk to you."

"Yes sir," she whispered.

"That's better."

He reached around to his back pocket and brought out a pair of silver handcuffs. "These are too big for your wrists, but they'll do nicely as shackles."

"No!"

But before Cassie could pull away, he slapped the cold metal bracelet on her right ankle. She made a feeble effort to kick him with her left foot, but he caught her leg and fastened the second cuff.

There was no way for her to run. However remote that possibility had seemed, it was gone now.

And in her heart she knew, she would never get home.

Twenty-nine

3:17 P.M.

Gaetke followed Matt Price into the captain's office and closed the door.

"Well, gentlemen?" Salcedo said, leaning back in his chair to gaze at them over his steepled hands. "Have we got anything to write home about yet?"

"We're working on it." Price gave Salcedo a thin blue folder. "The post on Kraft was at noon. The preliminary autopsy report won't be available before tomorrow sometime, but Dr. Soo is relatively certain that Rachel was suffocated. Like Lucy."

"Being suffocated is not among my top ten ways to die." The captain paged through the sheets in the file. "For her sake, let's pray it was quick."

How quick, Gaetke wondered, would be quick enough to spare the child from suffering?

"The toxicology results and drug screen are still pending, of course, but Soo seems to think both of them may have been drugged, and were unconscious at the time they were killed. I don't know if that falls under the category of wishful thinking or scientific conjecture, but I hope to hell he's right."

Salcedo nodded. "Anything else?"

"This time, there's physical evidence that Rachel was sexually abused."

For a moment, no one spoke. Salcedo closed the file and tossed it on his desk. "We knew all along it had to be something like that."

"Doesn't make it any easier," Price said.

"No, it doesn't. But— " the captain smiled bitterly "— it's definitely incentive to catch the slippery son of a bitch."

"As if we needed any."

"What about you, Billy? How's it coming?"

Gaetke glanced at his partner. "You had more, didn't you?"

"Not a lot," Price said with a shrug. "I got a DMV printout on the partial plate number Wilson gave me, and we've got thirty-seven actives out of a hundred possibilities registered here in the county."

"Any of them panel vans?"

"Not a one, but I have to tell you, I've come to the conclusion that the van angle is problematic, as far as I can tell."

"How is that?" Salcedo frowned.

"Let me put it this way, this guy's not stupid. If I were looking to grab a kid off a school playground in broad daylight, I sure as hell wouldn't park in plain view across the street."

"Good point."

Gaetke couldn't fault Price's logic, but it meant, in essence, that he'd banged the shit out of his knee for no reason. A lot of pain for no gain.

The captain twirled a pencil between his fingers. "Except why hasn't the driver of said van come forward to explain what the hell he was doing parked on Hillcrest that afternoon?"

"Who knows? These days we're perceived as the enemy, often as not, and it could be he's had a bad experience with the police— "

"And he's scared shitless he'll be made the fall guy,"

Gaetke suggested. "Maybe he's laying low until all of this is resolved."

"Or he hasn't put two and two together." Matt smiled his cryptic smile. "Come to think of it, none of us has had the time to sit down and do the math. There are a lot of things about this case that simply don't add up."

Salcedo inclined his head as if in agreement. "Which leaves us with . . . what? A van that may not be relevant to the case, and a license plate that is?"

"Your guess is as good as mine, Rudy, but I think we'd be remiss not to check out every possibility. We're tracking down the vehicles as quickly as we can, but it's gonna take time."

"Doesn't it always? Okay, Matt, sounds like you're on top of it. Keep me informed."

Batter up, Gaetke thought, as they looked to him. He cleared his throat. "The news coverage from this afternoon has been phenomenal. Danielle's on every station, every hour on the hour, describing this creep— "

"Do we have a composite?" Salcedo interrupted.

He nodded. "We had to call in a sketch artist to fill out the details; the face the Ident-i-Kit gave us was too generic to be of much use."

"But she says it looks like the guy?"

"As much as any of them ever do." Personally, he had difficulty with the one-dimensional quality of either approach. He would never have identified the Night Stalker, Richard Ramirez, from the composite they'd had back then, not in a million years.

"I assume it's being distributed?"

"Yes sir." Behind his back, he crossed his fingers; the gal in the city print shop swore the flyers would be ready within the hour, and faxed or otherwise transmitted no later than a quarter 'til, but he hadn't had a free minute to check on it.

"Good, good. Is everything in order over on Brighton Way?"

"We have the house under five-point surveillance
for the duration," Gaetke said, and ran through the
particulars of the operation as the captain jotted notes.
"Dispatch has assigned us a dedicated frequency—"

"Which is?" Salcedo looked up from his legal pad,
pausing in mid-scribble.

"Tach Six. No one will be able to get within a quarter mile of the place without us knowing. I walked
through the neighborhood twice, and I can promise,
there's not a blind spot anywhere."

Salcedo nodded his approval. "So all you need is
for the guest of honor to show up at your party."

Gaetke couldn't stop a grin. "At least we know the
invitation has been sent."

"And Ms. Falk, she's at the penthouse?"

"Yes sir."

"Who's guarding her?" Price asked quietly.

As angry as Matt had been last night, Gaetke expected—and more than likely deserved—to catch a little heat, but he detected nothing other than genuine
concern in his partner's eyes. A consummate professional, Price was. "I will be, tonight."

"She's not alone?"

"Dr. Harper was with her earlier, and there's a uniformed officer at the door." He consulted his watch;
it was getting late. "Who I'm supposed to relieve in
fifteen minutes. If there's nothing else, Captain, I'd
better head on over."

Salcedo dismissed him with a glance as he reached
for the phone.

"Be careful," Matt called after him.

"Will do."

* * *

On the way to the safe house, it occurred to him that he should feel bad about not being at the stakeout, after all the work he'd put into setting it up. To the contrary, he was secretly relieved that he wouldn't have to spend the night cramped behind the steering wheel of a car, unable to straighten out his leg for hours at a stretch, drinking brackish coffee and breathing stale air.

The truth was, he wasn't fit for street duty; all of the walking he'd done this afternoon had made his knee tender and slightly swollen. It was his own fault, of course, for not following doctor's orders and wearing the brace.

The pain was intense enough, just now, that he considered making a quick detour to go home and get it. On the other hand, all he really had to do tonight was make conversation. Not even that, if Danielle wasn't in the mood to talk.

He could make it without the brace. Put his leg up, slap an ice pack on his knee, maybe take half a pain pill to dull the persistent ache, then zone out and catch an NBA play-off game on TNT.

As one of the walking wounded, he was entitled to a little downtime.

The hell with the brace.

He found Danielle in the kitchen, dressed in jeans and a Dallas Cowboy sweatshirt, standing barefoot at the sink peeling an apple.

For a second he stood in the doorway, just watching her. Then he rapped his knuckles on the doorframe. "Knock, knock," he said.

When she turned, it was with a slight smile. "I'm glad you're here. Since Lauren left, Officer Richmond won't even hint at what's been going on."

"Consider the source," he said. He described the efforts underway, leaving out only the fact that there'd been a break-in at her house.

She listened without comment, and appeared to be taking it all in stride, considering that there were cops infesting her home. Citizens seldom appreciated the invasion of their privacy that resulted from a stakeout.

"What about you?" he asked finally. "Have you remembered anything more?"

"Unfortunately, no. Seems the harder I try to remember, the more elusive the answer is. Lauren told me not to worry about it . . . that it'll come to me."

"She's probably right." He took off his jacket and draped it over the back of a kitchen chair, then loosened the rib strap on his shoulder holster. "Oh, I almost forgot: I heard our beloved mayor has it in his head that we need to do another foot search, door-to-door, all over town."

"You don't think it would help?"

"The guy who's got Cassie isn't gonna simply hand her over to a cop at his door, because we ask nicely." Gaetke hesitated before adding, "In the worst-case scenario, it could provoke him to kill her."

Danielle leaned against the counter, apple and paring knife evidently forgotten in her hands. She closed her eyes briefly and took a deep breath before meeting his gaze. "And they say there are no monsters."

Thirty

Simon Avery sat at the cappuccino bar, sipping his latte and watching the ebb and flow of people through the mini-mall. Not that many people, in point of fact, and the flow was thinning.

Fifteen minutes ago, he'd watched that young cop limp his way across the lobby to the elevator, on the way up to where Danielle Falk was presumably in hiding. Shortly after that, the uniformed cop—relieved for the night?—headed for the street.

Earlier still, under the guise of a befuddled husband who seemed to have misplaced his wife, Avery had conducted a quick but thorough tour of the building to eliminate all of the floors on which Ms. Falk *wasn't* hiding.

The process of elimination had taken him to the top floor, discreetly labeled *P* for penthouse. When the doors opened to reveal the policeman seated at a desk in the private lobby, he'd feigned bewilderment and said, "Oops, wrong floor," and punched the button to go down.

The policeman didn't as much as blink.

Bingo. As they said in those war movies, Target Acquired.

He got a delicious thrill out of being here, now,

watching them, knowing they were ignorant of his proximity to their so-called hideaway and their precious witness. He'd had to resist an impulse to wave at the departing officer as the man crossed the atrium.

Not that Avery was happy, by any means.

He'd seen the coverage from the afternoon's news conference at least a dozen times. The News Breaks were flying, fast and furious, and each of them centered on the insulting composite based on the teacher's purported description of him.

Were she alive, his own sainted mother would not be able to identify him from that sketch.

There'd been a fierce battle waging inside his head for the past few hours, whether he ought to cut and run or hang tough by taking care of the nosy bitch once and for all. It was his misfortune that the only casualty to this point had been his own left thumb, which he'd slammed in the car door in the hurried confusion of the afternoon.

He didn't think it was broken, although it was nearly flattened and badly bruised. The knuckle was scraped raw and swollen, while the nail bed had turned an ugly reddish color and was exquisitely tender to the touch. Avery knew very well that he was bleeding inside his skin.

Bleeding.

The wretched word alone was enough to make him shudder, never mind the gruesome prospect of relieving the pressure beneath his thumbnail. He'd had a similar injury before, at the age of twelve, when he'd squashed his pinky carrying a stepladder the wrong way.

His dear mother had tended to him, claiming it wasn't worth a trip to the doctor. What she'd done was simple enough, but not easy to sit still for: she had straightened out a paper clip, and heated one end in an open flame. When the metal was suitably hot, she had quickly jabbed it into the middle of his fingernail.

The sterile paper clip had pierced the nail, and the collected blood spurted out. No more throbbing pressure, no more pain, other than the agonizing torture of having to hear his blood sizzling.

Oddly enough, the jab itself hadn't hurt.

He'd have to take care of it himself, this time, when the dust had sufficiently settled. Clearly, he wouldn't make the mistake he had back then, when he'd allowed his mother to perform the procedure within inches of his trusting face. He still had nightmares about the feel of blood as it splattered him.

Avery did not recall if that was the beginning of his aversion to blood— he suspected it went further back in his boyhood than that— but that incident most assuredly hadn't eased it.

Even now, the memory made the bile rise in his throat and saliva flow. Only the certain knowledge that he could not afford to waste his energy being ill kept him from giving in to the nausea.

And he dared not give in to his weakness at this critical juncture. Too much was at stake to wait passively for a resolution.

If Danielle Falk identified him, his secrets would be exposed, his privacy invaded. He'd done what he could to destroy any evidence linking him to the first two girls, but all he had to overlook was a single drop of blood, and the DNA match would be his ticket to Death Row.

Once in prison, *he'd* be the target. Pedophiles were reviled, he knew, subject to verbal abuse and physical attack from the other inmates.

He would never survive in prison, not for a day. With his delicate constitution, he could not endure the stress; he would be mentally crushed, psychologically ruined, reduced to a twitching mass of nerves.

If it came down to a choice between being incarcerated and death, he would rather die. And knowing the leisurely pace at which California executed its condemned, he would prefer to do so by his own hand.

For the time being, however, he was still in the game.

Taking a final sip of his lukewarm latte, Avery decided, without regret, that Danielle Falk needed to be eliminated, whatever the eventual outcome. At the moment, she was the only person who *could* identify him— young Cassandra didn't count any more than the other two had— and he could think of no other alternative but to get rid of her before she got the opportunity to do so.

The composite without a witness to substantiate it was worthless. Any value it had would be fully negated by Ms. Falk's tragic demise.

To that end, he stood, discarded his empty cup, and casually wove his way through the avant-garde sculptures on exhibit in the mall atrium, heading for a door he'd noticed earlier, marked Authorized Personnel Only. As expected, it was unlocked— the warning was enough to deter most people— and he slipped inside, unnoticed.

Also as expected, the door accessed an interior hallway, separating the individual shops from a storage area and the exterior doors.

The weak link in the building's design was the myriad of private exits on the ground floor. Virtually every store and shop had its own back door, perhaps as a convenience for the employees, who wouldn't have to walk the extra distance from the parking lot to the main entrance.

He selected five doors at random intervals, and stuck thick transparent tape over each door's self-locking latch bolt. The employees of the different stores presumably used separate exits, so if anyone were to detect that a door had been tampered with, only that door would be secured. Odds were at least one of the five would remain unlocked. On a hectic day like a Monday, it wouldn't surprise him if they all did.

That phase of his mission accomplished, he left via the fifth door.

He ran one last, essential errand on his way home, stopping briefly to purchase a security guard's outfit from the same store where the city's police officers bought their uniforms.

The long-sleeve shirt and slacks were navy blue in color, but looked black. He also selected a black nylon windbreaker to hide the fact that the shirt bore no insignia. There were arm patches available—he considered a California patch and one with the word Security on it—but he hadn't time to sew them on, and preferred not to rely on safety pins. As a kid, he was forever getting stuck with the safety pins his mother used to alter his clothes.

The pants were a trifle snug at the waist when he tried them on, and the shirt strained at the buttons across his belly, but this wasn't a fashion show.

The way he figured, it didn't really matter how he looked. He wasn't after a prize for having the best costume; his plan required only that the security guard getup fool the gimp cop for five to ten seconds.

Long enough to open the door.

After that, well . . . he also bought a canister of hot pepper spray. He hadn't the stomach for taking out a cop in any permanent way, and hoped to avoid that by using the spray. He'd read once that spraying someone directly in the eyes with pepper spray would temporarily blind them, and hence, hamper identification.

If that didn't work, as backup he bought a heavy-duty flashlight that could crack the hardest skull. Given the unfortunate tendency of head wounds to bleed, he ardently hoped it wouldn't be necessary.

Nevertheless, he'd made up his mind to do whatever it took to assure that the cop would be incapacitated and out of the way.

Everything was now in place.

All that remained was the lure . . . and she was shackled to the bed in the guest room.

The time had come to put her in play.

Thirty-one

"I brought food," a voice said.

Matt Price glanced up from the array of reports and printouts in his lap to see Dakota Smith holding a brown paper bag, peering in the open passenger window of the Taurus. He had parked two blocks beyond the surveillance area precisely to avoid being disturbed, and now this. He leaned against the headrest and closed his eyes.

Maybe there wasn't any justice in the world.

"Just a sandwich," Dakota said, her tone apologetic. "Ham, salami, some other kind of processed meat with enough preservatives to guarantee eternal life. I was going to get fried chicken, but I wasn't sure I'd be able to find you, and I didn't want it getting cold."

"How did you— "

"Find you? It wasn't easy." She opened the door and got in the car without waiting for an invitation. "A friend has a scanner, and I borrowed his car."

"Borrowed, huh?"

Dakota shrugged. "Whatever. So, do you want this or not?"

His usual diet of coffee and Coca-Cola, compounded by stress, wasn't doing much for his stomach lining. Or his disposition, for that matter. He collected his paperwork and tossed it onto the dash, then reached for the bag.

After unwrapping the sandwich, he lifted the top of the roll and removed a slice of American cheese.

"Aren't you going to eat that?"

"You want it?" he asked, offering her the triangle of cheese.

"I'm absolutely famished," she said, taking the slice and folding it into a wedge before popping it in her mouth. "Do you mind?"

"Nope . . . take the rest of it." He held the sandwich out to her and watched as she deftly removed every trace of cheese. "You can have the tomato, too, if you like. It looks a little anemic."

"That won't leave you with much."

He shrugged. "I doubt I'll starve."

"So," she said, plucking one last bit of tomato, "it must be getting hot and heavy for the kidnapper, don't you think?"

"It would seem to be," Price agreed.

She licked her fingers. "If I were him, I'd be hauling ass by now."

"That's always a possibility."

Dakota gave him an incredulous look. "You know, I've often wondered how much the city spends giving you guys all those lessons in equivocating? Just once before I die, I'd like a straight answer from you."

"That's as straight as it's ever gonna get." He took a bite of the sandwich.

"Listen, Matt— can I call you Matt?"

"No."

"Matt, I have to say I'm disappointed in your attitude. Far be it for me to upset the police department's anti-media apple cart, but we *are* on the same side, here."

Price raised his eyebrows at her. "Really."

"Yes, really, and to tell you the truth, I for one am getting sick and tired of being *used* by the police when it suits your purpose, and ignored when it doesn't. Oh, you're not above leaking information when you want to make a point, but heaven forbid we ask you to part with a scintilla of police intelligence— if that isn't a contradiction in terms— to our benefit!"

Bemused, Price laughed. "You're sure working up a head of steam."

"All I'm saying, Matt, is that a little cooperation goes a long way."

He considered that for a moment before shaking his head. "You're asking me to compromise the investigation and risk that little girl's life."

"I am not." Dakota frowned. "You think you're going to catch this guy? I mean, in time?"

"You never give up, do you?"

"Never have, never will. We have that in common." She indicated the jumble of paperwork with a nod of her head. "Mind if I have a look?"

He nearly choked at her audacity. "You're damned right I mind— "

"At the composite," she added hurriedly. "All I've got is a copy of a fax of a copy, and even that's at least twice removed."

"It's been all over TV."

"I'm *on* the TV news, Detective," she said icily, "I don't have time to *watch* it."

Price sighed. "Will you go away if I give you an original?"

"Probably not. But definitely not if you don't."

As he saw it, surrender was his only chance at peace and quiet. More to the point, he wasn't giving her anything that wasn't already in the public record. "What the hell, take one."

As quick as a rattlesnake strike, she grabbed an eight

by eleven composite from the pile. "Oh, this is much better, really. The copy I had made him look like the man in the moon."

"I'll alert NASA," Price said. "As for you, you can blast off any time now."

"Wait a minute, hold the phone." She squinted at the picture. "He looks *very* familiar."

"Sure he does."

"I'm not kidding."

He hesitated, recognizing the insistent conviction in her eyes. "Give me a name."

Dakota tapped a fingernail on the suspect's nose. "This is wrong, although I guess you couldn't tell from the front, but he's got more of a hook thing going, like a hawk maybe, or a vulture . . ."

"Who is he?"

"Avery," she said. "Simon Avery. This is crazy, but I saw him just the other day."

A faint bell was ringing in a corner of his mind. "Where do you know him from?"

"He runs NOD."

"What?"

"News On Demand. It's a video transcription service, like Burrelle's or Journal Graphics, only not as good. It's local. He was at the station on Friday."

Putting his sandwich aside, Price shuffled through paper until he found the computer printout from the DMV. He ran a finger down the registered owner column until he came to the sole business name, News On Demand. The license plate number listed belonged to a 1992 Chevrolet Caprice.

"This could actually be the guy," he said, not quite believing his luck. "Simon Avery. Where do I know that name from?"

"Well, his mother was Katherine Avery, who was a very wealthy woman, as in filthy, stinking rich. I know you've heard of her, she was always making bequests, although not to anyone *truly* deserving like me. She died last Valentine's Day."

"That could be the psychological trigger Lauren was talking about," Price interrupted. "His mother died in February, and a month or so later, Lucy Bosworth up and disappears."

"You really think it's him?"

"There's one way to find out." He tossed the paperwork in the back seat and put his half-eaten sandwich in the bag, his appetite gone. He fastened his seatbelt and turned the key in the ignition.

"Where are we going?"

"To catch a killer." At her bewildered look, he added, "You've just earned yourself an exclusive, darlin'."

Thirty-two

Danielle wandered restlessly through the apartment, pausing at each window to gaze out, a few minutes at a time, searching for . . . what? An answer of sorts, she supposed, to put a name to that face that now haunted her, oddly familiar and yet unknown.

The sun had disappeared behind the city's skyline, and shadows were gathering on the streets. To the west, the sky bore traces of the coming sunset, gold and pink reminders that, somewhere, daylight lingered.

There were, she noticed, only half a dozen cars in the rear parking lot. The building would soon be empty; the city offices closed promptly at five, and most of the stores were open no later than seven.

Downtown traffic was minimal, and from what she could tell, there were far more people leaving the area than coming in. An hour or two, and the city proper would be deserted, a virtual ghost town.

Even now, the rest of the world seemed far away. The dark would make the abandonment complete . . .

Danielle heard the floor creak behind her and although her mind reasoned that it had to be Detective

Gaetke, her mouth went dry and her heart began to pound as she whirled to face him.

"Sorry, I didn't mean to startle you," Gaetke said.

Evidently she wasn't hiding her anxiety as well as she'd hoped. "I startled myself, I think."

"Are you okay?"

"I'm fine." With her hand on her throat, she could feel her pulse racing, and she took a breath to steady her nerves. "Is there any word?"

"As a matter of fact, there is. I just got off the phone with Captain Salcedo. We've got a possible ID on the guy— "

"Who is it?"

Gaetke consulted his notebook. "His name is Simon Avery, and he's— "

Danielle felt suddenly faint. "Yes," she whispered, and closed her eyes, to better align the details of his face and the profile of the man as he'd passed the school that day. Katherine Avery's son . . . Simon had a reputation at Northcliffe of being a mama's boy. A quiet, nondescript man, more an object of pity than fear.

Could it really be that pathetic little man?

The two faces melded into one, and she knew beyond question that it *was* him.

"—they're outside his house," Gaetke was saying, "and they've got the place surrounded, but there's been no sign of him yet— "

"Surely they're going in," she interrupted rather breathlessly, feeling the color leave her face, "aren't they?"

"Any minute now."

"What are they waiting for?"

Billy Gaetke took her hand and led her to the couch. "You look like you're ready to pass out. Sit down, Danielle. We're gonna catch this guy."

With her legs threatening to give way, she sank to the couch, her eyes searching his face for any sign that he knew more than he was telling. "Will they be in time to save Cassie?"

He hesitated briefly, and then sighed. "I wish I could answer that, but the honest truth is, I don't know. No one does. I promise, though, it'll all be over soon."

She wanted desperately to believe him.

Thirty-three

The Avery estate presented a problem from a logistical standpoint, considering its impressive size. It had taken them an hour and forty-five minutes to put together the number of officers necessary to secure both the property and premises.

At first glance, the place looked impenetrable, with a heavy wrought-iron gate providing the only access to the property, otherwise surrounded by an eight-foot-high cinder-block wall. Scaling the wall had been nixed by Salcedo—the brass was a little gun-shy after the Los Angeles P.D. was crucified in the press for hopping a certain wall—and the gate, as might be expected, was securely locked. Regardless, it took their electronics expert less than three minutes to break the code.

The gate swung open soundlessly.

The house at the center of the grounds was totally dark. Was Simon Avery in the house, watching as they approached, or had he spooked and taken flight?

Matt Price fervently hoped Avery was home.

In the bright moonlight, they relied on hand signals to communicate, with Price directing various teams to different locations on the property. As a training exercise, he had orchestrated this type of silent urban invasion many times, but no matter how often the maneuver was practiced, the real thing was different in a fundamental way: there were lives at stake.

He felt a curious sense of exhilaration as he neared the house. The waiting was over.

At the front door, he paused momentarily to confirm that everyone was in position. Given the sprawling layout of the house, it was essential that every door and window be covered visually, if not physically.

An eternity later, he got the go-ahead over the radio, by way of three quick bursts of static made by the relay officer keying the mike in a patrol unit.

Price reached for the door handle and was surprised—and gratified—when it turned easily in his hand. Evidently Avery felt safe behind his eight-foot wall . . .

He held onto the door as he opened it, so it wouldn't bang into the wall. Moonlight spilled onto the polished wood floor.

He almost expected someone to rush at him from the darkness, but nothing moved. He motioned to the members of his own search team to hold their positions, as he listened for any sound from inside.

Nothing.

The plan was to conduct the initial sweep of the house under the cover of darkness. It was risky to do it that way, but with Cassandra's life very much on the line, their own safety was secondary.

He pointed his flashlight into the entry, and waved the members of his team in.

With the precision of a well-oiled machine, the room-to-room search began. The soft sound of their footsteps seemed to echo in the silent house.

The darkness closed in on them as they moved

deeper into the house, seeming to swallow the thin beams of light they aimed into it. Glancing over his shoulder, Price could only just distinguish the faces of his officers from the shadows surrounding them.

Somewhere in the gloom, a floorboard creaked, and he snapped his fingers twice— the signal to stop— then turned off his flashlight and listened intently. Ahead, down the hallway, he could discern a slight variation in the dark, as though a door was partially ajar.

Was Avery inside, watching and waiting?

There was only one way to find out. His back against the wall, Price closed the distance to the door, took a breath to steady himself, then kicked the door open and hit the lights.

They did not find anyone. Not Avery, and not, as Price had secretly feared, the body of Cassie Wilson.

"He's on the run," someone said. "Lucky son of a bitch got away."

"The game's not over," Price said grimly. He radioed to Dispatch to issue an All Points Bulletin for Simon Avery. A state-wide alert of airline carriers, bus stations, and train depots would be made, and with Mexico only a short distance away, they would also notify the Border Patrol.

"I think you'd better see this," Sergeant Weiss said.

Price followed the sergeant to a back bedroom where a floor-to-ceiling bookcase opened to reveal a narrow stairway to a basement-level room. Weiss did a slow sweep of the room with a flashlight. "What the hell?"

"See that?" Weiss asked. "The fucking furniture is

bolted to the floor, except for the toilet. The place looks like a prison cell . . ."

"Worse than that." Price turned his own flashlight on. "He kept them in the dark?"

"Must have, there's only the nightlight."

"This is unreal." He noticed a child's sweater hanging on a wall rack, a pair of girl's tennis shoes, and a crumpled pair of white anklet socks.

"And look at this." Weiss crossed to the bed and pulled back the covers.

At first, Price didn't comprehend what he was seeing. He moved closer, and identified what appeared to be tiny flecks of dried blood on the sheets. "If that's blood, there's not a lot of it."

"Hold that thought." The sergeant lifted the pillow, and pointed out a small, irregular-shaped white object. "Her grandma said she had a loose tooth."

"She just convicted the bastard," he said, with cold satisfaction. In spite of the gravity of the situation, he couldn't help but smile at the child's innocence. "After all she's been through, Cassie still believes in the tooth fairy."

"There's one more thing," Weiss said.

Price accepted the book Weiss handed to him, albeit reluctantly. It was an accounting journal, like those found in any office supply store. A black cover, with gold embossed lettering. Numbered and lined pages, also edged with gold.

He read:

There are others like me, I know. I am not alone in my obsession. The know-it-alls say we are intimidated by grown women and prefer girls since we can control them better, but the truth is women's bodies are so . . . cluttered, with breasts and hips, and, God forbid, *hair.* A young girl's body is pure and clean of line, the sweet swell of her buttock exquisitely shaped to fit the palm of my hand. I shiver with anticipation—

Sickened, Price slammed the journal shut. "This is one sick bastard," he said, handing it to Weiss. "Damn it, where is the slippery son of a bitch?"

Dakota Smith was sitting cross-legged on the hood of his car when he got to the street. The look she gave him was both expectant and full of dread. "Well?"

"Simon Avery is the doer, you were right about that, but unfortunately, no one's home."

"By that you mean, he got away, or he went to the store for a gallon of milk?"

"It would appear he got away," Price admitted, figuring he owed her that much, and added with absolute determination, "But not for long."

"How about the little girl?"

He shook his head. "No sign of her."

She unfolded her legs and slid off the car. "Do you have any idea where he went?"

"I wish I knew. But we'll find him. Now that we know who he is, we'll find him."

Thirty-four

The moment was at hand.

It was dangerous, coming here with the child, but if his theory was right, and there was a secure room within the inaptly named safe house, he might need Cassandra to lure the teacher out.

Avery walked along the shadowed side of the building until he came to the first of the doors he had fixed. It opened, which he took as a sign that his mission was destined to succeed.

He ducked inside, and began to hum "Lovely Rita Meter Maid" as he headed for the Phone Relay Room—not much more than a closet— which he'd noticed on his earlier walk-through. For obvious reasons, he hadn't dared fuss with it earlier, but it would be to his benefit if the phone lines were down.

Not that he thought for one minute that any cop worth his salt would *call* for help; dialing 911 wasn't exactly a macho response to danger. Officers were conditioned to act as protectors, not need them.

Danielle Falk, on the other hand, would surely rush to call for assistance, if she could. He figured the odds were fifty-fifty that she'd be close enough to a phone to at least try.

He'd prefer she weren't able to get through.

Again, technology was on his side; disrupting the phone system in the building was as simple as yanking out a dozen or so computer circuit boards. No wires to cut, no fuss, no muss, no error.

Everything was now in place.

Avery went outside to get the girl, his trump card in this high-stakes game. As he lifted her from the back seat of the car, he noticed her clothes were soaked through with sweat.

In the moonlight, she looked as pale as death.

"Cassie," he hissed, jostling her in his arms. She was lighter than he remembered, light as a feather; had she lost that much weight in three short days?

The child groaned and opened her eyes.

"Damn you, don't you die on me." He hefted her easily over his shoulder and, with a last glance around the empty parking lot, headed for cover.

The only sound was the soft jingle of the cuffs on her ankles.

Inside, he took her straight to the elevator. He had a bad moment when the floor indicator failed to light up after he'd pushed the call button— it crossed his mind that the machinery was shut down at night— but before he had time to panic, he heard the customary *ding* and the double doors slid open.

"Lucky me," he said, setting Cassie down in a corner of the elevator car. "Skinny as you are, I'd still hate to have to carry you up six flights of stairs."

Her eyes were puffy slits in her face. "Can I . . . please . . . have water?"

Avery frowned. "Did I forget to give you water?" There was a fountain, kitty-corner across the atrium—

he could see it from here— but he had nothing to collect the water in. Taking her to the fountain to drink was, he supposed, an option, but he was truly anxious to get this over with, and soon.

Her lips moved, forming the word please.

The Good Simon, silent throughout the day, needled him: *Do one nice thing, killer. She's no good to you dead. And who knows, maybe the devil will do the same for you, when you're burning in hell.*

"Okay, okay, okay." He picked her up, a bit roughly, and pulled the red Emergency Stop button. Muttering under his breath, he carried her to the fountain.

The child was too weak to stand on her own, so he positioned himself behind her. He pressed down on the silver bar, activating the stream of chilled water.

Cassie stirred, gave a little cry, and strained forward. She drank clumsily, as though she'd forgotten how, and water dribbled down the front of her overalls.

Watching her, Avery thought she might now forget to breathe. "You'll make yourself sick," he said. "Come on, that's enough."

Ankles bound, pouring sweat, and weak as a kitten, the kid still had a little fight left in her, resisting as he pulled her away.

"Don't make me regret being nice," he warned.

On the penthouse level, he stopped the elevator again with the Emergency button as soon as the doors were open. As he'd expected, the small lobby was unattended, the palace guard gone home for the night.

He glanced down at Cassie, huddled on the floor in the corner. The water seemed to have revived her somewhat; her breathing sounded easier, and there was a touch of color to her tawny skin. Her fingers were entwined with the chain linking the cuffs, but otherwise motionless.

Good girl, he thought.

"The moment of truth," he said, his tone hushed. "It'll be over soon, my sweet. And then we . . . we will go where no one will ever find us."

Girding himself for what was to come, he stepped out of the elevator. From his jacket pocket, he withdrew the pepper spray. Mindful of his sore thumb, he tightened his left-handed grip on the flashlight, and crossed the short distance to the apartment door.

Thinking it the kind of thing a security guard would do, he used the base of the flashlight to rap on the door. Just in case the cop looked through the peephole, he glanced away, averting his face. He held his breath.

He did not hear anyone approach the door from the other side, nor did he hear the distinctive sound of a dead bolt being disengaged, and so he was startled when the door just . . . opened. For a moment, he stood frozen, a deer caught in the headlights, and then all hell broke loose.

In the elevator, Cassie screamed—

The cop, reacting violently, started to shove him aside—

Simultaneously, he brought up the canister, aiming for the cop's eyes. The pepper spray hit the officer in the face, but with surprising quickness and strength, the cop grabbed hold of Avery's wrist and twisted his arm so that before he realized what was happening, he had squirted *himself* at point-blank range.

Indeed, blinded and gasping for air— his throat and lungs felt like they were on fire!— he swung the flashlight, flailing wildly. He hit something on the first swing, and was abruptly knocked down in return.

Someone fell on top of his legs, and he took an

elbow in the gut, which forced the remaining air from his lungs. Gasping still, he tried to squirm free.

Cassie screamed again, a bloodcurdling scream that sent shivers along his spine.

"Run!" the cop yelled.

Avery swung at the voice with all his might, and heard a satisfying *crack*. All at once, the cop was a dead weight on top of him. In his hand, the flashlight was slippery, as if wet with blood. Without thinking, he let go of it and heard it roll across the lobby floor.

He also heard someone run by them to the elevator, followed by the sound of the doors closing . . . and the elevator going down.

Avery staggered to his feet. Unable to see, he lurched toward the elevator, pressing his face against the cool metal doors.

The screaming had stopped, except inside his head.

"I'll get you," he whispered, his throat burning from the spray. "It's not over yet."

Thirty-five

In the final few seconds that passed before the doors closed, Danielle saw the blood on Billy's head and understood that she was on her own for now.

As the elevator started down, Danielle knelt on the floor to hug Cassie to her. Brushing the damp hair away from the child's face, she looked into Cassie's brown eyes, searching for the little girl she knew.

"Are you okay?" she asked.

Cassie's lower lip trembled, but she managed a ghost of a smile. "I want my grandma."

"I know you do, honey." In the circle of her arms, the child felt like she was burning with fever. "But right now, Cassie, we have to get away from here, to somewhere safe. And I need you to be brave, honey, because we don't have much time."

A tremor passed through the seven-year-old's slight frame, but she did not so much as whimper, instead asking solemnly, "Is he after us?"

"Yes." For a moment it seemed that she could actually hear the sound of footsteps echoing in the interior stairwell, but it was simply her imagination getting the better of her. "But we can get away—"

"I can't run, Miss Falk."

Danielle had seen the shackles on Cassie's ankles,

of course, and it nearly broke her heart, as did the despairing look of helplessness in the child's eyes. "Don't worry, I'll think of something . . ."

The elevator *dinged* as the red LED indicator displayed the number four. She wanted to bypass the fourth and fifth floors, because she assumed that no City office would ever be left unlocked overnight. The vivid memory of the dream she'd described to Dr. Harper now seemed to her to be a warning: Stay away from long, dark hallways lined with locked office doors.

That warning probably didn't apply to the third floor which, she recalled, was being renovated. It was possible that meant there would be no locks— or for that matter, doors— to keep them out, but neither could they shut anyone else out.

Still, in case the man was keeping track of the floors they stopped on, she pushed the button for three. At three, the doors opened, paused, and then closed. They started down again.

The ground floor offered the most logical way out of the building, but it would also be the first place Cassie's abductor would look. If, as she suspected, the main entrance required a key to open those tall glass doors, they would be trapped there, unable to escape.

She couldn't put Cassie through that.

There had to be another way out, obviously, or the man couldn't have gotten into the building, but her fear was that she would get them lost in a labyrinth of hallways that led to a dead end.

Better, she thought, to make a less predictable choice. She stopped the elevator again on two, and lifted Cassie into her arms.

Before she got out, she pushed all of the floor buttons just to muddy the waters a bit.

* * *

All of the stores on the second floor had sturdy metal gates that came down from the ceiling on tracks and could be padlocked at the sides. She walked quickly along the store fronts, until she came to one with a honeycombed gate that looked less substantial than the others.

Maybe, she thought, she could lift it enough so that Cassie could slip beneath it. Once inside, the child could scoot, crawl, or if need be, roll across the marble floor and hide behind a counter. In any case, she would be safe from *him*.

"Stay here," Danielle instructed, easing Cassie to the floor on the balcony side of the aisle, next to a planter filled with ferns. "Quiet as a mouse, okay?"

Cassie nodded mutely.

She tried to lift the door, straining until her arms and shoulders ached and the metal rungs dug into her sweaty hands, but she couldn't move it more than an inch or two. Desperate, she tried pulling it forward, free of the track, and failed again.

From somewhere in the building, she heard a thud. She crouched down to listen, trying to determine where the sound had come from . . . and how close he was.

How much time she had.

"Be smart," Danielle reminded herself, resisting the urge to grab Cassie and run, instead crawling across the aisle to peek over the balcony.

Both the ground and second floors bordered on an atrium, decorated with a jungle of lush greenery and modern acrylic sculptures, all of which were showcased by blue landscape spot-lighting. Aesthetics aside, the lights were largely ineffectual, beyond casting odd-shaped shadows in every direction.

Look too long, and the shadows came alive . . .

She saw him, then, a dark-clothed figure moving stealthily along the east interior wall on the first level, making his way to the entrance. He appeared to be carrying a rope or a cord, which he slapped rhythmically against his thigh.

Beside her, Cassie was shivering, even though heat radiated from her thin body.

Danielle gently stroked the child's cheek with the back of her hand. "Cassie," she whispered, "we have to find a place for you to hide."

"Can't I stay here?"

"I'm afraid not." Down below, the man was searching for them, patiently weaving his way between the plants and the geometric artwork. She was glad they hadn't gone down there . . . or he would be upon them now.

"Will you be hiding with me?"

Danielle hesitated, wondering how it was that kids always asked the hard questions. "Cassie, listen to me. He's looking for us. In a couple of minutes, he'll be up here. I want you to hide, honey, and let me lead him away from you."

"But I want to go with you— "

"You can't." Danielle tried to smile. "I'm not strong enough to carry you for any distance, and you can't walk with those on your ankles. The best thing, the smart thing, is to split up."

Cassie took a shuddering breath.

"It won't be for long, I promise. We've just got to hold on until the police get here to help us." The phone had been dead in the penthouse, but there was a panic button by the door, and she'd hit it before running out. "They'll be here any minute, but until then, we're on our own, honey. Okay?"

Cassie looked down and away, as if trying to conceal the tears welling in her wounded eyes. "What if they're not coming?"

It was a credible question, considering what the

child had been through. As would be, *Where were you when all of this happened to me?*

"They'll be here."

"But— "

"You'll have to trust me, Cassie." She looked around, her mind racing . . . and saw the perfect hiding place. "There's no more time."

Danielle carried the child to a four-foot-tall, cement waste barrel. On top of it was a brown metal lid that sloped inward to the center hole. The barrel was lined with a plastic garbage bag, in which there was a modest assortment of styrofoam cups, food wrappers, and single serving-sized plastic water bottles.

As quietly as she could, she removed the barrel lid and pulled the trash liner free from one side. She lifted Cassie and sat her on the rim, gave her a hug to reassure them both, then helped the child down into the barrel.

"I'll be back for you," she whispered.

After checking to make sure Cassie would be able to get enough air, she replaced the top. Standing a foot away, she saw nothing that would suggest the barrel was any different from the others on this or any floor.

The man would never find her, God willing.

Thirty-six

Simon Avery rubbed at his eyes— which still itched, although they finally had stopped stinging— and blinked rapidly. It took a second for his visual focus to return, but at least the tearing had stopped. He surveyed the lobby, and detected nothing amiss.

The front doors remained locked, inviolate. Outside, the streets were deserted.

He used a second pair of handcuffs to secure the push bar of the door marked Authorized Personnel Only to the handrail beside it, which eliminated the only other escape route.

Wherever they were, they were trapped and didn't know it. Oh, they might hide from him for a while, but eventually he would find them, and when he did . . . when he did there would be hell to pay.

Avery straightened the garrote between his hands. She didn't know it yet, but Danielle Falk would die this night. She would die, and the last thing she would see was him grinning wildly as her life faded and her eyes glazed over as death drew near. His laughter would follow her to her fate.

Not terribly polite, but who could blame him if he gloated at the end, after all the trouble she'd put him through?

He would take Cassandra then, and run. The child would slow him down, perhaps, but he meant to have his reward for the perseverance and restraint he'd shown through the past few days. And he'd be done with her soon enough that the delay would be inconsequential.

Afterwards, he'd disappear.

It was a shame to have to leave his inheritance behind, but money had never brought him any happiness, even *after* his blessed mother had died, and he was relatively certain he could survive on his own without it. As for where to go, this was a big country, full of wide open spaces, and it should be easy to hide.

Killers far more notorious than he vanished from sight all of the time. The Green River Killer came to mind, and that fellow back east, who'd slaughtered his entire family before melting away into the night. And Ted Bundy had run everyone in circles before he slipped up . . .

It could be done, absolutely.

But first things first. Avery snapped the garrote lightly, his eyes scanning the atrium for any sign of his prey. He moved among the shadows with a grace he'd seldom experienced in his miserable life.

He imagined the two of them, frightened and pathetic, huddled and shivering in some dark corner, helplessly awaiting their doom.

Avery smiled. Frissons of pleasure in his lower body suggested that he had truly found his niche. He would give some thought to adding a chase, the old hide-and-seek, to his game plan . . . if it could be done without risk of escape, of course.

There would be no escape tonight.

"Come out, come out, wherever you are," he whispered hoarsely.

Overhead, above the second-floor balcony, a banner

advertising 50% Off fluttered, as if stirred by an interior wind.

Or someone passing by?

Avery glanced up at it, and thought he saw the shadows move. "Are you that clever?" he asked softly, and started for the stairs.

Thirty-seven

Danielle followed the balcony wall to the stores on the west side of the building, away from the hiding place. She could hear that the man was humming, accompanied by the *whack* of the cord against his leg.

Crouched in the shadows, she watched him ascend the curving staircase to the second floor. Seeing him clearly for the first time as he neared the top, she felt a jolt of recognition.

It *was* Simon Avery.

Avery had been to the school many times with his mother. He was cordial, if withdrawn, a quiet man who had always walked a step behind Katherine and seldom spoke. His glance might linger on the children, but the rumor was his mother wouldn't permit him to marry. And Katherine was a strong-willed woman, used to having her way.

It was generally assumed among the school staff that the son's melancholy arose from a deep-held longing for a family and children of his own.

She'd actually felt sorry for him!

Stunned at how everyone had misjudged his intentions, she watched Avery pause at the head of the stairs. He was still humming, a bit off-key.

Danielle identified the song, then, the title and lyrics. "Here comes the sun," she whispered.

Only in this case, the son who was coming wanted to kill her and Cassie, as he'd murdered those two little girls in cold, savage blood. For all she knew, Billy Gaetke might be mortally injured—

She heard, in the distance, the faint wail of sirens, which rapidly became a chorus, or so it seemed to her. Her heartbeat quickened.

There was no way for her to tell how far away they were, or even if they were in fact headed this way, but she desperately wanted—or needed—to believe that help was coming.

Fifteen feet away from her, Avery fell silent, tilting his head to listen. He turned to face the front of the building, and took a single, hesitant step back down the stairs.

Through the window front, Danielle could see the street outside. At the nearest corner, the traffic signals blinked a cautionary red, but there wasn't a car or pedestrian in sight.

The sirens, however, were getting closer.

And there were a lot of them.

Avery went down another several steps and stood again, completely still, watchful. He snapped the cord straight between his hands, as if testing its strength . . . and glanced over his shoulder directly at her.

Danielle felt her breath catch painfully in her throat, and she could hear the drumbeat of her pulse racing in her ears.

She didn't dare look away from him, but with her peripheral vision, she saw the first flash of red and blue lights reflecting off the windows of adjacent buildings that promised help was very near.

His eyes filled with cold fury, Avery smiled at her, a terrible smile that froze her to the spot.

"Time's up," he said.

She thought he would run, try to get away before the police arrived, but instead he walked slowly and deliberately back up the stairs. After reaching the top, he moved along the balcony railing, away from her.

Towards the hiding place.

Afraid that any response from her might tip him off as to the child's whereabouts, Danielle remained still, but if he got too close, she would throw herself at him and try to knock him down.

If it came to that—

"Cassie," she said under her breath, "stay as quiet as a little mouse."

Outside, the first patrol car pulled up, the right front tire jumping the curb. A second car arrived a moment later, and in a heartbeat, there were two officers at the doors. One took his baton and swung hard at the glass, to no visible effect.

Danielle watched Avery, who trailed his fingers along the balcony railing as he walked along it. He had to know it was all over, she thought. For whatever reason, he hadn't chosen to run, but—

Avery stopped, a scant ten feet from the trash barrel where Cassie hid.

The street outside was filling with patrol cars, and there were at least a dozen cops gathered at the entrance. Two others ran up with a battering ram.

Danielle stood and began to walk towards Avery, who was too close to Cassie for comfort.

Avery turned to her and held up a hand, as though to ward her off. Then he began to back away.

Her first thought was that he was moving out of view so that the officers wouldn't be able see him. Down below, the battering ram hit, and this time she heard the glass shatter. Fifteen seconds, and they'd be in—

"Do unto others," Avery said suddenly, "as you would have others do unto you."

Riveted by the dreamy quality in his voice, Danielle could not take her eyes off him.

"My mother told me that, a million times at least." He laughed; it was not a pleasant sound. "There are exceptions, you know . . . some people can do whatever they want."

Downstairs, the sound of footsteps, running.

"If it's all the same to you," Avery hissed, *"I don't want anyone doing unto me—"*

Without warning, Avery took off running towards the railing, and vaulted it as if he were jumping a fence. His momentum carried him a good ten feet from the balcony, and to Danielle it seemed for a moment as though he were suspended in midair above the geometric shapes below.

Then gravity claimed him.

The instant before he hit, she turned away. She heard, though, the awful sound of his body as it landed on the apex of a pure white triangle.

She shut her eyes.

Later she sat at the foot of the stairs watching the medics load Detective Gaetke, his head swathed in gauze, into the back of an ambulance. Someone had given her a blanket and, feeling a chill, she pulled it close.

Cassie was already in route to a nearby hospital.

Before the first ambulance left, the paramedics had started an intravenous line on the child, who was dehydrated, and put her on oxygen. Her vital signs were stable, they said. Cassie would be all right.

Avery's body, still impaled, had been covered, hidden

from view. The pool of blood surrounding it looked almost black in the colored light.

Monsters, she thought.

Epilogue

December

The auditorium at Northcliffe Academy had been turned into a winter wonderland, curiously at odds with the typically mild Southern California weather outside.

The Christmas tree, at center stage, was a twelve-foot blue spruce, decorated accordingly with tiny blue twinkling lights and what appeared to be frosted crystal ornaments, also in hues of blue. Delicate clear icicles hung from the branches. The icicles looked so real, she could almost see them melt.

Brightly wrapped gifts were arranged beneath the tree, all dusted faintly with snow.

There were snow drifts all through the room, and the walls were covered with a blueish white substance that gave the auditorium the look of an igloo. And there was a small snow-covered slope with actual sleds for the children to ride down.

Dakota was impressed. "I hope this shows on tape," she said.

Rick, her hunky new cameraman, hefted the minicam onto his shoulder and plugged it into the battery pack. "Only one way to find out. What do you want?"

"All of it. Everything." In her position as weekend anchor at KNNX, she had a certain amount of flexibility in producing—and calling—her own shots. "But you'd better hurry and get the coverage we need before the party actually starts."

"Will do," Rick said, and wandered off.

Resisting an urge to try out the sleds, Dakota looked instead for the best place to do her spot. The station manager wanted this to be a sensitive and uplifting segment on the resiliency of children, a six-months-after kind of thing.

"Dakota, what a wonderful surprise."

She turned to Principal Maribeth Rifkin, who was virtually *oozing* good will, no doubt imagining that she now had the financial wherewithal to be an Angel herself. "Hi."

"It's *so* nice to see how well you're doing. Not that I ever thought otherwise—"

Clearly the woman had forgotten all those after-school detention periods in which she'd predicted *otherwise* by a factor of ten to the tenth power. "I'm sure that's what got me through, Maribeth," she said with a touch of impertinence, and walked away.

At the punch bowl, she spied Matt Price. "Hey there, stranger," she said, tugging on his coat sleeve. "It's been a long time. What are you doing here?"

"I was invited." Price ladled punch into a cup and handed it to her. "You working?"

"Oh yeah." She took a sip of punch. "Listen, I've been hearing rumors lately about videotapes of Avery's that the police found in a safe—"

"Don't even ask," Price said with a hint of a smile. "I don't have them, and even if I did, I wouldn't let you watch them."

"Some source *you* are."

"Whatever."

"I heard it was really perverted stuff," she persisted, "but there was also something about a television ad. You know what I mean? That Avery had taped that soap ad that has a little girl taking a shower— "

Price raised his eyebrows. "Who have you been talking to?"

"Why do you ask? Are you jealous that I might have another source? Hmm?"

"That'll be the day." He glanced down at his cup and swirled the punch to stir it. "The truth is, no one should look at that shit."

"Bad, is it?"

"The man deserved to die."

Something in his voice made her shiver. "Then it's best that he did."

"I won't argue the point." He put a hand on her arm. "Excuse me, Dakota, would you? There's somebody I have to talk to."

She turned to watch him cross the auditorium, which now was nearly filled. Price made his way through the crowd to where Evangeline and Zeke Wilson were standing. Cassie wasn't with them— most of the kids were backstage, getting ready to sing Christmas carols— so she decided not to approach them yet.

She couldn't help but notice that Zeke was looking pretty damned sharp in a dark gray pinstripe suit. Obviously working for the District Attorney agreed with him. He'd asked her out last summer, after the dust settled, and they'd gone out once or twice, but then she'd gotten swamped at KNNX, and he'd been hired by the city and that was that.

Such was life.

Not that she regretted the demands of her professional life; making anchor, even on the weekends, was a giant step in the right direction. Her pieces on Cassie had been picked up for national play by CNN. She'd even written a feature article on the kidnappings for the local newspaper; the word Pulitzer had been mentioned . . .

Okay, so *she* had been the one who mentioned it, whenever the opportunity arose, but things had come to a sorry pass if a girl couldn't toot her own horn, "Little Latin Lupe Lu" notwithstanding.

Her priorities were in order, but still, she would try to talk to Zeke later; if nothing else she could always use a reliable source in the D.A.'s office.

As luck would have it, Dakota was standing by the doors after the lights went down for the performance when Danielle Falk arrived, late. With Billy Gaetke, not that *that* was a surprise.

Even in the dim room, the diamond in Danielle's engagement ring seemed to catch the light. Given the size of the rock— how did the boy afford it?— it was no wonder.

On the stage, the kids were singing about a manger, just slightly off-key.

Dakota leaned over to Danielle. "Can I talk to you for a minute?"

"All right." Danielle whispered something to Billy Gaetke— who reluctantly relinquished her hand— and stepped back out into the hall.

"I'm sorry to bother you," Dakota said, and made a show of turning on her cassette recorder so there would be no mistaking that this was on the record, "but I wonder if you have any thoughts on how Cassie Wilson is doing after her ordeal, now that a little time has passed."

There was a slight hesitation before Danielle smiled.

"Cassie is fine. She's not in my class this year, but I see her every day at school, in the halls and on the playground, and . . . she's hanging in there."

"Is she?"

"I think so. She's made friends with a new student, a little girl whose family moved here from Texas, so yes, I'd say Cassie is doing great."

"What about you?"

Danielle blinked, as if startled. "Nothing happened to me. I— "

It was a hard question, but she was under orders to ask. "Have you forgiven yourself?"

For a moment, the only sounds were the whirring of the tape recorder and the muted voices of the children singing "Jingle Bells." Tears appeared in the teacher's brown eyes, but didn't fall.

"No," Danielle said quietly, "I don't think anyone who has had a child taken, *abducted,* while under their care can ever really forgive themselves for not keeping a better watch."

"Cassie came home."

"Not all of them do." She took a step towards the door, paused, and glanced back. "They're children for such a short time . . . how could anyone take that from them?"

Later, Dakota watched the children taking rides on the sleds, and there was Cassie, a radiant, beautiful little girl, awaiting her turn. In her blue velvet dress, with gold ribbons in her hair, she looked like any other child . . . unless you looked into her eyes.

About the Author

Dark Intent is Patricia Wallace's 17th novel for Zebra. Author of the Sydney Bryant Mystery series— *Small Favors, Deadly Grounds, Blood Lies,* and *Deadly Devotion,* and the forthcoming *August Nights*— her other titles include *Night Whisper, Fatal Outcome,* and *Thrill.* A former freelance Story Analyst, she has degrees in Communications/Film, and Police Science. She would like to hear from her readers, who can write to her at P.O. Box 50873, Sparks, NV 89435-0873.